SOLD TO THE MOB BOSS

A MAFIA ROMANCE (LAVRIN BRATVA)

NICOLE FOX

Copyright © 2019 by Nicole Fox

All rights reserved.

No part of this book may be reproduced in any form or by any electronic or mechanical means, including information storage and retrieval systems, without written permission from the author, except for the use of brief quotations in a book review.

❦ Created with Vellum

MAILING LIST

Sign up to my mailing list!
New subscribers receive a FREE steamy bad boy romance novel.

Click the link below to join.
https://sendfox.com/nicolefox

ALSO BY NICOLE FOX

Belluci Mafia Trilogy

Corrupted Angel (Book 1)

Corrupted Queen (Book 2)

Corrupted Empire (Book 3)

De Maggio Mafia Duet

Devil in a Suit (Book 1)

Devil at the Altar (Book 2)

Kornilov Bratva Duet

Married to the Don (Book 1)

Til Death Do Us Part (Book 2)

Heirs to the Bratva Empire

Can be read in any order

Kostya

Maksim

Andrei

Tsezar Bratva

Nightfall (Book 1)

Daybreak (Book 2)

Russian Crime Brotherhood

Can be read in any order

Owned by the Mob Boss

Unprotected with the Mob Boss

Knocked Up by the Mob Boss

Sold to the Mob Boss

Stolen by the Mob Boss

Trapped with the Mob Boss

Volkov Bratva

Broken Vows (Book 1)

Broken Hope (Book 2)

Broken Sins *(standalone)*

Other Standalones

Vin: A Mafia Romance

Box Sets

Bratva Mob Bosses (Russian Crime Brotherhood Books 1-6)

Tsezar Bratva (Tsezar Bratva Duet Books 1-2)

Heirs to the Bratva Empire

SOLD TO THE MOB BOSS: A MAFIA ROMANCE (LAVRIN BRATVA)

By Nicole Fox

An innocent girl like her... sold to a beast like me.

Nikita

As the boss of the Bratva, I live my life by a code: Always stay in control.

But I broke my own rule on the night I bought Annie.

She was so delicate and desperate up on that stage.

I'd pay any price it took to own her.

She says she can't be bought.

But she doesn't know how this game is played.

In my world, everything has its price.

And like it or not, she's mine now – my property, my possession.

I'll claim her. I'll break her. And I'll protect her until the end…

Even if it costs me everything.

1

NIKITA

The nights are always the same.

The thump of the bass from the DJ's music rattles the walls, even in the back of the club, much to my annoyance. But a club is the best way to do business. Or a butcher shop, for the old-school types. But the stench of uncooked meat and blood makes my stomach sour. I'd much prefer to be surrounded by scantily clad woman than lamb ribs and pork chops.

"Boss, we got a situation," one of the bouncers says, standing in the doorway.

With a low growl that rumbles from deep within my chest, I stand up from my desk and make my way to the main room. The blue neon lights, the thumping of the newest pop hit, and half naked girls who can barely hold their drinks crowd the room. When one of the drunken girls invades my space, I use my forearm to guide her away. These reckless college girls are not to my liking. Not in the slightest.

The bouncer leads me over to the bar where the lead bartender, Krissy, is mouthing off to a customer. My gaze travels to the man on the other side of the counter. Blood covers his face and broken glass is scattered over the top of the bar and on the man's shirt.

I groan and walk up to Krissy. "What happened?"

With flailing hands, Krissy glares right at the guy and answers, "Motherfucker felt it appropriate to grab my tits. So, I reciprocated."

"By cracking a bottle over his head?"

Krissy turns and meets my gaze, but doesn't shrink or falter. She's tough. It's one of the reasons I hired her. The other being that she's my cousin. Family protects family.

"You bitch. I'm going to sue you and this club," the bloody man spits, his face mottled crimson, his eyes popped, his tree-trunk neck strained. His words are spat out with the ferocity and rapidity of machine-gun fire.

Without wiping the spit from her face, Krissy leans closer, perfectly composed, and speaks her next words just millimeters from the man's face. "See if I give a fuck."

The man explodes with unrestrained fury. But Krissy doesn't care to stick around and watch him melt down. With a barely concealed smirk, she turns on her heel and walks away. My mess to deal with, now.

Always start with diplomacy.

"Sir, I think it's time for you to leave. Don't worry about the bill; your drinks are on the house." I hate giving away free shit, but it's better than being sued.

"You think free drinks are gonna stop me from suing this place?" the man staggers a bit.

I straighten my spine, my lips pressing tightly together. I can't stand dealing with drunken idiots. If he wants to be difficult, fine. I can deal with that just as easily.

When diplomacy fails, move next to the veiled threat.

"I can always call the police, check the cameras, and then you could be going to jail for sexual assault. Choice is yours, but choose quickly."

The man's face turns crimson once again, but no words come out of his mouth. Instead, his friends drag him out of the bar after giving me a nod of understanding.

The fool doesn't realize how lucky he is to have friends like that. Because I wouldn't have been calling the cops. No. Left to my own devices, the man would've disappeared, for good. No one messes with my business or my family. Hell, I would've had him killed if Krissy had come to me first. But of course she insisted on handling it herself. A smirk lights up my face. The Lavrin blood runs strong in her veins.

"Clean up the bar. I'm heading back into the office. And make sure Krissy doesn't get herself in any more trouble for the night," I say to the other bartender, before turning and walking back down the hallway.

Back in the sanctuary of the office, I make myself a glass of gin, just like my father used to do.

I've had so many thoughts of my father tonight. Very unlike me to be so sentimental. But murdered men have a way of remaining in the hearts and minds of their sons.

It's hard to forget my father when his presence is everywhere around me. The desk, the art, the chair I'm in—all of it was once his. I claimed this office after his death, just as I claimed his position at the head of the Lavrin family.

Right after I ended the life of every Scuderi motherfucker who took my father from me.

Our enemies, the Scuderis, spilled my father's blood, so I spilled theirs ten times over. Scorched earth. No survivors.

But the damage they did to my family was permanent. My father gone, my mother hospitalized with an emotional breakdown, never to recover quite fully. I did what I had to do to avenge them. And in the process, I taught this world one simple rule:

Do. Not. Fuck. With. Me.

Knuckles rap against the door again. Not even ten fucking minutes to myself. "What?"

Vinny and Tommy, two of my subordinates, drag in an elderly man and throw him in front of me.

For a moment, my breath catches in my chest. The man is facedown on the expensive rug that spreads from wall to wall. As he struggles to pull himself back to his feet, I have the strongest sense of foreboding.

The man looks exactly like my father.

But then he shows his face to me and the likeness fades away. It leaves a sticky, sour taste in its path, like blood on my tongue. I can feel a bead of sweat on my forehead. The ghosts in my brain are acting up tonight.

Vinny's voice cuts through the haze and drags me back to reality.

"Boss, he hasn't paid his protection dues for the past month," Vinny says, kicking the old man in the thigh.

"Mr. Lavrin, please," the old man whimpers. "Business has been rough. With the chain supermarket, I don't have as many customers coming in."

Fucking Christ. This is the one part of the business I can't stand. Part of me wants to help the man to his feet, dust off his jacket. He looks like he needs a night off, not a mafioso beating. But you can't run a business on mercy. The rules must be upheld.

"Not my problem," I tell him. "You asked for protection, so you pay for what you've been given."

"Please, Mr. Lavrin, I'm begging you."

I hold up a hand to silence him. "You knew the deal you entered. You have wasted my time and the time of my men who were forced to drag you before me. Bring me my payment by the end of the week—no, double it. A penalty for the frustration you have caused here tonight. Next time, you won't receive a second chance. If this happens again, your payment will be your life."

I nod curtly to my soldiers at the door. We are done here. The old man's eyes bulge and he cries out as Vinny and Thomas each grab an arm and pull him through the door and out of sight. I hear the sharp slap of knuckle on skin and the whimpering stops.

Silence takes over again after they're gone. The remnants of that haunted feeling still linger in my chest. For a split second, the old man looked just like my father ...

Another rap on the door. "Come in."

In walks Eitan Aminov, my top advisor. I throw back what's left of the gin in my glass. When it comes to Eitan, there's no chance I'll be enjoying my drink. He's all business, all the time.

"Nikita, so good to see you," Eitan shakes my hand and walks over to the chair by my desk. "We have much to discuss."

It's been a long night already, and there's still far more to come. But I just want to fucking go to sleep. Between Krissy and the old man, I'm not sure how much more I can take tonight. How did my father deal with this stress for so long? Everyone wanting things from me, all the time. I'm not even thirty and I'm looking forward to retiring.

"You okay, boss?" Eitan asks.

"Yeah. Krissy gives me a headache." I plop down into my chair and rub my temples.

Eitan laughs. "Girl's tough. One day, she might be running the business."

I snort. "She's too quick-tempered. She'd do something stupid and have the cops crawling all over the place."

Eitan nods solemnly in agreement. "Always start with diplomacy," he intones. My father's words. "So, to business. We need to discuss the auction."

The auction. Flesh trafficking. A highlight of the yearly calendar for the criminal elements in the city, and a hefty paycheck for the ones in charge—namely, me. When I was a younger man, I used to look forward to the auctions. So much beauty, all for sale to the highest bidder. But this time, I don't have the same excitement. This time, it's nothing more than business.

Opening up the spreadsheet on my computer, I scan through the list of names of those I invited. Those who possess the type of money needed to participate. "Who have you heard from?"

He begins to rattle off names. "Gino, of course. First one to respond. The Mendoninos. They always splurge. A few assorted businessmen of distinct taste," Eitan says.

I turn the monitor towards him and push the keyboard in his direction. "Just check off everyone you've spoken with."

Eitan taps at the keyboard while I massage away the headache in my temples. When he's done, I notice over three-quarters of the list have agreed to come. And high rollers as well. This might be the most lucrative year yet. But there's still too many moving parts that we need to handle.

"What about the venue?"

Eitan leans back in his chair and crosses his legs. "Checked it out myself. The downstairs room is very secure, with two emergency exits if we need to get away. Access to the club upstairs. Cops shouldn't know what's going on. Staff has been instructed properly; discretion, as always, being the better part of valor. No tolerance for violence on the evening as well."

"Good," I say.

Thank God for Eitan. The man has been with the Lavrins for a long time, since my father was a boy. He knows the ins and outs of our business as well as I do.

"What about the girls?"

Eitan blows out a long breath and runs his hand through the thinning salt-and-pepper hair on top of his head. "The Travoras are managing that aspect of the evening's operations. They assure me there will be no problems. But ..." He raises an eyebrow. "I've heard rumors of some struggles on that front."

My neck tightens in response to his answer. "What's the issue?"

"Supply, as usual. And apparently, some issues with a trade partner in the Eastern European block. There are always the drug addicts and runaways. But the pickings are slim and some of these girls ... not worth putting them up on stage," Eitan says. "I've sent men across the border in Canada to see what they can find," he adds.

"Good. Just make sure to keep on top of them. Last thing I need is for one of them to fuck up and get the FBI involved."

"I'll station some of the men in the club on the evening of the event. One never knows what may straggle in at the last minute." Eitan winks and folds his hands in his lap. "There is one last matter I want to address. You have an eager lieutenant, Augustin Molotov, who shows a lot of promise. He's chomping at the bit for more responsibility."

I tap my forefinger to my lips. "Molotov? I think I know the name."

"He handled the drug issue with one of Gino's men last month," Eitan says.

"Yes, that's right. Kid did a good job keeping the peace and getting our money." I click on the computer screen and open up my calendar. I'm more than happy to delegate some responsibility to those looking for it. "We have the Greeks delivering the weapons shipment next week. Let Augustin handle it. But make sure he understands how we run our business. And make sure he understands the consequences if he fucks up."

Eitan nods.

Weapons shipments aren't as easy as they look on TV. Something always goes wrong. Forget about the cops; half the time it's Mother Nature and her moody weather interfering with schedules. And once those schedules fuck up, all the precautions put in place get fucked up as well. Then there's the seller who always decides to haggle last minute, and of course that just ends with a dead body I have to get rid of.

"Be on call in case Augustin runs into any issues. The kid hasn't had to dispose of a body for us yet. First time's always messy, but there's no need to reinvent the wheel. You know how we clean up our messes."

"Understood." Eitan stands and pulls on his jacket to straighten it. "Have a good night, Nikita. I'll keep you updated."

"Good night, Eitan."

Eitan turns and walks out the door. Finally, some alone time.

But just as I start to lean back in my chair, there's yet another knock at the door. These interruptions are putting me in a foul mood.

"Nikita." Sophia pokes her head into the office. "May I come in?"

Sophia is one of my earlier purchases. She wasn't a runaway or a drug addict. No, she was an abused housewife looking for safety, though I'm still unsure what type of safety she felt a sex auction would offer. She's smart and drop-dead gorgeous. Even the skintight blue dress that shows off all her assets doesn't do her justice. And when I laid eyes on her, when I saw the mottled bruises circling her nose, I wasn't letting anyone else purchase her. And I'm glad I didn't. It doesn't hurt that the blonde can suck cock like her life depends on it. And she's been invaluable at keeping the rest of my harem in line.

"What do you need?" I'm so tired tonight. Weariness blankets me.

Sophia steps into the room and closes the door behind her. She's been with me for the past four years, and for the past three years she's been in charge of my harem girls. She knows when my door is closed not to bother me, so if she's poking her head in, something might need my immediate attention.

"It's Thursday." She smiles as she glides toward me, her long tan legs covering the distance fast.

Fuck.

"Ah. Right. I completely forgot. Eitan had me so busy with some upcoming business," I tell her.

"I figured. You look really stressed." Sophia stands behind me and runs her hands over my shoulders. "Maybe a quick massage while I update you on the girls?"

I'm not going to argue with her. My shoulders are tense, and Sophia is a licensed massage therapist, with skilled hands. She's one of the few in my harem I allow to run a business—as long as I get a cut.

Sophia's hands begin kneading my aching muscles and I let out a sigh. She giggles and then gets right to business. "The heat in the room on the third floor isn't working. Tina mentioned it to Vinny, but he slapped her and never fixed it. I stopped by and the place is freezing. I mean, isn't part of his job to be the super for any of the apartments the girls are in?"

"I'll talk to Vinny."

Sophia's hands travel down my chest, her nails grazing over my nipples. While I'm totally okay with a relaxing massage, sex is out of the question right now. I stir in my chair, attempting to sit up straight.

"Also, Lori was upset. Cried about how Vinny and Tommy beat some old man up at the little market down the street earlier. She said the old man looked dead." Sophia leans forward, pressing her ample breasts against my head as her hands extended down my abdomen.

I cringe. The old man.

I push myself out of the chair, away from Sophia's kneading hands, and pace around the room, running my fingers through my hair. Every nerve in my body fires and my blood boils. Fuck. Why couldn't the old man just pay? Why'd he have to wait until last minute to say anything? But I can't be weak. Not with everyone looking. I have no fucking choice.

Sophia walks up to me and presses her body against mine. Her fingernails gently scrape against my scalp as she licks her full lips. "Nikita, you're stressed. Let me take care of you."

Her hand runs over my dick and she holds my gaze. But I'm not interested. Not tonight, not with everything going on. Not with an old man—a man who looked to be about my father's age—lying beat up in the street. "Sophia, not tonight. If there's anything else about the girls, tell me now. Otherwise, you can go."

Sophia yanks her hand back, blinking rapidly as if I just smacked her across the face. She's not used to being turned down. Especially by me. She takes care of so much for me that a good fucking is the least I can do in return. Out of appreciation, if nothing else. But tonight, God himself could be standing in front of me demanding a hard-on, and I'm just not going to be able to perform.

"There's nothing else to report. Have a good night, Mr. Lavrin." With that, Sophia turns and walks out of the room.

Mr. Lavrin.

She knows better than to be openly disrespectful, but she can be subtly spiteful in her own right. She knows just how to walk the line between following my rules and letting me know when she's angry.

I'll have to buy her something tomorrow and make it up to her. The last thing I need right now, on the eve of the auction, is a mutiny taking place in my bedroom.

I walk back over to the gin and instead of pouring it into a glass, I put the bottle to my lips and gulp as much of the liquid down as I can, hoping the alcohol will ease my mind. And after a few minutes, it does. At least a little bit.

But the image of the shopkeeper on my floor still haunts me. I did that to him—I hurt him. I took his money.

Just like my father taught me.

2

ANNIE

I wrap my hair up in a messy bun, sling my bag over my arm, and head out the glass door of the math building. Finals are over. Thank God. But I'm not as relieved as I'd expected. I'm not sure if that's because this last accounting final made me nervous or if it was the way the TA ogled me that rattled my nerves. Either way, I'm out of the building and heading home for a nice, relaxing night of binge-watching my favorite medical drama.

I pull my coat tight around me and brave the heavy winds as I walk toward the apartment building I share with two other girls. I can't believe I only have one more semester left before I graduate. I swear, I thought school would never end. But my stomach churns at the thought of the real world waiting for me—adult life, a job, responsibilities. Of course, I've already met with my career counselor, and I'm lucky enough to have some people in mid-level accounting firms eager to interview me once I graduate.

But I know not to rest yet. Don't count your chickens before they hatch, yada yada yada. One step at a time.

I shrug the strap of my bag higher onto my shoulder and jog across the intersection. On the other side, I see a homeless man leaning against a dirty corner.

He gives me a broad, toothless smile as I approach. "Good evening, Mizz Thornton," he says in a raspy voice. "How'd your tests go?" Henry tilts his head and smiles. "You musta done good. You a very smart lady."

My cheeks heat at his words. "Thank you, Henry. I think I did well. But I still have to wait and see." I reach into my bag, pull out half of a turkey sandwich, and offer it to Henry. "I couldn't finish this with being so nervous about the exam. And I know how much you love turkey and mayo."

"Aw, thanks, Mizz Thornton. I truly appreciate your kindness." Henry smiles wider and takes the sandwich. "You betta hurry along, Ms. Thornton. It's cold tonight."

I frown and stare at Henry for a second. "Promise me you'll go to the shelter if it gets too cold?"

"For you, Mizz Thornton, I promise. I don't wanna see any worry in those pretty brown eyes."

I smile and wish Henry a good evening before continuing down the street toward the apartment. Tears fill my eyes when I wonder about who will take care of Henry once I graduate. Most of the college students don't pay him any attention. Hardly anyone offers to buy him a meal or give him a bottle of water. And once I graduate, I'm leaving the city. Henry will be left by himself.

I wipe my eyes as I climb the stairs to my building. Swiping the keycard, I push open the door and walk up to the second floor. Please God, I hope Wendy and Jenna are gone. I just want some peace and quiet.

But no sooner do I turn the key and push open the door than the shrill tone of squealing women floods my ears. At least they're down the hall. Maybe I can slip into my bedroom without them noticing.

I carefully close the door and tiptoe down the white hall, avoiding the creaky spot on the left side halfway down. This ain't my first rodeo. Ever so softly, I close my bedroom door.

Hallelujah. Unnoticed.

Sighing with relief, I let my bag slip to the floor before I shrug off my parka and hang it on the hook. I walk over to my bed and plop down onto the mattress just as Jenna bursts into my room.

"Annie, oh my God, why didn't you tell us you were home?!"

"Long day," I murmur as I curl up into my blanket.

"Oh, no, you don't, lady!" Wendy chirps as she walks in to join us. "You are *not* going to bed. We are going out to celebrate that finals are over."

"Guys, I'm super tired." I feign a yawn, hoping they'll just let me be. Dr. McDreamy and my bed are calling, and I am more than ready to spend all night long with them.

Jenna puts her hands on her hips and juts out her chin as she fake glares at me. "Nope, no way. These past four years all you did was study, study, study. And even when I went to visit you over the summer, you were taking extra classes at the local university."

Wendy crosses her arms in front of her chest. "Listen, Little Miss Bookworm. You are coming out with us. And if you try to back out, we're just gonna stay here and keep pestering you."

I groan and slam my hands down on the comforter. I've been through this routine before. They're in top form tonight, and when they get jazzed up like this, resistance is futile. "Fine."

The two girls smile from ear to ear as they bounce up and down on their toes. I can see it in their eyes already. They've been planning my makeover.

Ugh, what did I do to deserve this?

The last time they made me over, two years ago, I was hounded all night by drunken fools. I don't care for being the center of attention. Or attracting the attention of any man, really. Partying has never been my thing. I'd much rather wear my jeans and turtleneck sweaters over some skimpy dress that barely covers my butt.

But my two friends are the exact opposite. They're not brain-dead, like some of the hard partiers around campus, but they definitely do more than their fair share of getting dolled up and hitting the town.

Wendy and Jenna start whispering to one another, and I fling my legs over the side of the bed and sit up. Time to set some boundaries before this gets too out of hand. "Listen, the two of you: I agreed to go out with you tonight. But I don't want a repeat of the last time you both played fashionista with me."

"Don't worry, Annie. We promise to be a little more modest," Jenna says.

"Yeah, last time no one paid attention to us at all." Wendy rolls her eyes and pouts. "Do you know how gorgeous you are? I mean, you hide that killer body in oversized sweaters. Not to mention, I'd kill for your naturally wavy hair."

"Thanks, Wendy," I say, looking down at my feet. Heat crawls up my neck to my cheeks. Accepting compliments has always been hard for me. As if I've always believed them to be a lie. I'm not ugly by any means, but I just don't place importance on looks. Grades are what's important to me.

"Now, go get that butt of yours in the shower," Jenna says.

I hop off the bed, grab my robe, and stop in the middle of the doorway. "Where are we going?"

"Club Exposito," Wendy answers.

I groan. Of course. The two have been dying to go there for a couple of months. It's supposed to be the hottest place in town, meaning it's guaranteed to be absolutely packed to the gills. I shake my head and continue toward the bathroom.

Once inside, I lock the door and strip out of my clothes. I step into the shower, toes flinching as they touch the chilled ceramic floor. I turn the dial, old and metallic, and let out a sigh as the hot water trickles down my skin. I stand for a moment and enjoy the sensation. It feels like I'm rinsing away my hardest semester yet.

After the twenty minutes it takes to wash my hair and body, I slink into my robe and head to my room where Wendy and Jenna are waiting. "So, just an outfit, right?" I say tentatively. I wince, knowing that Wendy's reply isn't going to make me feel any better.

"Oh, we're going full-out, honey." Wendy holds up a blow dryer and pumps the trigger like a crazy woman with a gun. They both laugh. I just groan again.

Still, things could be worse, I remind myself as they set upon me like a pack of hyenas. While I might not like the idea of getting a sexy makeover, I'm not opposed to being pampered a bit. So while Wendy and Jenna go about styling my hair and makeup, I mentally begin to plan for the next semester.

Definitely need to meet with the advisor again and see if it's worth jumping right into a master's program or if I should keep pursuing the job hunt first. Some of the firms I've been perusing offer to pay tuition costs for employees. And that would help so much. My loans are already out of control.

"Stop frowning." Jenna smacks my shoulder, startling me out of my reverie. "You're screwing up the lip liner."

"Please don't tell me you're sitting here planning your future career," Wendy says as she twists a lock of my hair around the curling iron.

"I'm just trying to figure out what my next move should be. Besides, there's not much else for me to do except sit still while you psychos go to work on me, so I might as well be productive," I say.

The two huff and roll their eyes. When they're done, Jenna grabs a miniskirt from her closet and throws it on my bed while Wendy fishes out the cobalt-blue shirt I have in my closet. The one with the low V-neck and see-through sleeves. Of course she picked that one out—she's the one who made me buy it.

Grudgingly, I put on the outfit and slip my feet into the six-inch stilettos Wendy brought in. Why do we have to be the same size shoe? I swear the universe hates me. I make my way to the full-length mirror behind the bathroom door and gasp.

I don't recognize the woman looking back at me. The one with the fake eyelashes and dark red lipstick. The one with loose flowing locks of brown hair framing smoky eyeshadow. This is too much. It isn't me.

But ... I feel sexy.

Uncomfortable, extremely likely to trip over a sidewalk curb and break my ankle into a jillion pieces ...

But sexy.

"Thank you," I say to my two roommates, my sight blurring from the tears starting to form.

"Don't you dare cry. I don't have time to redo your makeup," Jenna threatens.

I chuckle and head out to the living room while the two girls continue getting ready, making sure my clutch has all the necessary items for the night, including cash and my portable phone charger. Jenna and Wendy are ready five minutes before the Uber is supposed to arrive. A miracle. Normally, the driver has to wait at least fifteen minutes for them.

"Start-of-the-night selfie," Jenna chirps. We pose so she can take a picture.

We head downstairs and jump into the car. About thirty minutes later we're standing on the longest line I've ever seen as we wait to get into Club Exposito. The thumping music is so loud, no one really needs to go inside to dance. Of course, there aren't any drinks out here, but at least the music makes the wait less boring.

"Annie, the cover is on me," Jenna says.

"No, no, no. I don't want you paying. Look how pretty you both made me tonight. I'm paying the cover for both of you," I say.

They both stare at me, hips cocked and lips puckered. But they know better than to argue with me. I'll win. So, with a dismissive wave of their hands, they turn and hand their IDs to the bouncer who allows us to enter. I gulp as I offer the cash to the cashier just inside the door—it's a lot of money.

"For a doll like you? Free tonight," the man drawls. He's got enough metal piercings in his face to be a danger to any magnets in the vicinity. He gives me a yellowed grin. I force a smile and we head inside before he changes his mind.

Once fully indoors, we head to the main area. Inside the club, it's like everyone is dancing under the northern lights. Smoke from dry ice swirls amongst an array of blue, green, pink, and gold lights. Bodies are fused together, moving to the beat of the music.

"Come on, let's dance." Jenna grabs my wrist and drags me onto the dance floor. "Loosen up, Annie."

Dancing isn't my thing. I'm stiff, awkward, and nervous as all get-out. I feel like a flamingo on roller skates. I'm envious of how simple and beautiful it is as Jenna rolls her hips to the music.

"Motion is lotion, baby," Wendy quips. We all laugh at her ridiculousness, but she's right. As I relax and let myself groove, I can feel the anxiety fading away.

The cavernous room is filled wall-to-wall with people dancing to the club music. It seems like there's no room for anyone else, but somehow, when Jenna, Wendy, and I hit it, the space magically clears. Of course, my roommates sandwich me, forcing me to dance with them, and encouraging the creepiest of guys to stare at us. But it doesn't matter.

We laugh and start dancing, twisting, turning, holding hands as we change sides. We're all sporting ear-to-ear grins, we look like idiots, and we don't care. Inside, we're just happy; happy, and more alive than I've felt in a long time. I have that feeling of knowing that I'll never forget this exact moment, that ten years from now, I'll still remember tonight as one single, perfect moment. Music, friends, not a care in the world.

The song changes and the feeling slips away, but I'm still buzzing and smiling. For once, I'm glad I let them drag me out of the house. "Let's get some drinks," Wendy says and heads toward the bar.

Jenna and I follow behind, elbows out to the sides to help push people out of the way. The three of us weasel into a clearing against the mahogany bar. Jenna calls over the bartender and orders a couple of whiskey sours.

"Having fun?" Jenna asks, shooting me a wide smile.

"Actually, I am." I wink at her and chuckle.

The three of us clink our glasses and huddle together. A trio of guys dressed in suit pants and button-down shirts with slicked-back hair walks over. They are very handsome, and they definitely know it. As they approach, they immediately split up, one coming up to each of us.

The tallest of the three men leans into me, his lips gently brushing my ear. "And what's your name?" His voice is a smooth baritone that slices right through the loud music like a hot knife through butter.

"Annie," I say and bite my lower lip as I shrink in on myself.

"Nice to meet you, Annie." The man pulls his head back and extends his hand.

I shake his hand and look back over to Jenna and Wendy. They're deep in conversation already. My man steps closer and his fingers gently grasp my elbow. "Annie, why don't you have a shot with me?"

"Um, okay."

The man walks over to the bar and waves down the bartender. Moments later, he's back with shot glasses for him and me. I take it from his hand. His fingertip brushes my palm as he passes it over. It feels like a spark leaps from him to me. "Cheers, Annie." He winks. It's the smoothest wink I've ever seen in my life. Somehow, it manages not to be corny or silly at all—just smooth, effortless, seductive. I almost shiver, despite the heat in the room.

I put the glass to my lips and throw back my head, forcing the acrid liquid down my throat. *Repulsive* is a massive understatement. I cringe and wrinkle my nose. The man smiles as I hold down a gag. I hand him back my glass.

"Another," he says firmly.

Before I can protest, he's already handing another glass over to me. I see the girls to my right throwing back drinks with abandon. Against my better judgment, I drink another.

"Another."

"Really, I can't," I cough, but again, he's too fast for me. My head is starting to spin a little, getting close to out of control. I try to refuse.

"Take it, Annie!" Jenna calls over. I see her peek around the bulk of the man talking to her and give me a broad smile and a thumbs-up. I groan.

"One more, but that's it," I warn the man in front of me.

He grins and shrugs. "Whatever you say, darling."

I throw it back. The last one is much smoother than the first. It slides down my throat and adds to the warm glow in my belly. I feel my hips swaying to the music as if they have a life of their own.

"I think that ought to do it for now. Annie, would you like to dance?" The man offers his hand.

"Sure." I fumble a little to place my hand in his, the alcohol taking effect. "By the way, what's your name?" I call as he leads us back towards the dance floor.

The man turns his head over his shoulder to meet my gaze. "Stephen."

We reach the edge of the mass of people and slip inside, the crowd parting like waves and then closing behind us, swallowing us deep within the hot, grinding bodies. Stephen pulls me into his embrace. In the dark, all I can see are his high cheekbones and shining eyes. We press closer together, bouncing and swaying to the hard bass pumping through the speakers. The white flash of his teeth is as bright as the lights above.

His body pressed against mine is rock solid, warm, and unyielding. I can feel the heat in my stomach and between my legs, rising up, boiling over. I can barely remember the old Annie, the one who wanted to stay in bed and watch people play doctor on television. I feel too alive for a night like that.

The club is electric, everyone feeding off the smiles and fast dancing. I could go like this all night long, never stopping. I move in my miniskirt like my hips were made to sway. The beat tugs at me like I'm a puppet on strings.

A perfect moment, one to remember forever.

That's when the nightmare begins.

3

ANNIE

Stephen pulls me up against his body and every nerve ending in my body fires off. He grinds against me, my arms wrapped around his neck. His hot breath on my skin is invigorating.

"You're very sexy, Annie," Stephen says. How is he getting away with being so cheesy and direct? If he were anyone else, he'd seem so cheesy, so lame. I don't know if it's because he's just that good-looking, or if he's casting a spell on me, or what, but whatever it is, it's working.

I bite my lower lip and duck my eyes to avoid his gaze, both out of shyness and because this close, my eyesight begins to blur.

We continue to dance, the smoke from the dry ice twisting artistically, forming curls as it's illuminated by the colored lights. My grip on Stephen tightens as the world becomes a carousel, gaining momentum.

"Are you okay?"

I nod slowly and look up at Stephen. "Just a bit too much to drink."

Everything feels like it's catching up to me suddenly. The pleasant heat in my hips is turning into a boiling inferno. I feel very wrong, somehow. Dizzy, sweaty, but shivering.

Stephen pulls me closer, his lips nuzzling the side of my neck. A flood of endorphins urges me to turn and kiss him, something that I would never do. But when I turn to meet his lips, my movements are awkward and my forehead clips his nose. I feel a sharp crack.

"Oh my God, I'm so sorry," I say, stepping back to give him some space as my hand flies over my mouth.

"It's ... okay." Stephen's words contain a hint of venom and something dark flashes in his eyes. It looks like there's a drop of blood on the rim of his nostril.

I struggle to walk forward, my legs swaying from left to right. It's as if I'm having some sort of out-of-body experience. God, I'm drunk. So very drunk. Why did I take all those shots?

Stephen grabs my arm and leads me toward a dark corner of the club. He spins me so the wall is to my back and steps into my space.

I force a smile against my growing nausea and lean into him. I'm trying to tell myself not to ruin this moment, but I don't know how much longer I can keep myself together. My eyes dart around the club looking for Jenna and Wendy, but I can't spot them. Just strangers, everywhere, sweaty and reeling.

"What do you do for work?" Stephen's question pulls me from my search.

"Oh, I'm a student still. I graduate in May."

Stephen's lips brush against my ear. "What do you study?"

"Um, accounting." The words barely come out as a whisper, the body contact stealing my voice.

Stephen chuckles, but something is off in the tone. Something sinister. The hairs on my neck prick for a moment and my hands slip to Stephen's chest to push him back a little, giving me some space.

But Stephen doesn't move.

"I need a little air. I'm going to find Jenna or Wendy and step outside for a bit," I say.

Stephen steps closer until he's pressing me flush against the wall. With his finger, he lifts my chin so that my gaze meets his. "Annie, you aren't going anywhere."

Adrenaline floods my system. My heart pumps and beats like it's trying to escape. My body wants to run fast for safety, but instead I remain where I am. Adrenaline surges so fast I almost vomit, saliva thickening in my throat, and beads of sweat trickling down my brow.

I don't feel sexy anymore. I feel like throwing up and crying, not necessarily in that order.

I take a deep breath to calm myself. Maybe Stephen didn't mean it the way I took it. Maybe the alcohol is causing me to panic. I mean, what can he really do? We're in a club with hundreds of people. Hundreds of witnesses. He's not going to kill me, for crying out loud.

But still, something doesn't feel right. I need to get away.

"Stephen, please. I feel sick. I drank too much."

There's a twinkle in his eyes, and he smiles wide, too wide. All his teeth show, as if he's a predator toying with his prey. "I said, you aren't going anywhere." His voice is laced with too much power and too much confidence, like a man used to getting his way.

I slap my palms against his chest with all the force I can muster. Thanks to being drunk, there's no real power behind the hits. Tears start to flow down my cheeks, my lips quivering. "Let me go. Stephen, move!"

Instead, Stephen grabs my arm. His fingernails press into my skin as he begins dragging me down the dark hallway that seems to appear suddenly to my right. I pull against his grip, digging my heels into the floor, but he's too strong. I try to fall, to crawl away, but Stephen reaches down and hoists me to my feet. "Shut up and be a good girl, Annie."

"LET. ME. GO." I slap him in the face and yank my arm once again. His fingernails cut into my skin and blood trickles onto my skin.

Stephen swings me around and slams me against the wall. It drives the breath out of my lungs. I'm gasping as he leans close into my face and says, "Bitch, stop giving me problems or else I'll just kill you."

Or else he'll just kill me?

What the hell is going on?

My heartbeat, already frantic, doubles again as Stephen grabs my upper arm again and drags me towards the exit. We slip through the curtain hanging in the doorway. The hallway reeks of urine. I turn to look over my shoulder, hoping to see my roommates, but no one is looking.

I swallow past the lump in my throat and try to come up with a way to escape. But my mind is hazy, the alcohol still affecting my brain. Stephen marches me down the hall.

A bright light hits my eyes when someone opens the exit door. My hand comes up to shield my sight as I blink rapidly. My legs refuse to move and my stomach lurches. It's had enough, and it won't stay still anymore. Puke flies from my mouth, splashing against the decrepit red carpet below my feet.

"Fucking gross," the new guy who's standing in the doorway yelps. He lowers the flashlight that was blinding me. Strings of vomit hang from my lips. I feel absolutely repulsive. "Not sure the boss will be happy with this slut puking all over."

"Shut up. You have the rope?" Stephen holds his hand out and I take advantage, throwing my weight at him and twisting free of his grip.

I attempt to run down the hall. Between the booze and the heels, I feel as if the universe and gravity are conspiring to fight against me. My hands tremble and my eyes water as I reach towards the wall to keep my balance. I race back towards the crowd, towards my roommates.

Towards safety.

But just when I've almost reached the main room, someone jerks me backwards by the hair. Pain erupts in my scalp as I collapse back into his torso.

"You dumb fucking bitch. I told you: you aren't going anywhere." Stephen's voice is too calm, too calculated.

He drags me back down the hallway by the hair as I continue to claw at him. I can feel his skin tearing under my nails, but his grip doesn't relax even the tiniest bit.

We get back to the exit door. "You going to help me?" Stephen's words are clipped as he spits them at the new guy.

"Augustin, if you fuck her up too much the boss is going to kill you."

"Augustin?" My voice cracks with each syllable. "I thought your name was Stephen."

Both men laugh as the new guy grabs my legs and the two drag me out the door. I fight back against them the best I can, but Stephen ... Augustin ... backhands me and my vision blurs. I sink to the cold asphalt as Augustin and his associate bind my ankles and wrists with rope. About five feet away is a light gray van with the engine still running. Bile creeps up my throat again.

My head swivels from side to side as I look for someone. Anyone. I need help. But the alleyway is empty. Suddenly, everything goes dark as a cloth is tied around my eyes.

"Please," I plead. "Please, let me go." I don't have much more fight left in me.

But no one answers.

My body is lifted and flung sideways. I land hard on cold metal and hear the squeaking of the van's shocks. Oh God. I'm going to die. I'm never going to see my parents again. Or my friends. I'm never going to graduate or have my own family. I should've stayed at the apartment tonight instead of trying to be something I'm not.

"Hurry up." Augustin's irate voice fills the van. "We're going to be late. This bitch put us behind schedule."

"You shoulda roofied her. Woulda taken the fight right out of the cunt," the other guy says.

"Then what? Boss would still have my head if she's falling all over at the auction, unable to stand."

Auction? What auction?

The van lurches forward and my face hits the floor. I struggle to sit up and then inch backwards so I can lean against the wall. It's cold against my bare shoulders.

The two men fall silent. My mind spins, trying to make sense of what's happening to me. The van hits a bunch of potholes and I bounce in the air a couple of times, landing hard on my butt. With my ankles and wrists tied, keeping my balance is hard, and whenever the driver makes a sharp turn, I fall over.

Eventually, the van comes to a stop. Someone opens the door. I swallow past my fear, waiting for what comes next. Still blindfolded, I have no idea where I am. A pair of large, calloused hands grip me and pull me forward. My heels strike the ground hard and my knees buckle, but whoever is holding me keeps me from falling over.

"Cute piece of meat," an unfamiliar baritone voice says.

"Yeah, that's quite an ass she's packing," another voice says.

"Fuck you." The words come out before I can stop them and I wince, expecting someone to slap me. But all I get are a couple of chuckles. A large hand palms my ass and squeezes. I hiss through my teeth and swing sideways, but no one is there and I stumble. Again, they laugh.

"She's got fight in her."

"Don't underestimate the bitch. Just get her upstairs before she causes trouble," Augustin instructs.

The man with calloused hands drags me forward while someone else shoves my shoulder from behind. I scream and scream, straining my voice, hoping someone will hear me and help. But nothing comes out, and no one helps. Instead, those around me just laugh more. Raw sobs wrack my body. I'm shaking like a leaf. With every second that passes, panic continues to consume every cell of my body.

If I want to live, I'm going to have to fight back.

I swing my leg at an angle, and connect with someone. The solid mass hurts my toes but I kick again. And again.

Someone jerks my head back by my hair. "Cunt, you better knock it off."

Augustin.

"Go to hell, Augustin. I hope you fucking die." Each word I spit out at him contains as much venom as I can muster.

"Oh, Annie. With what's going to happen to you, that wish is something you should be making for yourself. Death would be far preferable to the future waiting for you after tonight."

I shiver at the icy venom in his voice. He means every word he's saying. For the millionth time since they threw me into the back of that van, I wonder why this is happening to me. Who are these people?

"Ain't that right? With those lips, who wouldn't want to fuck her mouth?" the man with the baritone voice says.

"She'll probably earn a pretty penny. Especially from some of the customers who like a feisty girl they can smack around," another man says.

Oh God.

Auction.

I'm up for auction. This is a sex-trafficking auction. I've heard of this before, but I never really believed it existed. Just trumped-up housewife gossip, or so I thought. But if I'm right, then Augustin is right. Death would be kinder.

I go limp again. This can't be happening. This kind of stuff isn't real … is it?

"Pick up your feet." Augustin's voice is threatening. I do as he says.

The climb up the staircase is more difficult than it should be and I'm not sure if that's because of the lingering effects of the alcohol or the adrenaline coursing through my body. Maybe it's both, but my legs are shaky and barely support my weight. After a few more steps, someone shoves me from behind and I fall to my knees before being hoisted up again.

"Shoulda kept her on all fours. Hottest fuckin' thing I've seen all night," one of the men says, and my stomach curls in disgust.

"Your balls on a serving tray would make my night," I growl. The alcohol is definitely fueling my loose lips. I've never spoken like this before. I've never been this angry or afraid before, either.

In response, someone slaps me on the back of the head. Head spinning, I'm hoisted up and placed back on my feet. My heels slip a little; the new surface is slick. Something leathery wraps around my neck, too tight to be comfortable, and I squirm to get away. But it's no use. Metal clicks around my wrist and cuts into my skin. I yank to try to free myself only to hear the clank of metal on metal.

A collar and handcuffs.

I hear the murmurs and shuffling of a crowd. Then, whatever material Augustin used to obstruct my vision is unceremoniously ripped off my head and I'm left staring at a room full of men and women.

Augustin is off to my right. Now that I can see him, I sneer in his direction as I tug against the handcuffs. My head swivels around the room as I take stock of my surroundings. I'm up on a stage, surrounded by other women who are also restrained to their own poles. The dim lights create a seductive but terrifying atmosphere, and my eyes go wide as I face the crowd again.

A man gets on stage, microphone in hand. "Ladies and gentlemen, here are the lovely ladies up for auction tonight. Enjoy, and happy bidding."

The crowd breaks into hoots and hollers and applause.

My heart thunders in my chest as if attempting to break free from its bony cage. My breathing becomes shallow as I gasp for oxygen. All I have are questions.

Where am I? How the hell do I get out of here?

And what is about to happen next?

4

NIKITA

I lean back in the chair as my gaze lingers on the brunette giving my men a hard time. The corner of my lip curls up into a slight grin when she tries to kick Augustin. She's a fighter, and although she looks like a deer caught in headlights, she also appears to be a deer ready to take on said automobile. She's unlike the other girls on stage, or the ones that were already sold in the first batch a half hour ago.

The previous group was the usual trash—addicts, desperate runaways. Boring, boring, boring. Nothing I would want close to my finger, let alone my dick. I had one of my lieutenants dispose of a girl because of the way her eyes rolled up into her head. I can't make money on someone who might die five minutes after she's been sold. And I couldn't exactly let her traipse out of here. Who knows where she'd go running off to, blabbing about things she should never have known?

My attention focuses back on the beautiful girl on stage. Her legs have some meat, yet remain thin with a slight muscular undertone. Probably a runner. My gaze travels up the length of her body to her breasts. Perky, full. A perfect mouthful. Her olive skin is clear and smooth.

"She'll sell for a lot of money. Hopefully, enough to make this night a success," Eitan says. "I told you Augustin would deliver someone worthwhile."

Sweat drips from the man's hairline. I can't help but smile every time a groan or grunt passes his lips. My advisor is a bit on the pale side. His eyes dart between the stage, the customers, and the screen of his iPad. He's a weasel and a snake, but he's *my* snake. The only one I trust, though even that has its limits.

I glance around the room, taking in all the customers. Everyone is focused on the girl. Some are whispering to their lieutenants. Eitan is right; she will certainly bring in a lot of money. But where the hell did Augustin find this rare creature? She's definitely not an addict. And I can't imagine her being a runaway. She's far too innocent to have been on the streets. I pray that she isn't some rich brat who wanted to piss off Mommy and Daddy; otherwise, I'll have the cops crawling around. But that won't be my problem once she's sold. It's one of the terms in the contract the winning bidder has to sign—they take on all responsibility, and no refunds are given.

I take her in once more. Her hair is a lovely shade of whiskey. The way the locks frame her eyes makes her look innocent and beautiful at the same time. But those lips, those damn lips, are cock-sucking lips. Full and plump. My dick jerks at the thought.

I clear my throat and straighten in my seat. This is my show, my income. I'm the boss here, and showing any interest or any emotion isn't an option. Especially with potential enemies in the room. In this world, every mob boss and lieutenant is just waiting for a sign of weakness to jump on so they can take over.

"Eitan, how much have we made so far?" My attention bounces between the highest bidders in the room as I wait for him to answer.

"So far, about seventy-nine thousand." Eitan sighs, his shoulders slumping. He pulls a handkerchief from his pocket and dabs his hairline "I'm hoping this next lot pulls in the rest of the cash we need."

I grunt in agreement. I can't afford to lose money tonight.

The auctioneer returns to the stage. The first time we met, I pulled a gun on him for trying to duck out of one of my bars without paying his tab. But he managed to talk me out of killing him for it. Instead, I had him beaten to within an inch of his life, then I gave him a job. It turned out nicely. The man is good and has helped keep my auctions successful.

The auctioneer taps the microphone to get everyone's attention and I sit back, ready to enjoy the show. "Ladies and gentlemen, first up in lot five is a lovely Hispanic beauty. Bid starts at three thousand."

A hand goes up.

"Three thousand. Do I hear four thousand?"

Another hand goes up.

The auctioneer and the bidders continue their dance until the Hispanic woman is sold for twenty-five thousand to the wife of the Dinotto family. Finally, we've hit one hundred thousand in revenue. But to make this night a success, I want about three times that. I pull at my jacket and watch as the next girl is auctioned off, trying to avoid looking at the beautiful creature Augustin managed to drag in.

Eitan continues to keep track of the winning bids on his tablet. My lieutenants bounce between their security patrols and gawking at the women on stage. At least they're behaving professionally. Nothing I hate more than one of my men acting like an uneducated prick. They represent me, and I don't tolerate people making me look bad. There are no second chances and they know it.

"Damn, what I wouldn't give to run a train on that brunette bitch."

Of course, one of the newest lieutenants has decided to open his fucking mouth. My blood boils in an instant and I turn around and grab the lapels of the man's jacket. "Shut the fuck up before I put a bullet in your head."

My nostrils flare as each breath comes out rushed. When the man doesn't respond, I inch my face closer to his, my eyes unblinking. "Acknowledge."

"Sorry, boss." The man ducks his head and slinks backwards.

I turn back around to face the stage but can see the rest of my men staring at me. What the hell did I just do? The kid spoke quietly enough that none of the other families could have heard. And his comment was hardly the most offensive thing I've ever heard. But the moment he completed his sentence, an image of his vile fingers violating that beauty flashed in my head.

I close my eyes and take a deep breath to calm myself. When I open them, my men are facing forward, spines straight, and they're back on alert. They know better than to fuck with me, or question me.

My father was a kinder man. Eitan reminds me of that every day. He'd probably have laughed with my lieutenant, or even high-fived the kid. But that kindness got him killed, and I won't allow anyone to take advantage of me.

I grind my molars together as memories of my father swirl around in my head.

∽

Years ago

"Sure is hot today," Dad said.

I grunted and trekked up the small hill. "Hot doesn't even cover it. I thought the trees were supposed to keep things cool."

My father chuckled. "Blame it on global warming."

I took in all the air my lungs could hold and expelled it slowly. The air was rich with the fragrance of leaves and loam. The path twisted in front of us, snaking around the trees. The roots crisscrossed, gnarled and uneven. These hikes with my father were like a trip out of my everyday life. It was the only time all year I got to spend time with him by myself.

The ground was smooth under our shoes and the light of the sun filtered through the tree foliage on each side of the trail. We were barely a third of the way into a three-hour hike and I was already drenched in sweat.

"So, your mom told me you came home late a couple of times this week. Or, I should say, she claimed you came in during the early hours of the morning." Dad quirked his brow at me as he waited for my response.

"Went out with my friends."

"You know, you're graduating soon. I need you to be more responsible." Dad grabbed a tree branch and hoisted himself over a fallen log. "I need you ready to take over the business. I need you to take things more seriously instead of running around nailing every girl you come across."

"I said I was partying, not fucking." I cringe instantly. Sometimes I forgot to curb my vocabulary when speaking to my father. "Sorry, sir. I didn't mean to curse."

"At least a certain level of maturity is present," he sighed. "But son, you aren't a child anymore. It's time to grow up and be responsible. You can't just go running around doing whatever you want."

I stopped and turned toward the old man. "I help out at the office, I help with the books, I lie to the cops. I'm not even twenty yet."

"And yet there are some younger than you who are lieutenants running parts of the family businesses. I need you to step up your game."

I felt my temper rising in my chest. "What's next? Are you going to tell me I'm not a man yet?" My feet stomped into the dirt trail and I kicked a stone. This was supposed to be our annual bonding time, not a lecture.

My dad took a deep breath and shook his head. "There's more to being a man than age. Maturity and responsibility have a lot to do with it. But so does experience. And so does looking at the bigger picture, and seeing the areas of gray that exist. Son, you still see only in black and white. Right or wrong. You beat someone up for looking at you the wrong way without ever questioning why they looked at you in the first place."

Again, with this. I'd barely hurt the guy. Some blood, some broken bones. He was fine. And he shouldn't have looked at me like that, anyways. He started it, if you asked me. My temper ratcheted up another notch.

"What? I'm supposed to let some punk disrespect me? You weren't there." My voice rose and my temples throbbed as I thought back on the incident my father was referring to. Sure, I'd lost my temper and put some kid in the hospital. But my father, of all people, should have understood, especially with who he was. Hell, he had had people killed for not respecting him.

"The dumb kid made fun of you." My father turned to face me, his eyes narrowed and his lips pressed tight. "He was a dumb kid. You should've let it go. He didn't threaten you. He didn't pull a gun on you. He was some insignificant kid. Nikita, part of being a man—part of maturity—is learning to choose your battles."

I raked my fingers through my hair and sighed. This argument had gone on for two weeks now and no matter what I said, he just wouldn't drop it. "Dad, I apologized to you. Hell, I even dropped an envelope of cash off at the kid's house. What more do you want from me?"

But before he could respond, the sound of crunching leaves caught our attention. My fists balled immediately as a burst of chirps filled the air and a nearby bush shook. My father inched toward the bush, crouching low to peer between the branches. "A bird is stuck."

I could see it now, a little bluebird hooked on thorns at the base of the shrub. The closer my father got to the bush, the more the bird frantically flapped its wings. But there was nowhere to go. Every flap only drew more blood and got it entangled further. My father swung his backpack over his shoulder and placed it on the ground. He unzipped the bag, reached inside, and pulled out a pair of gloves. "Nikita, come help."

I dropped my own backpack to the ground and walked over to my father. It seemed hopeless to me. Even if we got the sucker out, it looked like one or both wings were broken. The thing was a goner. "Dad, there are tons of thorns. You're going to get all cut up. Leave the bird."

"Son, the poor creature needs help. We're not leaving it to die." He stepped toward the bush with a small knife in hand and started cutting branches out of the way.

I watched the frightened bird as its tweets and chirps became hysterical. Its wings beat as if attempting to fly away with the bush in tow. My father whispered to it as he kept working. Slice by slice, the thorny whirls fell away, until finally there was a clear path to the bird. My father reached in and took gentle hold of the small creature, pulling the bird from its thorny prison.

He stood and pivoted towards me, keeping the bird cupped in his hand as he inspected it. I was wrong about the broken wing. Free of the bush, it looked relatively intact, if a bit bloodied and ruffled. It seemed content to sit in my father's hands for now. "Little guy got off easy. No real cuts, nothing broken." He smiled and slowly opened his hand further. The bird flapped its wings once, twice, as if testing to make sure it was okay. Then it flew off through a gap in the branches overhead. We watched it go.

My father turned to look at me. "Nikita, being a man sometimes means putting yourself in harm's way to do the right thing."

∽

Someone coughs and pulls me from my thoughts. My eyes are wet. I grit my teeth, shake my head, and compose myself again.

I look back to the stage. There are only three girls left, including the beautiful woman who first caught my attention. My brows pinch together as I watch her head swivel from side to side. She yanks at her restraints. Her chest rises and falls at a rapid rate.

Just like a bird caught in thorns.

But when she turns to face the crowd once more, she's anything but the bird from my memory. Instead of fear, her eyes are hot with an angry blaze.

I turn my gaze from her and focus on my hands, my thoughts shifting once again to my father. The man was too kind and good, and that's what got him killed. He gave people too many opportunities, trusted too easily. And that's all the traitor needed.

Anger boils deep in my body, as hot as lava. It churns within, hungry for destruction, and I know it's too much for me to handle. I allowed the darkness to swallow me whole the moment I thought about my father. My fists clench so hard my knuckles turn white. But it's all I can do to keep from losing control in front of everyone.

"Nikita, sir?" Eitan frowns as he lays his hand on my forearm. "Is everything okay?"

But it's too late and the thoughts take over.

The traitor.

The bastard from my father's inner circle. The one who betrayed my father, kidnapped him, and then sold him to our enemies. Of course, it took days for us to find out what happened. But I knew instantly the first night my father didn't come home that he would never step foot into the house again.

I'd wanted to be the one to find my father. I wanted to have a body to bury, to give him the funeral send-off he deserved. And I wanted for all that to happen so my mother didn't have to be the one to find him. Because if that happened, I knew I'd lose her, too.

It didn't take long. Not even a week. One of my father's lieutenants came across his body strung up in a warehouse that we used to store weapons in. I got the call after midnight and raced over to the place. The men had left him in the position they found him. Seeing my father like that, my father who had set a small bird free, broke my soul.

I didn't shed a tear. I felt nothing that night. No pain. No anger. I was just numb as I cut him down and covered him with a sheet. As I stood over his dead body, the same memory from the mountain came to mind.

My father had told me it was my responsibility to free the bird. But it was the wrong lesson. The lesson was not to free the bird.

It was to never become the bird.

Instead, I became the thorny bush, trapping and destroying those who threatened my business and my family. I would never be as weak as he was. No one would ever think to betray me. And I'd never afford them the opportunity either.

It has been ten years since that night. I've clawed my way to the top. Anyone whose loyalty I question is killed—whether by my hand or my command.

Sparing the life of the old man earlier tonight was the most sympathy I've shown in a decade.

Eitan is the only person I've allowed to be close to me. And truth be told, I bugged his house years ago and still listen in.

Trust is a luxury I can't enjoy. Especially with the newest weapons shipment coming in.

"Eitan, is everything set for the meeting later?" My fingers drum against my thighs.

"Most of the bosses were told to keep a cool head during the auction, that we have important business to discuss. But you know some of them don't really listen. I expect Dino might be a problem," Eitan responds.

I snort. "He always is. I still don't understand how the man hasn't been imprisoned yet. The FBI has been on him for years."

"He plays the game with them. A great showman. But my gut says they feel he's low on the pecking order. Too dramatic. Not to be trusted."

Eitan's right, and it's one of the reasons Dino and the Tratatori family are always on my radar. I'm not one to underestimate him. Hell, I'd love to put a bullet in his head most days, but he's got a strong network. One I can and have used.

"We'll go over the inventory expected, pricing, and narrow down the times. Remember, don't let the exact time slip. No need for anyone to slip and give the feds the heads-up. Remind our men as well," I say.

Eitan nods.

I breathe in and out slowly. I've been working on this deal for a while—been burning the midnight oil to make sure the operation runs smoothly—because this massive weapons shipment will guarantee power and control for a long time to the Lavrin family.

And to me.

5

ANNIE

My head isn't throbbing as much and my legs feel steadier. Thank God the alcohol is finally leaving my system. But now I can see more of the predicament I'm in, and just how dangerous this situation is. In front, one of the final women is up for bidding. That leaves just me. Her dark hair is frizzy and curly over bruised mocha skin. Her silver dress sparkles in the lights from the stage. She's missing one shoe and her knee is bleeding.

The crowd hoots and hollers, but tears stain the woman's face. My brows pinch together. She looks younger than me. Do these people go around abducting young woman? How can they get away with this? Families have to be searching for these girls.

And someone has to be searching for me ... right?

The woman hangs her head down, her shoulders shuddering as the man holding her chain hoists her dress up to show the crowd her goods and spins her around. Some creep in the front row jumps up and slaps the woman's ass, cackling like a crazed lunatic. In that instant, the woman looks up and our eyes meet. Her eyes are full of terror and hopelessness. Her mascara mixes with tears, black tracks running down her full cheeks. Her bottom lip is swollen, a trickle of blood running from a split in the middle.

"This is some beauty. That ass has enough cushion to take quite a pounding," the guy from the crowd says.

"Bidding will begin at six thousand dollars. Do I have six thousand?" The auctioneer starts up his spiel again. "Six thousand. Do I hear seven thousand?"

My blood begins to boil once again. I'm not going to let anyone bid on me like I'm some piece of meat. And I won't be sold to some fucking creep just so he can screw me to get his sick rocks off.

No. Fucking. Way.

I have to get the hell out of here and now—by any means necessary. Judging by the bloodlust in the eyes of the men in the front row, I'm beginning to think I'd rather have them kill me than be subjected to whatever the winning bidder has in mind once he gets his filthy hands on me.

The bodyguard to my right is too busy looking at the spectacle going on with the girl's bidding. He's tall and broad, like a linebacker. But he's currently distracted, so I take advantage and I make a break for it. But suddenly, I'm snapped backward and my feet go up in the air as I crash to the ground, landing hard on my backside.

I forgot about the collar.

Every eye turns to me. The room breaks out in a cacophony of laughter and claps. One guy turns beet red and slaps his thigh. I'm mortified, frozen to the spot on the ground I landed. I can't believe this is happening, and that everyone in the crowd finds this amusing. I clench my jaw tight as I take in the cruel laughter, my head beginning to spin once again.

"When's she up for bidding?" someone yells, and I want nothing more than to become invisible.

"Gentlemen, let's focus on our current bid. We will get to the lovely lady who's been providing us with an unprecedented level of entertainment in a few minutes," the auctioneer says.

I remain seated on the cool floor. Terror sinks its claws deeper into me. There's no way I'm going to make it out of here, no way I'll ever see my family again. What did I do to deserve this? Why has my life ended up in this nightmare? I pull my legs up to my chest, balling myself as tight as I can, wishing I could shrink even smaller and just disappear. Why did I have to go out tonight?

The crowd gets louder as the bidding continues once again. An argument breaks out, but the auctioneer keeps the two men in control. Finally, the bidding on the woman ends at forty-five thousand dollars. Sweat drenches my skin, my eyes throb uncontrollably, and my heart thumps in my chest like a herd of stampeding horses. My fingers curl into a fist, nails digging into my palms. My breathing is ragged and shallow. Fear churns my stomach in tense cramps.

I'm next.

I scurry backwards, as far away from the front of the stage as I can. But a pair of large hands comes from behind to lift me to my feet. I whip my head around to find the linebacker goon with a foul smirk on his face. My legs are shaky and I stumble a bit as I attempt to find my balance. I choke back a sob and close my eyes as I take a deep breath, silently praying for a miracle. Praying for a way out of this nightmare.

The man's calloused skin scrapes up my shoulders and pulls me back to my horrific reality. He stops near my neck. Maybe he's going to unhook my collar. Maybe this is my chance to get away. My miracle.

Instead, the unmistakable sound of tearing of fabric fills my ears. The front of my shirt falls to my waist, exposing my bra and cleavage.

"Oops, clumsy me," the man behind me drawls, the unmistakable hint of humor lining his words.

The crowd roars in appreciation. Some people stand and applaud. One man waves a handful of cash in the air while another sticks two fingers in his mouth and whistles. Even the auctioneer turns and smiles, his pupils dilating as he focuses on my breasts. His gaze runs the length of me and the tip of his tongue grazes across his crooked teeth.

I curl my shoulders forward, trying to hide, but it's no use. My heart aches. My stomach churns. My skin is drenched in cold sweat.

The goon behind me unclips my collar from the pole and pushes me toward the front of the stage, holding onto the chain as if it were a leash. As if I'm a dog who needs someone to lead me. When I try to hold my ground, the man jabs me in the back, forcing me forward. When I'm where they want me to be, the auctioneer circles around like a shark waiting to feed. His creepy eyes devour me.

"Where am I?" The words squeak from my lips without permission. I wish I could take them back.

The crowd once again breaks into a bout of laughter. I hate being a source of entertainment for all of them. They're demons. What other explanation is there? How could any human do this to another person?

A fat man, bald and sweaty, in the front row glares at me. His bloodshot eyes twitch. Bloody red stitches climb his crooked neck, under his leering grin. A cackle erupts from behind his chipped teeth that slant in every direction like broken piano keys. He's crouched awkwardly, and for some reason it reminds me of a tarantula, the way he clings close to the ground, all pent-up kinetic energy and whirling, watching pupils.

Then he springs forward and runs his slimy tongue across my foot.

I flinch and yank my foot away, bile crawling up my throat. "What the fuck is wrong with you all?" I gasp. "Where am I? What is this?" My last wisp of courage is gone now, and in its place there isn't anything left but pure, wide-eyed panic. I want out. I want home. I want my mother. I want to be anywhere in the world but where I am right now —trapped, chained, and about to be sold to a beast.

The man who tongued my foot looks at me, eyes bulging. As if he can read my mind, he licks his lips and says, "Baby, you're in the underworld. And we're the devils who live here."

It's like he said the magic words that unlock a whole new level of unfiltered lust, of dirty energy that now expands to light up the eyes of every man in the dark room. The crowd erupts into cheers, fists pumping into the air.

I know the man is telling the truth. I'm in some kind of hell. A hell where men like him buy women like me. A hell where strangers rip open my clothes to expose my breasts to onlookers. A hell where a grotesque bastard licks my foot without permission.

The goon behind me unlocks my handcuffs and leads me closer to the auctioneer. But the creep from the front row jumps up on stage, reaching his hand out and squeezing my breast. "Just want to test the merchandise."

Without thinking, my free hand comes up and my fist connects hard with the guy's jaw. There's an audible pop, and the crowd falls silent. My hand is hurting, but the adrenaline muffles the edge of the pain. All I can think is how good it felt to hit back. To not be helpless. To go down swinging, if it turns out that this is indeed the end of me.

For one brief moment, I'm in control of my own life.

Then it's gone. I look at the man. His sneer has vanished and now his lips press into a tight line. Before I can react, he cracks me backhanded across the cheek. My head jerks back and I stumble. Stars flash in front of my eyes.

"Dumb bitch."

Tears cloud my sight, the blow making me dizzy. The stinging pain is familiar and before I can stop it, the floodgates in my mind burst open. Memories rush in, unwanted but unstoppable.

I haven't been slapped like that since my father was still alive.

∼

Years ago

"Mom, what time is Daddy coming home? I need his help with this school project."

"I'm not sure, Annie. I know he has a meeting with his bosses. Is there anything I can help you with?" Mommy laid a hand on my shoulder.

"No. We're writing a story for Father's Day in school and there's an interview I have to do with Daddy." My shoulders sagged as I put away the assignment sheet and grabbed my math homework. Hopefully, my dad would be home before bedtime. I wasn't sure what I'd say to my teachers this time if he didn't show up.

Mom kissed my head and made her way back to the stove. "I made some mac and cheese, honey. I know it's your favorite."

I forced a smile. Mom was always trying to make me feel better, ever since Daddy had started this new job that kept him away at all hours of the night. His mood had changed, too. He was more nervous, more tired than he ever had been before. And when he was here, things were different. Darker, somehow.

He wouldn't tell us what his new job was, only that we couldn't tell anybody about it and we couldn't ask any questions about the people he brought over. The men who came home with him sometimes were cocky and rude, bossing my mom around, cursing or slapping at her if she got their drinks wrong. She told me to stay out of sight when Daddy had guests, but I couldn't help peeking at them, with their cigarettes dangling from their fat lips and dirty shoes propped up on the coffee table. Mommy always yelled at me if I put my shoes on the furniture, but for some reason she never said anything to them. She seemed scared of the men my father worked for now.

A crash sounded from the living room and my heart stuttered as I jumped out of my chair. I tried to look out into the hallway, but Mommy forced me behind her. We inched to the doorway and peered into the living room where the noise had come from.

Shattered glass was strewn across the floor. In the middle of the mess was a brick. I looked up and saw a huge hole in the living room window. Mom huffed and straightened her spine. She turned to me, her hand pushing my hair back from my face. "Annie, please get the broom and dustpan."

I nodded and turned toward the kitchen as my mom walked towards the front door. I wasn't sure what was happening, but it seemed bad. Why would someone throw a brick through our window?

I brought Mom the broom from the kitchen closet and stood silent in the corner as she swept up the shards of glass. Neither of us said a word. I held the dustpan for her until the mess was cleaned up.

Then Daddy walked in just as we finished.

"What happened?" he growled.

"Someone threw a brick through the window!" I blurted. Mommy glared at me, like I'd given away a secret.

Daddy's brow furrowed. He raked his hand through his hair, walked over to the couch, and plopped down, pouring himself a big glass of whiskey from the bar table next to him. "This is my fault. My bosses are angry. I'm not meeting my quota." He leaned forward and pressed his face into his palms.

I'd never seen him so upset before. It was weird and uncomfortable. I wanted to ask questions, but before I could open my mouth, my mother cut me off.

"Annie, go to your room so your father and I can talk." She sounded like she was about to cry.

"But—"

"*NOW.*"

I didn't dare resist. The warbling edge in her voice was frightening.

I made my way back down the hall to my bedroom, closing my door but pressing my ear against the crack in the bottom.

I didn't hear everything they said to each other, just bits and pieces.

Drugs. Packages. Bratva. Money, someone owed someone, and someone was going to get hurt if they didn't pay someone. Bricks, warnings. It didn't all make total sense, but by the time I heard my mother pad past my room, I knew enough to be afraid. Daddy had gotten us mixed up in something really bad.

That wasn't the first brick through the window, either.

But I would've preferred a thousand more bricks, a brick every night for the rest of my life, compared to what came next.

It was a few months later. Things were worse than ever. I walked on eggshells when I was at home, terrified of making my dad even angrier than he normally was. My mother had stopped eating and was wasting away to skin and bones. Whenever I asked about the bruises on her arms after she and Daddy had been up all night arguing again, she just snapped at me and told me it was nothing.

"Annie!" I heard her calling me from the kitchen. "Annie, go check the mail!"

I walked outside and saw a package leaning up against our doorframe. Picking it up, I noticed the bottom was sticky and wet. It must have been raining outside.

I walked into the kitchen and set the box on the crowded countertop, then went over to the sink to wash the cardboard residue off my hands. I noticed the water turned red as it rinsed my skin.

"Mom, the box is leaking something."

She came over, picked it up, then sat down with it at the kitchen table, knife in hand to slice the tape off.

Then I heard the knife clatter to the floor. My mother screamed. My heart froze.

I ran over to her. "Mom, what, what is it?" Her eyes were wide with terror, face pale, hands trembling. I looked down at the opened box.

It was a finger.

A bloody finger.

Bile clawed at the back of my throat. I pulled away from my mother and ran back to the sink to puke. Tears fell from my eyes as I retched again and again. Was that my father's finger? We hadn't seen him for two days.

"Is Dad dead?" I looked up to see she hadn't moved from her seat at the table.

It took her a long time to answer. "I don't know, Annie."

Neither of us slept that night.

Eventually, my father did eventually come home, bloodied and beaten, scabbed-over stump where his right middle finger had been. He'd been tortured by the Bratva for failing to sell enough product once again. How much longer could this dark secret persist? What would happen to him if he couldn't make things work? What would happen to us?

Fate decided that for us. And our dark secret became public news when we woke up after another night without my father home, to find his face plastered over the front of the local paper.

Arrested. Charged with racketeering, intent to distribute, possession of a mind-boggling amount of illegal drugs. No bond. No hope.

We lost our house; assets were all frozen. With no living relatives left to help and no friends willing to open their doors to the family of a criminal, Mom and I had to move into a homeless shelter.

Mom eventually found a job as a secretary and we made some ends meet. A new city helped us put some distance between the bricks and bloodied fingers that still haunted my dreams. I buried myself in my studies to try and forget.

But forgetting was impossible.

My father ended up dying in jail. It was no more and no less than he deserved for what he did to me. To my mother. To our family.

I swore I'd stay far away from the kind of men who had taken everything from us—the men with cigarettes and dirty shoes on the coffee table. The men who slapped my mother if she messed up their drinks. The Bratva was no sexy fantasy—it was a living, breathing beast. And it had ruined my life.

∼

I look around the room from the stage once more. So much for my promise to myself, because the reality is that my past has come back to haunt me. I'm once again in the belly of the beast I've spent my whole life trying to escape.

But this time, there's no getting away.

6

NIKITA

I swallow hard, hypnotized by the scene up on the stage.

The beautiful brunette continues to pique my interest. Her fighting spirit, still scrapping even though there's no way out, is admirable. And her innocence. So rare. Two traits that shouldn't naturally blend together but, in her, they do. Marvelously.

The delicate skin of her breasts is similarly captivating. But her fire is what holds my attention. She holds a hand to her cheek, a red handprint visible even this far back from where that fool in the front struck her. And while a mix of tears and makeup streams down her face, she recovers and glares at the man who even now lingers on the stage.

I fight to keep up the appearance of complete control and utter disinterest. But the truth is the girl has touched a nerve in me. Too much. It's becoming harder to look away. I turn to Eitan. "Where did Augustin get this woman from?"

He shrugs, his attention on his iPad. "Not sure. I know he scouted a few clubs tonight with some of the other men. She must've been at one of them."

"She's too innocent to have been a hooker. Maybe a runaway?" I steeple my fingers and press them to my lips. I run my eyes over her body for the millionth time tonight. While the miniskirt and stilettos scream experienced, the basic bra says otherwise. Almost as if the woman on stage isn't the woman she truly is. There are mysteries to be unraveled. Undressed.

Eitan finally looks up from the computer to the woman. I register a note of concern in his voice. "She's too clean. Her skin too perfect. And look at her hair, clean and shiny. Most of the runaways and addicts have dry skin and their hair looks like shit—brittle and broken strands. And not one would have thought to punch a mobster. Even a low-level charmer like our friend at the front of the stage."

Eitan and I chuckle. She has guts. And she must not know who she's dealing with, otherwise she wouldn't have slugged the man. Or maybe she would have. My lip twitches at the thought. From the corner of my eye, I can see Eitan looking at me, a hint of worry still on his face.

So, what if she belongs to someone? What if they come looking for her? I shake my head. Once she's sold, it's not my problem. I won't have to worry about the feds or her family looking for her. And I would hope one of my men would know better than to kidnap someone that others will be looking for.

Because I don't take kindly to costly mistakes like that.

The auctioneer grabs the microphone, walks up to the girl, and stands next to her. He faces the crowd and grins. "Bidding for this wild filly will begin at ten thousand dollars. Do I hear ten thousand?"

A hand immediately goes up. The auctioneer moves to fifteen thousand and another hand goes up. From the back of the room, I watch as every boss in the room vies for the girl, her value rising with each passing second. Eitan tracks each hand waving for the next bid and smiles wide. "I knew this woman would sell for a lot."

I nod and continue to watch the action up front. The woman's head whips around as she tries to follow each person bidding on her, terror taking over her features the higher the number gets. Such a shame. She should be proud about how much everyone in the audience values her. As to what ends they will use her for ... well, it's better not to think of it.

The back-and-forth continues on until only two men are left in the bidding war. One of them is Gino DeLuca.

"Looks like our friend Gino has his heart set on the wild one," Eitan says.

I grunt.

The DeLuca don is a constant thorn in my side. I wish he would have passed on the invitation tonight. Actually, I didn't want to invite him. The man is unhinged and deceptively sneaky, and he's starting to drift outside his lane. Gino controls much of the drug traffic in the city, a fact I've been fine with, up to a point. But lately he's been making noise about moving into weapons. And weapons are my key line of business.

My blood begins to boil and my eyes narrow on the Italian. I watch him lick his lips as the bidding swirls around him. "Gino's not blind. He wants what everyone else in this place wants: fresh meat," I finally respond.

"One thing's for sure: the bid on the girl is up to sixty thousand dollars, so we just met our quota for the night."

He's right, but the thought of our payday is far from my mind. Something is brewing in my chest. A dark, unfamiliar feeling. Hatred for Gino, lust for the girl ... I grind my teeth. What I wouldn't give for someone to whack the guy. But when it comes to Gino and the Italians, diplomacy over violence has been my policy. There is no telling what a street rat like Gino will do if backed into an uncomfortable corner. Most of the time, I feel that it's better to keep him fat and happy—where I can see him.

But tonight, that strategy doesn't sit well with me.

"One hundred fifty thousand dollars," Gino shouts as he stands up.

"Jesus Christ," Eitan mutters, nearly dropping the iPad. "He's out of his fucking mind. Not that I mind the money, but he's fucking crazy."

My gaze falls back on the girl, her eyes as wide as a doe's—whether from fright or from the staggering sum, I'm not sure. She begins to thrash against the collar again, furiously trying to break free. I don't blame her. Gino will break her, maybe even kill her. It wouldn't be the first time he's killed a slave.

"One hundred fifty thousand. Do I hear one hundred sixty thousand?" The auctioneer looks around the room as he walks back and forth across the stage. "One hundred fifty thousand going once."

The girl looks at Gino, then around the room. She yanks on the chain, although she, I, and everyone else in the room knows it will not yield to her. She swings out her leg to kick my lieutenant. She's not giving up, full of fight instead of flight, even if she's going to end up dead for it.

Then, out of nowhere, like a ghost whispering in my ear: *"Son, the poor creature needs my help. I'm not leaving it to die."*

When I look back to the stage, I see a trapped bird. The same bird who kept fighting against the thorny bush. And I can't turn away from her. Something inside me wants her in a way I don't understand. It wants to help her like my father helped the bird.

My pulse quickens until my temples throb. I need to move, not be stuck sitting in this chair. But pacing isn't an option, not in present company. *Control. Control. Control yourself.*

But it isn't meant to be. My eyes swivel to the auctioneer and before I know what I'm doing, my hand is up in the air. "One hundred sixty thousand dollars."

Fuck.

Every head in the room turns to the back. To me. I look straight ahead and avoid the glances from those around me. I fight to keep my expression blank, controlled, all business. No chink in my armor must show to these people, though I know by jumping in I have just caused a stir in the atmosphere, especially since I never act on impulse.

Everything I do is calculated. Everyone knows that about me. It's my lone trademark, the calling card that has taken me to the top. I'm just hoping that, instead of seeing a moment of weakness, they're wondering what game I'm playing.

My eyes fall on the girl once more. The slight tilt of her head and the way her eyes narrow suggest she's trying to focus, to see who I am. But I'm all the way in the back of the room. There's no way she can see me through the glare of the lights.

"One hundred seventy thousand dollars," Gino growls.

I'd almost forgotten about Gino for a moment. This is far from over. The man relishes a fight. And whatever his interest is in this girl, I know if he ends up winning, her life will be over. I won't let her die.

Besides, I've just spoken up in front of a crowd cluttered with the city's underworld elites. I can't second-guess myself, can't show weakness, can't waver.

"Two hundred thousand," I counter, refusing to look Gino's way.

Eitan places his hand on my shoulder, his fingers gripping me hard. "Nikita, this isn't a good idea. Going head to head with Gino is only going to piss him off. And remember, we still have the weapons meeting later. We'll need his cooperation for that. Let him win the girl."

Everyone in the room is murmuring. While Eitan is right, I can't back down now. Not that I would, anyway. Not to Gino. But with the city's worst surrounding me, I have to finish out the game I've hurled myself into the middle of. If I'm lucky, they'll think I'm toying with Gino to continue to drive up the price. After all, the fool made a stupid move by offering such an outrageous bid.

Gino stands up and turns toward me, his face red and his brows pinched. "Two hundred ten thousand."

"Two hundred twenty thousand." The corners of my mouth curl up into a wicked smirk. Watching Gino's face contort in a fit of anger is quite pleasing. After years of appeasing the asshole, it's nice to finally strike back in a way.

The crowd gasps. It's not every day they see the city's two most powerful men go head-to-head over something so small and petty as a new slave. But I'm not backing down. A fire has lit inside me. One I'm not about to let die.

The girl is coming home with me tonight.

"Mr. Lavrin, are you truly interested in the slave or are you simply looking to pad your pockets with my money?" Gino sneers in his thick Italian accent. He's careful not to disrespect me too openly. But malice trickles underneath his words. The crowd falls silent as they await my response.

Eitan clears his throat loud enough for me to hear, a clear warning to be careful. But I know Gino is baiting me, and I need to be careful with my response. "A slave willing to punch a made man could be useful. And a spirit like that would be interesting to break, wouldn't it?"

Tension. Silence. I don't blink. Neither does Gino. His eyes are endless black pits.

Then, just as suddenly as it began, the moment ends. Gino growls but doesn't say another word. Instead, he sits down. The auctioneer repeats my bid and asks if anyone is willing to go higher. Gino turns and looks over his shoulder but doesn't raise his hand.

"Sold, to Mr. Lavrin," says the auctioneer.

And just like that, the girl is mine.

I've bought myself a new slave.

I can feel Eitan glowering at me. So much for hitting our quota when I'm the one who just wasted a mountain of money. But it's also a reminder to everyone in the room:

I'm Nikita Lavrin, and I'm not to be underestimated.

At least, I hope that's the message they take away from it. Deep down, I'm nearly trembling. It isn't often that I lose control like that. I did a stupid thing, and there may yet be consequences for it.

"I hope you know what you're doing," Eitan says, his voice ripe with concern and frustration.

"I do," I snap. But when I meet my advisor's eyes, they're full of questions. Questions I'm not answering. Still, he knows better than to question me. I stare back, silent and defiant. He just grunts and turns back to his iPad.

"You know how much that just set us back, right?"

I wave my hand at him. "I have the money."

When Eitan doesn't press the issue further, I turn my attention back to the beautiful creature on stage. Her body trembles and she bites her lower lip, her chest rising and falling at a rapid pace. The men around me continue to gawk at her. I can feel anger rise in my chest. How dare they look at what's mine? They need to respect their boss.

I turn. "Jimmy, take some of the men and get the girl cleaned up. I want her off the stage as soon as possible. No need to have Gino staring at what he lost. I need him calm for the meeting later."

"Yes, boss."

But the way Jimmy's eyes narrow, like a predator focusing on his prey, tells me he's interpreted the situation wrong. There have been times I've purchased a slave or two and turned her over to my men as a treat. A good boss likes to keep his employees happy. And for all their hard work, my men deserve to be rewarded. But the bird on stage isn't for them.

She's mine and mine alone.

"Jimmy, get her cleaned up and have Sophia pick out a dress. Something ... elegant. She'll be joining me for dinner," I say, making sure that it's crystal clear the new slave isn't for them.

One of the men to my side coughs in surprise. Eitan's head whips in my direction so fast, I'm momentarily afraid he may have hurt himself. Jimmy glances at me, his mouth pursed. His gaze bounces to Eitan for a second and then back to me. He blinks as if to refocus.

While no one questions me, I do understand where their confusion comes from. Normally, a slave I purchase for myself—like Sophia—is cleaned up and told to wait naked in my bedroom. I've never asked for a slave to be prepped to attend dinner with me.

"Am I understood?" I repeat. I let a dangerous coolness creep into my voice.

"Yes, boss," Jimmy says quickly.

The men straighten and head toward the stage. My attention turns back to Eitan, who's staring at me like I've grown a new head. I can tell he wants to ask just what the fuck I think I'm doing. But he would never dare question me like that.

I don't give him the chance. "Are we ready for the meeting?" I ask, standing.

"Are we not going to discuss what just happened?"

I pull at the lapels of my jacket. "No explanation needed."

"Nikita, this is out of character for you."

"I understand your concern. But I'm the boss, and while it's your job to advise me, it isn't your job to question my actions," I say. "*Ever.*"

He sighs and stands. I almost feel bad for being harsh with him. He's been with my family for so long. But the laws of our world must be respected. And that means no one gets to question the boss.

So I turn to Eitan before we leave. "And, Eitan ..." I say. "If you ever challenge me again like that, I'll put a bullet in your head myself. Is that clear?"

He doesn't dare to look me in the eye. "Yes, sir," he murmurs.

We exit. Time to get everything back under control once more.

7

ANNIE

Dread owns me, pushing against me like an invisible gale, attempting to reverse my steps backward and as far from the crowd as possible. The fear has my stomach locked up tight, and sets my face stiff like rigor mortis, my teeth locked together. But unless I can turn back time, there's no escaping the hell I'm in.

Every time I've tried to fight back has resulted in failure and if what the foot-licker said is true, I'm stuck in the worst place possible. I know what these people are like. I remember what they did to my family, to my mother and me. I know there's no escaping them. And I know if I try to fight back anymore, I'll only get hurt or even killed.

So, I shut up and try to dissociate. I run through some of the problems from my last final, cross-checking the numbers. I run through a checklist of things I need to get done this weekend so that I'm all set for graduation in a couple of months. And I run through the list of bills I need to pay that aren't set up for autopay. Anything to take my mind away from this nightmare.

But I can't believe what just happened.

No matter how hard I tried, I couldn't shut out the voices from the crowd. Especially as they grew louder. I opened my eyes to the crowd swiveling its attention back and forth between two men in the back. The tension was palpable.

"One hundred seventy thousand dollars."

Wait, what? Was that a bid for me?

"Two hundred thousand," a baritone voice from the back of the room called out.

They were warring over me. I knew I should be afraid, and I'm terrified still, but curiosity started to seep in then. My eyes darted between the man in the front and the voice in the back, the voice that rattled my bones—not in fear, but something else, something I couldn't quite wrap my head around.

The crowd no longer paid attention to me as they, too, focused on the bidding war going on. This must not be normal. Between the muffled whispers and occasional gasps, whatever was going on was far from what was expected.

The man in the front, with his Italian accent, pulled me from my reverie. I missed what he said, but he was pissed, if the scowl he was wearing was any indication. The deep red shade his skin turned was a sharp contrast with his gawdy gold jewelry. Didn't anyone bother to tell him how tacky he looked?

Still, something about him frightened me. He looked like a man who was way too comfortable with violence.

"Please God, if you can hear me, please don't let the hideous scarface win." I whispered the prayer over and over. But when I squinted to focus beyond the lights to find the owner of the baritone voice, I was no longer sure if my prayer was such a good idea.

The man in the back was dressed in a black suit. His expression—what little I could see of it through the spotlight glare and the shadows beyond—was arrogant and cold as ice. But there was something about him I couldn't put a finger on. I continued to watch as the two men brawled back and forth, but over and over again, I found myself drawn to the mystery man in black. His shoulders were broad, his hair dark and slicked back. His features were sharp and angular. He was ... handsome. Incredibly so.

Christ almighty.

I must've still been a bit drunk. How in the hell was I even considering some creep who was bidding on me as a sex slave to be handsome? No, he was a pig. A monster. A devil.

A handsome devil.

Dammit. I bit my lower lip and waited for the bidding to be over. I clenched my fists tightly until my nails dug into the palm. A metallic liquid flowed across my tongue and it took me a second to realize I'd bitten my lip so badly that it was bleeding.

Then came the voice. "Sold!" the auctioneer screamed out. And just like that, it was over.

My thoughts are panicked and confused now. What am I going to do? What are *they* going to do *to* me? My breaths become shallow and I know I'm about to panic again, but I don't know what to do. I'm lost.

"Who ... who won?" The words leave my lips in barely a whisper.

The auctioneer turns to me with a smile that's all business as he points to the man in the back.

"You're his now."

The crowd claps—hesitant and uncertain, I notice—and the entire demeanor of the room is different than when I first walked in. I glance to the man in the back one more time. He's just sitting there, straight-faced. But the way everyone is reacting must mean he's someone important.

And in this world, that makes him someone to be feared.

The auctioneer and the man holding the chain attached to my collar start shoving me off the stage and into the back. My skin breaks out into goose bumps from equal parts cold air and panic.

"Please help me. Let me go. I don't belong here," I plead. I turn and look the auctioneer right in the eye. "They kidnapped me. Please let me go. I beg you."

But he just uses his forearm to move me out of the way and walks down the hallway and out of my sight. I grab hold of a railing as the goon tries to drag me and hold on for dear life. "Let me go! I swear, I won't tell anyone anything."

No one responds. No one shows any interest, much less any sympathy, though the goon and another man definitely are starting to appear frustrated. The one guy walks over and starts to pry my fingers from the railing. He doesn't say a word to me nor does he look at me. Truth be told, it's as if he's doing his best to avoid looking at any part of me, like I'm firmly off-limits even to his gaze.

Who the hell is the man who purchased me?

When I'm no longer gripping the railing, the goon holding the chain yanks me and I fly forward, landing on my knees. "What the hell is wrong with you?"

I gingerly push to my feet, my knees aching from colliding with the cement floor. A trickle of blood travels down the length of my calf. I glance around, hoping to find Augustin. Not that the jerk will help, but at least I pray he will give me some answers. Like, why the hell did he pick me? But he's nowhere to be found.

The goon stops when we're a few feet from the back door and turns to the guy behind me. "Give her your jacket. Don't want the boss gettin' mad with her being all exposed."

The man grunts and shrugs off the black jacket and drapes it around me. While I hate to admit it, the jacket offers some warmth and I slink my arms into the sleeves. This is the first kindness I've received all night.

"Thank you," I mutter automatically. Neither man responds.

The goon jerks the chain once more and we head out the door into an alleyway. A lamppost provides a dim light to illuminate the eerily quiet area. Dumpsters line the sides of the small road and most of the windows of the buildings are boarded up. I don't recognize the area, not that I've spent much time exploring.

The frigid air bites at my skin and I shift from foot to foot in an attempt to keep warm. "I'm begging you, let me go. I don't belong here. I didn't do anything to deserve this."

Again, neither man replies. The one who gave me his jacket taps his phone screen and huffs. Moments later, an all-black Bentley Continental pulls into the alleyway and stops in front of us. The man behind me opens the door while the goon shoves me into the back and slams the door shut.

He walks toward the passenger side and nods at the driver before turning around to reenter the building. I pull the coat tight against me and press back into the leather seat, curling my legs up until I'm a tight ball. The car is warm and, while this entire experience is terrifying, the quiet hum of the motor relaxes me.

A click from the door grabs my attention and I realize the car has just been locked. *Wait a second. Where the hell are the door handles?* I whip my head to the other side of the car and notice that neither door has a handle. Tears stream down my face as the car starts to move. These men are professionals. They know exactly what they're doing, how to keep me trapped in here.

And I'm utterly, helplessly theirs.

The driver pulls out onto a main road. In a couple of minutes, we're on the on-ramp of a highway. One that I know. *Okay, time to pay attention.* Maybe I can figure out where I am. We pass exits I'm not familiar with, but the numbers are getting smaller so we're definitely heading closer to the city.

I decide to try my luck with the driver. "Sir, I really don't belong here. I'm a college student. I'm begging you, can you just let me out? I won't say anything," I promise.

The man doesn't even turn his head.

"I don't have a lot of money but I'll give you whatever I have in the ATM."

He still says nothing. He just stares out the windshield and keeps driving deeper into the city.

I sigh and rest my head against the cool window. My eyes drift up to the skyscrapers, all lit up. The city is beautiful at night. And this could be the last time I get to see it. How could one night of fun end up so bad? Why did this have to happen to me? I've suffered enough. And now I'm going to vanish. I'm going to become one of those missing people whose face is on a flier.

Then I think to myself: *No.*

I will *not* disappear and be forgotten. I'm not going to just vanish off the face of the earth. I'm not going to let some handsome devil in a suit make people forget I ever existed. One way or another, I'm going to get away from these bastards.

I need to start by figuring out more about my enemies, starting with the man in the back. I lick my lower lip the instant I think about the man who purchased me. A fancy car like this must cost a lot. More than I would ever make as an accountant.

So, who is he?

Who is the man who spent over two hundred thousand dollars to own me?

8

NIKITA

The auction is over. The girl is escorted off the stage, Jimmy trailing behind. She fights back, crying out for help, but they lead her into the back without any incident. Everyone's too smart to get involved, though not smart enough to stop gawking at her exposed chest.

Gino glowers as his eyes track her every move and I want to hit him. But I won her. He has no claim. And that fact is both satisfying and calming. As the crowd begins to disperse, Eitan and I stand and head to the right toward the meeting room.

Others are on their way as well, Gino among them. He shoulders past the crowd, not giving a fuck who he slams into. Of course, no one complains. Not after what happened just a few moments ago. And with the intensity of his scowl increasing, most of the patrons are heading toward the nearest exit to escape the Italian's possible psychotic break.

I rub my temples.

Jumping in and outbidding Gino wasn't a good idea, not with this meeting on the line. Hopefully, the fool will be able to keep calm enough so that business isn't ruined. I turn to Eitan and tell him,

"Text the men. I want extra security in the room and outside the door. No telling how Gino may react tonight."

Eitan quirks a brow. I can tell what he's thinking. *Are you finally second-guessing what you pulled back there?* But after my warning, he doesn't dare say it aloud.

I stare straight ahead, not saying a word. I push open the solid wood door and enter the room. Most of the heads of the various families are there, as well as some of the key biker club presidents. I snort. It's not every day you see bikers dressed in suits and all cleaned up. But proper appearance is a rule at the auction, and exceptions are made for no one. Rules are what separate us from the animals.

Besides, it amuses me to see them uncomfortable. They're in my element, playing my game. And it will take a violent uprising indeed before I relinquish my seat at the head of the table.

A moment later, Gino bursts into the room, sweating and beet red. He narrows his eyes to mere slits as he walks past me, and takes his place at the far end of the mahogany table. Eitan heads over to the bar on the left and pours himself a scotch. Some of the men are already seated, sipping at their rum, and of course, there are the few who are snorting cocaine.

"Want a scotch?" Eitan asks, holding up an empty glass. I nod.

"Shiiit, Nikita. You feel like burnin' a whole pile of money tonight, or what? What the fuck were ya thinking, spending so much on a slave?" The East Side Boys MC president shakes his head and laughs.

"You coulda just snagged her up before she even went on stage. Ain't this your damn event, anyhow?"

"Sure is. Coulda gotten that pretty pussy for free," one of the other bosses chimes in.

I smile coldly and ignore them. Eitan places my drink down in front of me and takes a seat at my side. I glance over to Gino, who's stiff-lipped and silent. Gazes bounce between him and me, causing my stomach to roil. I pray that none of these impudent motherfuckers rile him up. He's a live wire, dangerous and unpredictable.

Four of my lieutenants walk in and stand around the room. This meeting is semi-regular and used to conduct business and keep the peace. Any street warfare is supposed to be approved by the council before it can take place. This safeguards the families, and ensures that all of us make the appropriate adjustments to our businesses at the appropriate times in order to keep the police from peering too closely at our end of the city. In that sense, our interests are aligned.

But in another sense, this is a room full of sharks, deciding whether it might be more filling to take a bite of each other instead of our usual fare.

I swirl the liquid in my glass, listening to the chinking of the ice cubes, breathing in a fragrance that only years in an oak barrel can achieve. It's my one vice and I make a virtue of it. I savor it as I sip and roll the liquid across my tongue, eyes closed.

"Eitan," the East Sider continues, "Why'd ya let the kid waste all his money on that slave?"

My eyes snap open.

Eitan wisely demurs. "Mr. Lavrin can make his own decisions about what he wants to spend his money on."

"'ey, Lavrin, what d'ya think about renting her out? Maybe make some of your money back. After you break her in of course," someone else cackles.

Other voices start to rise, jesting at my expense. I slam my glass back down on the table with a crystalline thunk.

"Enough."

The man who spoke last, a reedy bastard with nasty-looking face tattoos, laughs nervously and falls silent. The others shrug and mumble under their breath, but no one dares to go farther.

Except for Gino.

Gino holds still, staring at me, eyes locked with my own. There is a wrinkle in his nose, promising danger, like a dark cloud on the horizon. His jaw is clenched, a slight tick visible every couple of seconds. His nostrils flare with every breath.

"You really needed another fucking whore?" he grinds out in a raspy whisper.

"I haven't purchased a new slave in a long time. I wanted something new." I pick up my glass and take a slow sip with all the casualness I can muster. We're like two jungle cats in the wild, prowling and sizing each other up. Violence is in the air.

"Just something new? Or were you trying to show me up?" Gino's lips pull back over his teeth. "Because, for the amount of money you just spent, I would say your aim was to embarrass me."

I set my glass down once more, holding Gino's gaze and never blinking. "I'm not sure why you're taking this personally. We have bigger things to discuss."

Gino slams his fist down on the table and everyone turns toward him. "Bigger things to discuss? How about we discuss your lack of respect for a member of the council? How about we discuss what the consequences should be?"

My eyes narrow and my men step closer to the table. My fingertips drum against the mahogany surface as my gaze bounces between the members of the council, all of whom remain silent. One of the bikers grabs his drink and kicks his feet up on the table like he's about to watch a movie. But everyone else is tense.

It's taking every ounce of willpower I have in my body not to rise to Gino's bait. He wants to get me riled up, but I won't let him play me so easily. *Calm. Control. Breathe.* I feel the rage start to simmer back down, and my fist slowly unclenches.

Then Gino goes one step too far.

"Cat got your tongue, Nikita? You're as silent as your dead old man."

Big. Fucking. Mistake.

Burning fury hisses through my body. Inside, I'm a volcano erupting, anger pouring off of me like a wave. How dare this Italian fuck even mention my father? A million visions run through my head—slicing Gino to pieces, bleeding him out, dragging him down the highway behind my car—a million slow, painful deaths for his insolence, none less than he deserves. I want to lash out, to hurt him again and again.

But losing my temper is exactly what Gino wants. I'm an inferno on the inside; outwardly, I keep my features calm. My voice is acid as I ask him, "What did you just say?"

"Maybe it's time for the Lavrin reign to end." Gino sits back and cracks his knuckles. "I think it's my turn to show you who you're dealing with."

The tension in the room is so thick, you could cut it with a knife. And after that threat, it takes me but a moment to realize every man's hand is on his gun. Gino is obviously goading me, but tonight isn't the night for eruptions. No matter how bad I want to put a motherfucking bullet in the fucker's head.

I stand from my chair and place my palms flat on the table before I lean forward. "Nothing is done without the council's prior approval, Gino. You got something you want to bring up, something you want to start over a fucking cheap whore? You want to start a war? If so, speak now."

Gino smiles and holds his hands up in the air in mock surrender. "Relax, Nikita. I'm merely speaking aloud. On second thought, given the money you lost on that bid, I think we're even."

I stand straight and pull on the lapels of my jacket. I take a couple of deep breaths to try and calm myself down. Truth be told, the entire room needs to calm down. Gino might have started this, but tension-filled cokeheads with guns are likely to be more dangerous than him right now.

I push back my chair and head over to the bar to add more ice to my glass. Not that I need more ice, but if I keep standing—or start pacing—everyone is going to continue to remain on edge. The peace between the families, between the elites, must be kept if I want to pull off the weapons shipment I have coming in. I need their full cooperation.

Eitan clears his throat and speaks up, beginning the normal process of the meeting. The tension has eased somewhat, but no one's hand has strayed too far from his weapon of choice. "To business now, gentlemen. First item on the docket: Lenny, you still have use of the docks in two nights, correct?"

Lenny, the Devil's Canyon Motorcycle Club president, runs one of the largest clubs in the city and they're all business. Hell, Lenny used to work for a Fortune 500 company, and he took what he learned and incorporated it into his club. The man runs a tight ship. The thought of bikers using spreadsheets still makes me laugh.

Lenny nods. "Double-checked everything this morning. Going to have a talk with the guys to make sure everyone knows what they're doing."

The meeting goes on, Eitan confirming with the other members of the council that protection and distribution are in place, that the proper police and port authorities have been paid off. Lenny runs over statistics and details about the docks, which of his men will be helping, points of entry we need to keep an eye on in case the feds get tipped off for any reason, and myriad other aspects including getaway plans that incorporate the dock layout. When everything has been checked off, the conversation turns to other upcoming projects being undertaken by various family heads.

The whole time, Gino smokes cigarette after cigarette, exhaling a continuous stream of foul smoke in my direction. I hate the stench. The odor somehow finds a way to permeate my suits and even the dry cleaner can't fully remove the smell.

I wonder what Gino could be cooking up. It's not as if I'm vulnerable, my performance at the auction tonight notwithstanding. My power in the city is untouchable. I have the advantage in cash flow, number of loyal soldiers, weapons—the list goes on and on. And yet, something in my gut tells me that he will do something stupid. It would be just like him to launch a suicidal attack he has no chance of winning. Though I'd almost surely come out on top, it would be costly, not to mention the undue attention it would draw.

The fool isn't more than a common thug. He's just showing off for everyone. If there's anything the man loves more than money, it's attention. I turn my attention back to Lenny, who is finishing an explanation of the dock schematics on a laptop.

Once we're done going over all the specifics, I give Eitan the go-ahead and he transfers over the cash. Gino leans forward and puts out his cigarette by dumping it into the glass of whatever he was drinking earlier. He says nothing, just sits there with his arms crossed.

I stand and hold my glass in the air. "Thank you, gentlemen, for coming tonight. I hope you enjoyed yourselves. Cheers to future success."

"Cheers," the voices in the room ring out, and everyone finishes their drinks.

I hustle out of the room without another word. It's been a turbulent evening, and I need to take the edge off. I get in the back of the luxury sedan waiting outside for me.

"Take me to the penthouse," I order the driver. We peel out at once.

There's a new slave I'm quite eager to meet.

9

ANNIE

The car pulls into one of the most expensive apartment complexes in the city. The driver descends deeper into the parking garage and pulls up to the elevator entrance. Another suited goon is waiting there. He strides forward and opens my door, yanking me out by the arm.

"Do none of you morons know how to be gentle?" I spit.

He doesn't even acknowledge me. He just closes the car door and leads me toward the elevator. The vehicle pulls away and we stand there in silence until the ding of the arriving elevator cuts through the dead air. Inside, the floor is covered in red carpet. The walls are metallic and the place smells floral. The whole thing is dripping with classless luxury, fancy just for the sake of being fancy. The bodyguard inserts a key and hits the button for the top floor.

Penthouse.

I shouldn't be surprised. The man spent over two hundred thousand dollars on me. Where else would he live? I gnaw my lip. I still can't believe I'm in this mess. But maybe this man will listen to reason and let me go. Maybe I won't end up dead.

The ride up to the penthouse is even longer than I expected and when the doors open, my jaw drops. *Holy crap.* My eyes fixate on the window ahead of me, so large it reminds me of a storefront but instead of merchandise it displays constellations against an inky black sky. The bodyguard nudges me forward and my heels click against the ceramic tile. I close my mouth and continue to take in the grand space.

In front of the window is a huge mahogany table. Two tall, silver candelabras command attention from the center of the table, holding smooth peach candles whose wax has never dripped. Above hangs the most beautiful crystalline chandelier. Simple yet elegant, it perfectly complements the table beneath it.

The bodyguard jabs me again to move down the hallway. I turn my head over my shoulder and glare at him. "You could just tell me where to go instead of prodding me like cattle."

"Shut up."

He brings me into a large bedroom and stops in the doorway. The floor is carpeted and the walls painted a gentle cream color. The bed is centered against the far wall with an elaborate headboard. On top of the mattress is a dark blue dress. I walk over and take in the garment. If they expect me to get dressed up like a dancing monkey, they've got another thing coming.

"I'm not wearing this."

The dress—if it could even be called that—barely covers a thing. If I even attempted to bend over, my butt would be hanging out. The material is nearly see-through, and there is no breast support. Not that I have large breasts, but still.

The bodyguard growls and steps into the room. "Put it on now."

"No. I'm not wearing this. I'm not a whore."

He steps forward again, close enough for me to feel his breath against my face. I realize suddenly how tall he is, how broad, like a boulder with arms. I'm a little ant in comparison. "You can put it on yourself or I'll put it on for you. But, one way or another, you're going to wear the fucking dress."

I swallow hard. This jerk would enjoy putting the dress on me against my will. But after the night I've had, no one is touching me anymore. No one is ripping my clothes again. "I can dress myself, thank you," I say through clenched teeth.

Satisfied for now, he turns and stalks back to the doorframe, where he stands observing me with crossed arms. I narrow my eyes at him. "Turn around or get out. I said I'll dress myself but you aren't getting a show. And if you keep harassing me, I may just let your boss know."

The man's face goes rigid, blotchy red spreading over his skin. He looks like he wants to lunge across the room and strangle me, but I've clearly said the magic word—'boss'—because instead he steps through the doorway and slams it shut behind him without saying anything.

With a sigh, I take a second and sit on the bed. It's soft and I just want to lie down and close my eyes. My night has been hell on earth and my body is drained from the stress. Sleep would be a blessing. But I can hear the bodyguard tapping his heel impatiently against the wall outside. I don't want to piss him off too much. There's no telling what he might do to me—what any of these people might do to me, really.

I undress, peeling off the oversized suit coat, my torn blouse, and my leather miniskirt. I pause for a moment and look down at myself, clad only in a pair of sheer lace panties. My pale elbows are mottled with bruises where Stephen/Augustin squeezed me at the nightclub. It feels like that was a million years ago. With another heavy sigh, I slink into the blue dress and pull it up around me. The material is surprisingly soft, but truth be told, I just want a warm pair of pajamas right now.

"I'm done," I say. The door is yanked open and the bodyguard stomps in again.

"Let's go."

This time, he doesn't poke me, but leads the way to an outside terrace. The area is almost as large as the inside of the penthouse. In the middle of a cast iron table is a beautiful centerpiece made up of lilies and surrounded by candles. Wine sits in a silver bucket of ice and two entrees of seared steak and a medley of potatoes and fresh vegetables lie waiting. The smell of the food makes me realize how hungry I am. When did I last eat? I can see the steam rising from the food into the cool night air. My mouth is watering and I feel weak all of a sudden, like I might fall down if I don't eat right this second.

Then a cough pulls me from my daze.

I turn to meet the gaze of the man from the auction.

He's standing behind one of the chairs at the table. He gestures at the other as he says in a smooth, low rumble, "If you would, please join me for dinner. I'm sure you must be hungry."

I don't reply. I just stare at him, as if he sprouted a new head.

He steps forward towards me. My first instinct is to jump back. He must see my fear, because he smiles and raises his hands as if to show me he means no harm. I almost laugh out loud. The man who bought me, who abducted me, who might very well end this night by tossing me off the fortieth-floor balcony—he means no harm. Just a nice guy, really, I'm sure. Loves his mom, donates to charity, saved a kitten from a tree once. The whole thing is a sick, cruel irony.

He comes around to the back of the second chair and pulls it out for me. "Please, take a seat."

Part of me wants to argue, but the part of me that's famished chooses the path of least resistance. I hesitantly sit in the chair he's offering.

He makes his way back across the table and takes his seat. "What is your name?" he says politely.

"What's yours?" The words rush from my mouth before I can stop them.

He smiles and says, "I'm Nikita Lavrin."

Nikita Lavrin. I say the name inside my head. It's a strong name, and the way he says it is so confident, like it's the most valuable of all his riches. He says it like I should know who he is, although I don't have the faintest idea.

All at once, my anger comes boiling to the surface. 'Angry Annie,' my grandmother used to call me when I'd lose my temper. It didn't happen often, but when it did, I was a terror and a half. And if anyone has ever deserved the full brunt of my wrath, it's this rich pretty boy smiling at me from across the table.

"So, Nikita Lavrin," I spit, "What makes you think, after getting kidnapped, dragged around, and damn near threatened with rape for half the night, that I'm in the mood for a steak dinner and small talk with someone who *purchased* me? Do you think I'm having fun? Do you think this is enjoyable? You're a monster, and you need to let me go right now, or I'll call the police."

The words pour out of me in a big rush, but as soon as I'm done speaking, I immediately regret it. I shouldn't have said any of that, especially not with so much venom. And especially since I have no idea who I'm actually dealing with.

He doesn't say anything. His eyes are dark and unreadable. This is my first time seeing him up close and personal like this. At the auction, the room was too dark and although I could make out some of his features—and that he was handsome—it didn't prepare me for how beautiful he is up close. His lips are pale and thin and his nose slender and rounded. His eyes are the green of fresh dew. A prominent jaw drawn in a graceful slash reveals the strength of his neck, wrought with twining cords of muscle. He's an Adonis ... and I'm in trouble.

Then he smiles again.

"You've had quite a night," he says. "Please eat. There will be time for answers after you have some food in you."

And just like that, my outburst is over. His voice has a weird effect on me. It's equal parts calming and invigorating, like a splash of cold water to the face while my core heats up. My anger disappears completely and in its place once more is the throbbing hunger that's been killing me since the second the scent of the steak first hit my nostrils.

I pick up my fork and poke at the tender meat on my plate. Caving, I take a bite and nearly exclaim at the explosion of flavor that floods my taste buds. The meat is savory, tender, and has the faintest hint of pepper. I moan as I chew. God, I've never tasted anything so delicious.

Satisfied that I'm eating, Nikita takes a bite of his own. I watch him carefully from the corner of my eye as I keep devouring the food on my plate. He reaches over and pours wine into my glass and then passes the breadbasket full of warm dinner rolls. I grab one and plaster the fakest smirk I can muster on my face. I hope the bastard doesn't think he's impressing me.

"Would you mind telling me your name?" he says after a few silent minutes have passed.

"Annie," I growl in between bites.

"Well, it's a pleasure to dine with you, Annie. I'd like to learn about you. Who are you? What do you do?" Nikita pats his mouth with his napkin and then places it on his lap, patiently awaiting my answer. His whole aura exudes this powerful sense of control. Every movement, every word, down to the pitch and pronunciation, is calculated for maximum effect. He reminds me of a panther in the jungle stalking his prey—me.

I huff. *Is this guy for real?* I shake my head and swallow before responding. "Majoring in accounting and supposed to be graduating this June."

His eyebrow quirks. "You're in college?"

"Yeah."

"What do you do for fun?" He lifts his glass of wine to his lips and takes a sip.

"What is this, twenty questions?" He raises an eyebrow and says nothing. I scowl. "Let's see, I like to read, hike, and occasionally, I volunteer at an animal shelter." I scoop up mashed potatoes a little too aggressively and bite down on the fork on accident. The tang of metal reverberates painfully through my teeth. "What about you?"

"You could call me an entrepreneur. I own a couple of businesses."

"You mean you're a criminal."

"Most of my business is legitimate."

"But not all of it." I place my utensil down on the table and wait for him to answer.

Once he's done chewing his food, he inhales and closes his eyes for a second. He picks up his glass of wine and swirls it, looking at the red liquid as if he's trying to come up with an acceptable answer.

"I do what needs to be done to make my businesses and my family successful."

I snort. Yup, he's a thug. A criminal. Someone who belongs in jail.

We fall silent again. I go back to my food. The steak has got to be the best thing I've ever eaten, but the rolls are pillow-soft and so warm. I want to keep eating this same meal forever, over and over again. I can't imagine ever getting sick of it. Nikita seems content to stay silent and chew slowly, thoughtfully, carefully, taking small sips of wine between bites.

After a while, he speaks up again.

"Tell me, Annie ... when was the last time you got fucked?"

The potatoes fall off my fork at the same time my jaw drops. I blink rapidly as I try to process his question. I'm honestly stunned. No one has ever said anything like that to me before. I'm taken aback and confused, and a little annoyed at the flash of heat that runs through my legs when those words come out of his mouth. I don't like the effect he's having on me, not one bit.

"When was the last time you got slapped in the face?" I retort.

He chuckles, seemingly satisfied with my answer. I look down at my plate to focus on something else. If the jerk thinks I'm some sort of whore who randomly sleeps with strange men, he's dead wrong. And if he thinks I'm going to roll over and play dead, he better think again.

"Accounting, then? How are your grades?"

I take a sip of wine as I struggle to make sense of what is going on. It's not every day that someone jumps from my sex life one moment to my grades the next. More heat crawls up my chest to my cheeks, his question still at the forefront of my thoughts. "Top of my class."

The seconds tick by. Stars wheel overhead. Nikita finishes his meal in silence, but his gaze is constantly on me, studying me. And even though I try to finish my food, all I can seem to focus on is him. His body. His voice. And his question. No matter how hard I try, that question makes my skin tingle and every time I glance at him, my body heats up even more.

After a few more minutes of eating, with no more questions about when I last got laid, something changes in the air between us.

Nikita places his napkin on his plate and stands, then makes his way over to me. This close, I can smell his cologne, and the musk of man underneath it. His scent fills my nostrils completely, overwhelming me.

I stare at his chest, refusing to look up, refusing to acknowledge what him being this close to me is doing to my body. But he lifts my chin gently so our eyes lock. His eyes are dark, almost black, and swirling with a ferocious intelligence. The image of a black panther is even more powerful now. He stares into my soul. When he speaks, his words are quiet, whispered.

"You do understand that I own you now, Annie?"

I'm silent for a moment. But I won't let this cocky bastard intimidate me into quitting. There's a lot of fight left in me, even if I don't see right now how I'm going to get myself out of this situation.

"No one can own a human," I snap. "Not anymore."

He continues to stare into my eyes and my pulse quickens. Without another word he releases his grip and walks away into the penthouse. The thump of his shoes against the floor stops and his baritone voice cuts through the air. "Until tomorrow night."

Then he's gone.

Left alone, I grab a dinner roll and shove it into my mouth, shredding it to pieces. Since I can't take out my anger any other way, I guess being overly aggressive with a piece of bread is better than holding my feelings in. The heavy thump of footsteps alerts me to the fact I'm no longer alone and when I look up, I find my new friend. The jerk bodyguard is once again by my side. To hell with him if he thinks I'm leaving before I'm done eating.

"Hurry up and finish."

I stare right at him and shovel more steak into my mouth, overemphasizing a moan of delight as I chew. Then I shoot him my best 'fuck you' smile and take another bite. I swear, he looks as if his head is about to explode but he doesn't manhandle me. Guess he has orders.

When I'm done eating, the bodyguard leads me back to the guest bedroom I was in earlier. I slam the door in his face and lean against it to take a deep breath. I guess tonight I'll be staying here.

I just want to go home. I want to go back to my bed in my apartment with my roommates. But I have no idea how the hell to even get out of this place. Between the bodyguard and the key I would need for the elevator to go down to the ground floor, I'm trapped. And who knows what I would run into in the lobby. Do non-mob people live here? Plus, I have no money, nor do I have my phone, since those were taken by Augustin.

Asshole.

I slink over to the drawers and open them. There has to be something to wear to sleep in. Something I can use as pajamas. Nikita is rich, powerful, and controlling. And if he's into abducting people, he should be smart enough to leave them something to wear to sleep in because God knows, this dress isn't it. But of course, there's nothing.

I walk over to the door and yank it open. My new favorite friend is standing right outside. "Hey. What am I supposed to sleep in?"

"Not my problem."

"Make it your problem unless you want me to speak to Nikita." I cross my arms over my chest, glaring at him.

He glowers and stalks off down the hallway. While he's gone, I take the opportunity to tiptoe down the other end of the hall. There are a couple of closed doors and when I turn the corner I spot the elevator. The only exit.

The heavy thump of men's shoes against the tile catches my attention and I scurry back to my doorway. No need for the bodyguard to find me snooping.

He rounds the corner and tosses me an oversized shirt. "Here."

I retire into my room and close the door once again in his face. I smile wide and start to laugh when I hold up the shirt. I'm not sure what I find so funny. Maybe it's all the emotions catching up to me. Or maybe it's the simplicity of the XXL white T-shirt that must belong to the bodyguard himself.

Either way, I slip out of the blue dress and into my makeshift pajama before climbing into bed. As I rest against the pillows, I contemplate what I'm going to do. How I'm going to get out of here. The only thing I know is that I need to get control of the elevator. I need the key. And that's going to take time to obtain.

So, I guess for now, I'll do what I'm told as I wait for an opportunity. But no way am I giving up. No way will I let this Nikita own me. And if he thinks elaborate dinners will change my mind, he's dead freaking wrong.

The thought triggers another. The dinners ... Actually, that's it. Nikita has to have a key on him, right? Maybe if I get him drunk during dinner tomorrow night, he'll pass out and I can steal his key and get away.

I run over various scenarios on how to make that happen. But my eyelids grow heavy, too heavy, and before I know it, the world fades into darkness.

∽

There's a faint knock at the door and I sit up in bed. The moonlight filtering in through the window illuminates Nikita, who is shirtless and stalking toward me, slowly and carefully. But I'm not afraid. Instead, my pussy grows wet and eager as I wait for him to reach me.

Nikita gets to the bed and rips the covers off me. But when he touches me, he's gentle. His fingertips glide from my cheeks down the side of my neck. He leans in and kisses me, his mouth all-consuming.

"He saw her, like the sun, even without looking."

Oh God. He's quoting Tolstoy and touching me. I moan. I skim his jaw with my fingers and thread them into his hair. It's soft and thick.

I press closer, but it's not enough. My focus lies on the feel of his hands on my skin and the warmth of his mouth on mine. He breaks the kiss, and his lips travel along my jaw, warm and wet on my skin. "Is this okay?"

"Yes."

He grabs the swell of my ass, squeezing gently. "And this?" *His full bottom lip begs for attention, so I give it a nibble and a suck.*

"Yes."

He pulls my body closer, shifting his hips at the same time. "What about this?"

And there it is—the friction I've been looking for. It feels so good. So much better than my own fingers because it's a big damn dick and all I have to do is shift against it. "Fuck me." *The words come out on a breathy groan.*

I release his hair to explore the rest of his cut body. Muscles tense and jump under my touch. I've never been this close with someone in such amazing physical condition. Below his navel is a smattering of dark hair leading to a rock-hard erection. God, he's so thick, massive even. I wonder if he might break me with it—and I wonder if I might love just that.

As soon as he reaches my breasts, his thumbs sweep over my nipples, ripping a long moan from my mouth. My face and chest heat up. He closes his lips around the taut nipple and sucks gently. I bite the inside of my cheek in an effort to derail the sound forcing its way up my throat and manage to keep it to a whimper.

His kiss is all soft lips and sweeping tongue. The thick head probes low, and Nikita makes several unhurried passes until we're both panting again. Propped up on one arm so his eyes are on me, he eases his sheathed cock inside me. When he pauses, I tighten my legs around his waist to urge him on until he bottoms out.

He eases back and rocks forward. With each measured thrust, I lift to meet him. Everything turns suddenly intense as he pulls out—way, way out—and pushes in again. As heat and need expand to consume me, I urge him to go faster and harder.

Without the slightest bit of warning, my entire body flushes. The spark ignites, bursting into flame. I grip his shoulders as I come; his name a scream on my lips. He bites out a choked grunt and buries his face against my neck as he pumps erratically, chasing his own release.

Spent, Nikita collapses on top of me. I run my fingers through his damp hair, both of us breathing hard, our hearts beating double time.

10

NIKITA

Fucking Christ.

I barely sleep the rest of the night. Even though I came into the office early, my concentration is off, thanks to Annie. All I can think about is the way her skin flushed when I asked about the last time she was fucked. And her quick retort amused me. She's the perfect mix of porcelain and fire. Of meekness and fury. And it makes my cock jump for joy.

But in the harsh light of day, outbidding Gino seems unwise, to say the least. I can only hope that my moment of foolishness doesn't come back to bite me in the ass. All the council knew something was up. None of them have ever poked fun before. Most are too scared. But their openness—asking to rent out Annie—was too brazen. I should have stopped it in its tracks. Another mistake. So very unlike me.

But the thought I come back to, again and again, is that I don't give a damn about Gino or the council, and especially not about my fucking money. Every cent spent on the girl was well worth it. It's been a long time since I've been excited about anything, since something or someone has kept me up all night. Every time her soft lips parted, to snap at me or devour her food, my gut twinged in delight. I wanted so badly to ravish her then and there.

Not since the night I took over the Bratva have I had this kind of energy racing through my veins.

I remember when I finally sat down behind the desk in my father's office. My body hummed, every nerve ending firing as I sat down in his chair. The room sizzled with a force I couldn't see. And when I looked out the window, down onto the city, my pulse raced at the realization of all the power I had at my fingertips. Power to control the city. Power to destroy my enemies. Power to do whatever the hell I wanted.

The memory pumps me full of adrenaline. I want to race back to my penthouse and take her now. Right fucking now.

But giving into one's desires makes a man weak. I force myself—for now—to only wonder how she'd handle my hard cock. After all, control is everything in the life of a mob boss.

And I damn near lost it on the rooftop.

The way my blood surged and my dick throbbed, I almost gave in to the adrenaline—to the raw fucking need—to fuck Annie right there out in the open for anyone to see. It was a dangerous moment, a crisis narrowly avoided. One mistake begetting another.

A knock at the door grabs my attention. "Come in."

Eitan enters, along with a younger man who is dressed in a navy blue suit. His chestnut hair is cropped and slicked back. A scar above his eyebrow accentuates his harsh features. His nose is just a tad too big for his face and slightly crooked, as if it's been broken on more than one occasion.

The man doesn't look around the office as most normally do, but focuses on me instead. The look in his eyes isn't that of a subordinate

—it's the look of someone who thinks himself my equal.

No one walks into my office as if they own it. I'm the king. I run this city. My gaze shoots to Eitan, who quirks an eyebrow in my direction. But I keep my expression neutral, my mask of calm firmly in place. "Good to see you, Eitan. Hope you're well rested."

"Indeed, I am," Eitan says as he and the new person step closer to my desk. "Nikita, I wanted to introduce you to Augustin. We spoke about him a couple of days ago."

"Good afternoon, sir," Augustin says, extending his hand out to shake. The arrogant look I saw in his eyes is gone now, replaced with the appropriate deference. I wonder if I imagined it. He bows his head towards me.

I shake his hand and everyone takes a seat.

"Shall we?" Eitan asks. I nod my head and he begins. "I wanted to bring Augustin to the meeting to keep him in the loop for the incoming weapons shipment. As you know, everything will be going down in the next couple of days," Eitan says, crossing one leg over the other.

"Where are we on security?" I ask him.

To my surprise, Augustin interjects. "Eitan and I put together a team. We went over logistics with ten of my best guys. I figured it would be best to keep it small, since the East Siders MC will have some of their members there and too many people might raise suspicion." His voice is fast and raspy, like oil on asphalt.

"Well done," I say. In spite of myself, I'm impressed. He speaks with the confidence of a natural-born leader. The intelligence behind his dark, beady eyes is obvious. It mirrors my own.

"Have you spoken to our contact on the police force?" I ask. "We need to manage our friends in blue."

"I spoke to him. So far, the police are in the dark. The docks aren't even on anyone's radar," Eitan responds.

The shipment is big and I know there will be some glitches, but so far everything is going according to plan. I take a deep breath. "And what about Gino's threat?"

Eitan squirms in his chair. "There are more rumors floating around today that the DeLucas plan to muscle in on our guns business."

A low growl rumbles deep in my chest. Of course Gino would want to make a move. I can't blame him. Most of the bosses want all the power. "Explain."

"Word is that Gino is coordinating his own shipment with more upgraded guns. M-9s, grenade launchers, armor-piercing bullets, even some 3-D printed guns that metal detectors can't pick up. And …"

"And?" I raise an eyebrow.

"… And there is also another rumor about him looking to heist your shipment."

I snort. "That can't be serious. He wouldn't be so dumb as to move against the entire council like that."

Eitan clears his throat. "Rumor or not, we have eyes on him and have noticed he's been increasing his numbers."

My jaw tightens. I like this less and less.

Augustin speaks. "Mr. Lavrin, I think maybe we should put together a team to track Gino, especially during the shipment. This way there won't be any surprises. Maybe we could come up with an alternate route that only you know about—or that only the three of us know about—until moments before we arrive at the docks. That way, Gino won't be able to intercept," Augustin says.

Not a bad idea. And not just for Gino, but for anyone possibly thinking of hijacking my shipment, including the bikers. They've been allies for a long time, since my father's days behind this desk, but I'm still not fond of having another group involved with that much influence over the proceedings.

Once again, I'm impressed by Augustin's sharp grasp of the situation. He has Eitan's stamp of approval, and his suggestions so far have been sharp and actionable. Perhaps a future right-hand man in the making, when Eitan retires. "Agreed. Augustin, go ahead and start putting a team together to track Gino."

"Yes, sir." Augustin stands and shakes both my hand and Eitan's before exiting the room. Eitan waits until the door is shut before looking at me again.

"What do you think?" He tilts his head slightly, awaiting my response.

"Impressive. He shows promise." I thumb through some papers on my desk, grinding my molars. Gino still weighs heavily on my mind, that impulsive Italian bastard. "So, what do you think about Gino's threats? Is he just running his mouth or do you think it deserves more attention?"

"I'm not sure. Right now, I think we just run business as usual. If the team picks up on anything or if Gino makes a slight misstep, then we handle it quickly," Eitan says.

"Agreed." I have never been one to sit idly by, but no better option seems to be presenting itself for now.

Eitan says his goodbyes and heads out, leaving me to focus on my normal tasks. The rest of the day flies by, though I do little but stare at endless rows of data in spreadsheets. Anything to avoid thoughts of Annie.

Finally, as the sun slides through the blinds hanging over my window, I decide to leave. Shutting off my computer, I make my way down to the car to head home. The ride isn't long, yet it's long enough for my mind to wander to Annie, and as soon as it does, my dick hardens.

Fuck.

Just the thought of the woman sets my body ablaze. The driver pulls up to the elevator entrance and I adjust myself before stepping out and heading up to the penthouse. I force myself to stay patient. Going to her right away would be giving into my desires. No matter how badly I want to fuck her senseless, the move is to wait. And wait. And wait.

After a quick shower, I change into a white shirt and gray slacks and stand in the mirror. I think, not for the first time, that I look like my father. My mother used to keep a photograph of my father in the living room when I was growing up. It's a shot from him in his younger days—not much older than I'm now, actually—from the day he purchased his first car.

I close my eyes and picture it. He's tall, broad-shouldered, dark-haired, a confident slope to his nose. Those Lavrin eyes—piercing, stormy, proud. I open my eyes, look in the mirror, and see the same features. I see him in me. I'm his legacy.

A faint aroma of penne a la vodka drifts into my room. It's time. Dinner. Annie. I groan as my dick begins to harden once again. That body, that innocence ... I won't deny myself another time.

Tonight, I won't stop myself from ripping off her dress and burying myself deep inside her.

My cell phone vibrates against the nightstand and I grab it, dreading a possible development with Gino. But when I click open the message I'm met with a picture of a pair of naked breasts. A text from a girl I used to sleep with. The phone dings again with a follow-up message, asking me to come over.

Her body is flawless, but it's nothing to me anymore. The prize I'm after is waiting down the hall.

My fingers click against the screen as I inform the slut to lose my number—I'm done with her.

Annie awaits me.

11

ANNIE

I can't believe my luck. I found a small bottle of laxative pills tucked in the medicine cabinet of the bathroom attached to my quarters. I slipped one into Jimmy's morning coffee when he wasn't looking. It didn't even take five minutes before he was running off to the bathroom, leaving his suit jacket draped over the chair he was sitting in ...

With the elevator keycard in the pocket.

I don't have time to waste. One second could be the difference between making it out of here, and getting dragged back in by the suited brutes patrolling this place. If Jimmy comes back and finds me halfway out of the penthouse, there's no telling what he'll do, especially with the boss not around to keep him from laying his hands on me.

So I have to go now. *Right* now. I race across the tile barefoot and slide the keycard into the slot, smashing my finger over and over into the button while I beg the elevator to hurry the hell up. This is my chance at freedom. My chance to escape. And I need to get out of here if I want to survive. The electronic display with the floor numbers ticks up, one by one, agonizingly slowly.

"Where the hell do you think you're going?" The baritone voice cuts through me like shards of glass.

Nikita.

I thought he was still away from home, gone to wherever he goes during the day. Do mob bosses have offices? I'm not sure. Not that it matters now. I turn my head over my shoulder and spot him at the far end of the hallway. He looms in the doorframe, tall and broad, a silhouette of dark power.

He starts to stride towards me.

"Hurry up, hurry up," I mutter to the elevator as I mash the button again and again. I can hear the gears whirring as the cables guide the car up towards me, but it's not going fast enough. I hear Nikita's feet pounding into the marble floors as he races towards me. It's a long hallway, but not that long.

Ding.

The doors slide open. I jump inside. My breath is coming in ragged gasps as I whirl around and frantically search for the button to close the doors. Moments pass me by, too fast, like sand falling through my fingertips no matter how hard I try to keep it cupped. *He's going to stop me, he's going to stop me, he's going to stop me ...*

I find the "close doors" button and press it. The doors start sliding closed. I'm going to make it. I can feel my heartbeat drumming in my rib cage, a million beats per minute, a billion, I can't breathe ...

Then Nikita's hand thrusts between the doors.

They shudder to a stop and reverse direction, revealing him in all his dark Russian rage. His brow is furrowed, and one black lock of hair has fallen out of place over his forehead. He smooths it back as he stares at me. There are storm clouds building in his eyes. He's angry. Very, very angry.

But even in the middle of this scary moment, where I feel like he might just kill me for this little stunt, I can't help but notice how utterly beautiful he is.

I don't have long to focus on his sex appeal, though, because with one step, he crosses the distance between us, wraps one strong hand against my throat, and slams me against the back elevator wall. He presses his forehead up against mine, and I can see deep into the storms swirling in his dark irises.

"You aren't going anywhere," he hisses.

I'm not sure whether I want to kiss him or kick him. I'm not sure which one he would prefer, either. Something tells me this man likes a little fight in his women.

The desire to keep resisting wins out. "Like hell I'm not," I spit. I try to pry Nikita's fingers off me, wriggling to escape his grasp, but it's no use.

Keeping his hand on my throat, he spins me around and pushes me back into the penthouse. He grabs the keycard from the slot and the doors close. The elevator hums as it plunges away, without me in it. I feel like I'm watching my dog get run over by a car, and I'm just here, mere feet away, completely and utterly helpless. Nikita stands between me and the only way out. And he's not moving anytime soon.

I reach a hand up to my throat, where Nikita's fingers have left a painful red mark. The air-conditioned oxygen surging into my lungs is sweet, but not as sweet as a breath of fresh air outside would've been.

"Do you think you're going to take me down, Annie?" he smirks.

I look down and realize I've fallen into an aggressive crouch. My hands are balled into fists and adrenaline courses through my veins. But Nikita's arrogant question takes the fight right out of me. I sag, defeated. We both know that there's not a snowball's chance in hell that I can overpower him, take the keycard, and manage to get away before his guards arrive.

He sees the fighting spirit dissipate and smiles again coolly. "I will not punish you for trying to get away this time," he says. "But I won't look kindly on a second attempt. Don't try to leave. You belong here now. This is your home."

I snarl back, "No, it isn't. It will never be."

He steps closer, wary and smooth, like the jungle cat he is. I freeze as he raises a hand to gently stroke the side of my face. Up close and personal once again, the aroma of his cologne wafts into my nose. The woodsy blend suits him. And the heat radiating off his body further floods my senses. Because the dream I had last night wasn't enough, now I have to stand this close to the sexy devil. And damn my traitorous body for responding to him. My nipples pebble under his gaze and I clench my knees together.

He looks like he wants to say something. But instead, Nikita steps back. The anger I saw rising in him is gone now. The mask of calm control has settled back in place. "Let's eat." The faint Russian accent on the edge of his voice sends an unusual chill down my spine.

I have no choice but to follow him out onto the porch. There's no way I can escape right now since he has both keys, but maybe there will be an opportunity later in the night. I still have my original plan, to get Nikita drunk enough to make a mistake. But that will take some time, and some acting skills. I need to get my mind right if that route is going to work. That means getting some food in my belly for starters. And honestly, I could do with some fresh, cool air right now. My skin is sizzling and I don't need my hormones undermining my escape plans.

The terrace is decorated in luxury once again. The spread smells delicious and my mouth waters. One thing I can't deny is that whatever cooks Nikita employs sure are talented. I've never tasted food so good before.

We sit down. A staff member comes to serve us soup and bread. The bread is a whole-wheat focaccia, covered with garlic, olive oil, and generous quantities of rosemary. The inside is stuffed with creamy goat cheese.

A few silent moments go by. I refuse to look into Nikita's eyes at first, until I remind myself that I need him to relax if I'm going to succeed in getting him drunk. That means I need to be pleasant, on my best behavior.

The server comes back to refill our wine. When he's gone, Nikita asks, "Where's Jimmy?"

Despite myself, I snicker as I shove a piece of bread in my mouth. Given Jimmy's current circumstances, I'm not sure the topic of his whereabouts is proper dinner conversation, but I can't help myself. "Crapping his brains out," I snort.

Nikita chokes on his wine, his eyes going wide as he stares at me.

I shoot him a wicked smile. "Gave him a healthy amount of laxative with his coffee. If the jerk thinks I'm his gopher, I sure hope he learned his lesson today."

To my surprise, Nikita laughs, a full-bellied laugh, slapping the table with his hand. "That's how you got the keycard?"

"He barely made it down the hall. I wish I had my camera. The way he clenched his butt as he ran would've gone viral."

We both laugh for a long time. It feels strange, but it's been so long since I laughed or even smiled that I just give in to the feeling. I can hardly catch my breath and I clutch at my stomach to try to calm down.

The staff brings out the next course and I dig in. Nikita is more relaxed tonight. He asks me about my day outside of my chemical attack on his bodyguard and I huff. "Boring. I'm trapped up here. At least the weather was nice enough that I got to sit outside but there's not even a book for me to read."

Nikita takes a sip of his wine then places the glass down on the table. "What sort of books would you like to read?"

I swallow my pasta and wipe my mouth with the cloth napkin. "Fantasy. Or sci-fi."

"Are you a fan of Scalzi?"

My mouth opens and closes but no words come out. Before this moment, I would've bet a million dollars that this man had never read any book ever, much less the books of my favorite author of all time. It seems too out of left field to be true. But his smile seems genuine, and the question is innocent enough on the surface.

I don't want to give him the satisfaction of knowing anything more about me, but I can't stop myself from blurting out, "I'm a huge fan."

Nikita smiles. The conversation that unfolds from there is like something from a different life. In another world, I would've thought I was on a first date that was going really well. Nikita is more well-read than I ever would have guessed. We go from topic to topic—sci-fi to robots to the ethics of cloning, on and on. I'm surprised at every turn by his wit, his charm, his panty-melting smile.

Who is this man?

∼

It started as acting, but before I know it, nearly four hours have passed and I can't believe I'm having ... fun. How is that possible?

"I'll leave the *Exforce* books for you to look at. I really think you'll like them."

I almost thank him. Then, like a spell is suddenly lifted, I look in his eyes and realize who he is. I realize where I am. I realize that none of this is fun, none of this is funny, and I'm not free to leave.

I'm this man's prisoner.

My gaze falls to the table and I take a deep breath. I know what I want to say. I want to tell this monster that I don't want his books or his kindness or his maddening, flirtatious charm. I want to tell him that I want to go *home*, not to his library. I want to tell him that I'm not his slave and I never will be.

But I have to stick to my plan.

For tonight only, I will be the perfect date, the perfect slave. That means swallowing what I really want to say and instead picking up my wineglass, giving Nikita the brightest smile I can muster, and saying, "To Scalzi."

He doesn't reciprocate at first, just raises an eyebrow. I wonder if he can see the internal struggle taking place in my brain, this fight between my desire to get the hell away from him and the competing urge to let his perfect lips trace patterns over my body.

Whatever he sees in my face must satisfy him, because then he picks up his glass and clinks it against mine. "To Scalzi," he echoes.

We both drain our drinks.

Nikita's server comes and opens another bottle for us, pouring fresh red wine into the glasses. I go to grab mine again, but Nikita waves a hand, cutting off the flow of alcohol.

"Let's drink," I urge, smiling.

But Nikita shakes his head. "There will be time for that later." He turns to the bodyguard who is standing at attention by the terrace doorway. "Luca, turn up the music." Turning back to me, he stands up and offers a hand. "Let's dance."

A soft violin spills out of hidden speakers, filling the air with gentle chords and a brassy beat. Nikita pulls me reluctantly to my feet, guiding me away from the table.

Go along with the plan, I remind myself for the umpteenth time that night. *Keep him happy.*

Above us, the stars are out, dotting the sky. The air is crisp but warm enough I don't need a shawl. Nikita wraps a hand against my lower back and pulls me in close to him. His body is solid as marble, radiating a heat that seems to seep into my bones. I shiver in spite of it—not from the temperature but from the effect this man is having on me despite my very best efforts. I feel slightly woozy as he spins me slowly across the paved terrace.

The music pulses and swoons as we revolve. My hand feels tiny in Nikita's grasp. He's an excellent dancer, effortlessly in control of both of us. I risk a look up and find him staring at me with a hint of a smile on his lips.

"Are you enjoying yourself, Annie?"

"Yes." I duck my chin again to avoid his intense gaze.

"You move well. Are you a dancer?"

"No. Actually, I don't dance much." I bite my bottom lip. I always wanted to learn to dance. Always wanted to go to dance class after school like the other girls. But my parents couldn't afford it.

"Well, you're a natural." Nikita bends closer, his breath tickling my ear. "I wonder what else you're a natural at?"

A surge of heat zips through my body. My nipples pucker against the dress' material and I grow wet between my legs. One sentence and this man has my body running on overdrive. He's dangerous.

His hand on my back slips lower as we dance and when he pulls me tight against him once more, I feel his erection dig into my hip and moan. Audibly.

It's a mistake, and instantly, we both know it.

The game I've been struggling to play is over. I feel like a mouse caught in the cat's gaze. With one piercing glance, Nikita knows everything that's been raging in my brain. He sees the fight and the desire. And he knows damn well which one is winning.

I'm not going anywhere.

His voice is soft but direct. "Do you like that, Annie?" He doesn't blink.

I try to pull away to create more space between us, but he's too strong. When I look up, his pupils are dilated and his jaw thrums with tension. My lips part for a moment until my gaze lands on his breast pocket. The keycard. Maybe, just maybe, there's a chance I can salvage this situation. If we could just sit down at the table again, if I could just get him to drink a little more…

But that window of opportunity is closed. I know it, he knows it—hell, the waitstaff probably knows it. His taut body, his solid erection, and the power he exudes without even trying is making my body a puddle of need. It feels like my lips are disconnected from my brain.

"I, I …" I stammer.

Nikita smiles. He knows he has me. He knows what I want.

"I'm done waiting, Annie."

In one sweep of his arm, he knocks all the remaining dishes from the table and sends them crashing to the floor. Shards shatter and ricochet on the concrete slabs, shooting in every direction. He flings me on top of the table like I'm a weightless rag doll.

"Nikita," I whimper, but nothing else comes out. I'm at a loss, my mind shutting down and giving over to the need between my legs.

Stupid, stupid girl, screams a voice inside my head, but it's like it's talking to me from down a well, it's so faint and easy to ignore. The blood pounding in my ears, on the other hand, is overwhelming.

And so is Nikita.

My dress catches on the edge of the table when he throws me and hikes up to the tops of my thighs, exposing me to his touch. Nikita leans over me, nipping at my neck with his teeth. One of his hands slides up to where my legs meet. The other reaches up and cups my breast through the thin fabric of the dress. He gently squeezes as his hot tongue snakes around to the base of my throat. My hands find their way to his hair as his fingers push aside my thighs and find my clit. He rubs gently at first. I can feel my wetness soaking his fingertips. Nikita expertly drags his finger from my clit to my opening, drenching it in my juices. He lifts his fingers and pushes them onto my lips, the smell of my own saltiness gently wafting in my nostrils.

"Taste yourself," he growls, his emerald eyes intensely staring at my lips.

I open my mouth cautiously and he slips his finger into my mouth, my tongue instantly picking up the foreign taste: salty, primal, hot, with a hint of a metal. He removes his finger from my mouth and cups my other breast, squeezing both of them roughly. His thumbs push across my erect nipples and my body quivers and bucks forward on its own.

Nikita pulls forward one of the chairs, sits down, and pushes my legs apart, exposing my pussy to him even more as he leans in, his face inches away from it. He dives in, his tongue splitting my lips apart and lapping up my juices.

"Feels ... so good," I groan.

My back arches in anticipation. He swirls his tongue over my clit, building up my oncoming orgasm, making me moan louder and raspier, rhythmically licking, and finally inserting two fingers into me, stroking the special spot on my walls. My hands find the back of his head once again and as my hips grind against his soft tongue, each stroke and lick send bolts of uncollected desire through my body, make my back arch, and cause my hands to tug harder on the roots of his hair.

Nikita stops, drawing a gasp from my throat as the cool air wafts between my legs. He stands and leans over me, his clothes brushing against my exposed center. My stomach churns for more. He smiles and takes off his jacket and shirt, revealing his broad, tan chest and shallow abs.

In one swift movement he flips me over onto my belly. I look over my shoulder and see him unzip his pants and drop them onto the ground. As his erect cock bounces up from his boxers, I can't help but stare. It stands at attention, jaw-droppingly massive, with a gentle curve that threatens to tear me apart. Blue veins trace over the thick girth. When he takes his erection in his hand, stroking so gingerly that I can see the precum gathering at the tip, I can't help but imagine him masturbating. The thought sends my need ratcheting up to an even higher level.

"You want this, Annie?" he taunts, taking the tip and slowly rimming my opening and clit. Each touch is overwhelming on its own; altogether, it's enough to keep me from forming complete sentences. I let out another stifled moan, backing my ass up slowly, signaling to him that I want him in me as soon as possible.

After a few more long moments of teasing with his member, he plunges it into my pussy, sending thousands of pleasure ripples through my body as his whole cock pushes against my walls, making them squeeze it even tighter. I close my eyes and my hips move on their own, hungrily taking his cock and slowly releasing it, the ripples turning into tidal waves pounding through my body.

"Fuck ... You're so tight ..." Nikita breathes unevenly between thrusts and low, lustful grunts. His hands squeeze hard into my hips, directing me exactly where he wants.

I turn my head around as he grips me tighter and fucks me harder. He throws back his head and lets out a low and raspy growl of his own. Our eyes meet and his flash with lust and greed. Nikita lifts his hand and quickly slaps my ass, making it sting and making me groan out of frustration and hotness. The sharp and sudden pain adds a delicious edge to the rumbling tension building deep in my core. One of my hands finds its way to my clit and quickly rubs with the rhythm of his thrusting. Abruptly, he takes me by my hips again and starts pounding quicker, groaning with each pump.

"Nikita ..." I struggle to breathe out as the pleasure builds up. I turn back to look at him again and he stares back, his eyes darkening. He's about to cum as well. My eyelids flutter as my pussy pulsates around his cock. I shudder and all my muscles tighten.

I open my eyes again. Nikita growls, pulling out his penis, his hand quickly stroking his hardened cock. He releases his cum, hot and salty, all over my breasts and the top of my dress as he lets out the lowest, longest moan of ecstasy yet.

12

NIKITA

What just happened should terrify me.

No words can describe the orgasm I just had with Annie. I've had countless women in my lifetime. They flock to the power, the money that my position brings. But this ... this was different. It feels like I gave part of my soul to her when I came. In that moment, I would've traded everything I've ever owned for just one more second inside of her.

In other words, I lost control. And that's a dangerous, dangerous thing.

I dress quickly, fighting to steady my breath and regain my composure. The last thing I want is for her to see the weakness she just revealed. I can feel my cock, still hard and throbbing as I zip up my suit pants.

Annie coils up, her eyes focused on the ground, a faint flush to her soft skin. She chews her bottom lip as she uses a napkin from the table to wipe my cum off her breasts. I can't help but eye her body as she does. Her curves are lovely—not the surgically enhanced fakeness I normally favor. The natural shape of her body is something different, something more intoxicating.

As the glow fades from my skin, I can feel the familiar coldness settle back in. I may have lost control, but I won't make that mistake again. And right now, I need to reassert the power dynamic here.

I fix Annie with a sharp gaze. "Fix yourself up," I say as I grab my shirt from the floor.

She slinks off the table. Once standing, she adjusts her dress to make sure she's covered. She runs her hand through those luscious brown curls and ties them back with a band. Her neck bears a faint hickey.

She looks at me, and the heat that had taken over her eyes while we danced is dissipating. I see the same hardness I saw over dinner. She thought she could fool me, manipulate me, as if I wasn't expecting her to try some new plan of escape. Her ploy with Jimmy caught me by surprise, but I'm not the type of man to make the same mistake twice.

She isn't getting away again.

She can see that I know it, that her chance to slip away is long gone. The feistiness is dying a slow death, but it's dying nonetheless. Maybe she'll accept her fate soon. Maybe she'll finally realize that's not going anywhere.

"I shouldn't have done that," Annie says as she tucks a stray lock of hair behind her ear. She stares at the ground, and her voice is hushed and almost mournful. She raises her gaze to meet mine. "I still want to go home."

My lip twitches and I focus on the hickey. For another dangerous moment, I feel a twinge of sympathy. Maybe I should let her go. She's far more innocent than the girls who usually come through the auction, the ones who know that they were destined for a grim fate. This one refuses to buckle, despite the odds she faces.

But she's marked. She's mine. I paid a fortune for her, and now I've claimed her with my cock. I refuse to let her go. Besides, a girl with fighting spirit like her won't disappear if I send her home. She can pick me and half of my lieutenants out in a lineup, and I wouldn't put it past her to go straight to the station with a nasty story and the bruises to prove it.

No, despite the unusual thoughts running through my head, I can't afford to be weak here. I need to make her understand the situation. And even more than that, I need to reassure myself that I'm still in control.

When I answer her, I choose harsh words. I want this new reality to sink in for her. "I don't think so, kitten. It was a nice fuck. And I will have you again. Get it through your head … you're mine. There is no going home, so don't let me catch you trying to escape again."

I watch her face closely, but she doesn't react. She merely blinks, then looks away to where the moon is cresting over the horizon. She's an interesting character. There's far more to her than meets the eye, I think.

I frown, deep in thought as I finish buttoning my shirt and reach for the jacket on the floor.

Suddenly, the hairs on the back of my neck stand on end. Something isn't right. As I straighten, I glance around. Nothing appears out of place. But I've learned to trust my gut. In my line of business, paying attention to the body's signals helps one stay alive. My focus turns to Annie, who stands next to the table in silence, wringing her fingers and avoiding looking at me.

The terrace is silent.

The music has stopped.

"Stay here," I order. I head inside, tossing my jacket on the table as I walk by.

Jimmy still hasn't appeared, but Nikolai should've been standing guard. My men know to give me privacy when I fuck, but they're never too far. I stride deeper into the loft. Maybe he's sitting at the bar by the radio controls. He might've grabbed some spare food and decided to eat while I took Annie.

I turn the corner and all the air rushes from my lungs. Nicolas is lying facedown on my floor in a pool of his own blood. I hurry over to him and bend down next to the body. A long slit runs across his throat, blood flowing thickly from the gash. In the light of the penthouse, it's a grotesque crimson, sticky to the touch.

"Oh my God."

I jump up and spin around. Annie stands there with her hands covering her mouth, tears in her eyes. Real blood is nothing like movie blood, just as real death is nothing like movie death. There is no amount of horror that can prepare a person for seeing the life ebb from a dying body. Nicolas' eyes are wide and vacant. He's long gone.

Annie takes tentative steps toward me, her eyes focused on the body. She doesn't scream or try running for the elevator. I'm thankful that she hasn't yet made too much of a fuss. Something very bad is happening.

I stand and sprint back out onto the terrace, grabbing Annie's forearm and dragging her with me. We need to get out of here, but the keycards to the elevator are in my jacket sitting on the table outside.

Just as we cross the threshold, mercenaries swing over the edge of the rooftop.

They're clad in all black, teeming with weapons and aggression. One of them steps forward in a cocky saunter. "Nikita Lavrin," he drawls.

My hold on Annie tightens as we stop in our tracks. "Annie, stay close," I whisper.

"So, this is the whore Gino is going crazy over." He rolls up his ski mask to take a closer look at her. His tongue shoots out and runs across his lips like he's savoring a hot meal. I feel an irrational anger curl in my gut. The men level their guns at us.

"Why have you come to my house?" I say. As I talk, I'm inching towards the large plant to my left. "If Gino has a problem, he should have taken it up with the council."

The man snorts. "Gino prefers to handle his business himself. He doesn't need to ask permission from anyone to obtain what was stolen from him." The mercenary leader takes a slow stride forward to close the gap between him and us. He walks around Annie, trailing a gloved finger over her bare shoulder, across the back of her neck, sizing her up. "Especially a morsel this tasty."

I can feel Annie stiffen in my grasp at his words. The soldiers circle us and cut off my path to the keycards. The elevator is no longer an option. But the fire escape behind us could work, if we can manage to turn and run without catching bullets in the back. It should work. It has to.

I tense my hand. I'm closing the distance; the plant is just a foot away to my left.

"The council won't take this attack lightly," I warn. A little farther. I'm almost close enough to make my move.

"No, they won't. But no one will be around to let them know it was Gino."

In one smooth motion, I throw Annie across me, behind the large stone pot that houses the plant. At the same time, I stoop and grab the gun I keep hidden among the roots, then swivel to wrap my arm around the leader's throat in a chokehold. I press the gun against his head. "You might want to rethink what the fuck you're doing," I hiss in his ear. "Tell your men to stand down."

The man snickers. "You'll never make it off this roof alive," he says. Even with a gun pressed against his temple, he's a cocky asshole. But he's right—we're vastly outnumbered. I just need a distraction.

My eyes scan around the terrace, looking for something, anything that could help us. A few seconds is all we need to turn and make it to the fire escape over the edge of the roof behind me. The mercenary soldiers all have their guns pointed at me as they step slowly closer, but they don't dare to shoot for fear of striking their leader, who is still caught in my chokehold.

Then I see it.

There's no time to hesitate. I release my chokehold and kick the leader a few feet forward. One quick pull of my trigger finger is one quick bullet to the back of his head. Before his dead body has even hit the ground, I'm already swiveling up and to the right. I take aim and fire.

My second bullet hits a light, casting a warm glow out over the terrace. I had it specially installed three months ago. It's a special gas fixture—expensive, and highly flammable.

The shot causes a small explosion. Shards of glass lance outward, and the rush of heat sends a few of the men stumbling backwards. For now, it's enough.

I turn and grab Annie's upper arm. We sprint to the edge, where a low wall runs along the border of the roof. I fire a few blind shots over my shoulder, hopefully accurate enough to keep the advancing soldiers at bay for just a moment longer.

"Jump!" I shout.

"What?!"

"Jump over the side of the wall!"

"Are you crazy?" Her eyes are wide like a doe's.

Before I can answer, a bullet flies through the foliage of the plant and grazes my shoulder. A light spray of blood erupts and I roar in pain.

I turn back to her. "Now!"

The cold rage in my voice is convincing enough. She swallows hard and jumps over the side. I follow. We crash into the metal platform below. I immediately feel a searing pain lance through my knee, but I ignore it. I can't afford to succumb to pain now. We get to our feet, and race down the stairs. Annie slips and tumbles down a flight of stairs. I reach her, drag her up, and pull her after me.

My knee is screaming at me as we race down the sidewalk. I'm still holding Annie's hand. We sprint down the wet pavement littered with garbage, across the street, and sprint in front of a passing bus that lays on the horn. On the other side of the road, Annie stops and bends over, hands on her knees, breath coming in ragged, painful gasps.

"We can't stop. Keep moving."

She nods in exhaustion and pushes forward. When I glance down, I notice she is barefoot and tracking blood with every step. She must have stepped on broken glass. But she doesn't complain, just looks to me for direction.

"Do you need me to carry you?"

"No," she mumbles. "It'll just slow you down. I'll keep up."

We race into the night as fast as we can manage.

∼

Finally, nearly three miles away, we come upon a cobblestone building: a Bratva safe house. Annie and I stumble up the steps and I use a keypad to open the door, shoving her in first. When the door is closed, I triple-lock it and head up to the next flight where Annie awaits.

"There's a change of clothes in the room down the hall. Throw something on, now," I say.

She nods and races off while I head to the closet in the other end of the house. Throwing open the closet door, I'm met with myriad guns and weapons. I grab some new weapons and start to pack as much ammo as I can into my pockets.

Footsteps pad down the hall towards me. Annie enters. She's dressed in a pair of sweatpants and a sweatshirt. "There should be some women's shoes in the closet to the left." She opens the closet door and starts digging. I return to my task, making sure the bullet magazines are all full. God only knows how long it will take Gino's soldiers to show up. We didn't exactly make an inconspicuous scene—a limping, bloodied couple in fancy dinner clothes sprinting through the city—and there's no telling how good Gino's intel is. If he knows about the safe house, then we need to get the fuck out of here as fast as possible.

I go to tuck a knife in my pocket and the motion sends a sudden lightning bolt of pain piercing through my injured shoulder. I drop the knife and a groan escapes my lips.

Annie is next to me instantly.

"We should take care of that."

"There's no time. The only way for anyone to get up to my penthouse is if they had the password to my security system."

Annie gasps. "That means ..."

I nod.

My blood boils. It means that someone from inside my own circle betrayed me, just like they betrayed my father. The only difference is that I got out alive. When I have time to plan, I will rain hell on everyone involved with this mutiny. But right now, Annie and I need to get to safety. We need to get away from everyone until I can figure out how deep the betrayal goes.

Annie takes off down the hall once more.

As soon as she disappears, a new thought pops into my head. Is she involved? She was different from the other girls, too smart for her own good ... Have I been a fool? Did I buy my own betrayer? The idea makes my blood run cold. I squeeze the gun between trembling hands and raise it.

When she comes back around the corner, I'm going to put a bullet between her eyes.

I hear her footsteps approaching. I release the safety and level the sight. Three, two, one ...

She reappears mid-sentence. "If you aren't going to let me fix your wounds now, then I was grabbing some supplies to fix them up when we get to wherever ...."

She freezes. The gauze and ointment she was holding—supplies to take care of my wound—clatter to the floor.

And in that instant, I realize I was wrong. The terrified innocence in her eyes says this is as much a nightmare for her as it is for me. She isn't the one who stabbed me in the back. She's just another frightened bird, caught in a thorn bush she can't escape.

The feeling that rushes into my gut almost makes me vomit. It's shame, the kind of shame I haven't felt in God knows how long. I lower the gun and turn away before she can see the embarrassment surging in my face.

Her voice trembles. "You were going to shoot me."

I don't face her as I reply, "I thought you might have been responsible for this. I see now that I was wrong."

She says nothing. A few moments pass, pregnant with tension. I wish I could take back my actions. Regret, shame, emotions that are so foreign I don't even know where to begin with processing them, are clouding my brain. I swallow hard and turn to face her. She hasn't moved.

"I'm sorry," I whisper.

A single tear drips down her cheek.

I cross the room and grip her shoulders between my hands. My gut twists again. I look her in the eyes and say with all the seriousness I can muster. "Annie, no matter what, I promise to keep you safe. I will not let you die. I promise on my father's name."

She nods, once, unsure whether or not to believe me. I can hardly blame her, but there is no time for anything else. I stare into her eyes for a second longer, searching for something—forgiveness? Trust? I'm not sure.

I stoop and grab the things she dropped. "Thank you," I say.

Then we leave, running out the door and racing for our lives.

13

ANNIE

I don't want to die.

Nikita's grip on my shoulder is tight as he propels me down the hallway. Every step sends a stabbing pain into the sole of my feet. I'm doing my best to ignore it, but the painful heat is growing step by step. We make it outside, and the concrete steps on my bare skin are the last straw. I can't suppress the whimper that comes out of my mouth.

Nikita whirls around, keys in hand, to study my face. After a quick once-over, he takes a quick step towards me and hoists me over his shoulder.

I yelp. "Are you for real?"

"You can't walk and we need to move. This is our only option."

I just close my eyes and try to ignore the pain. Each step we land on jars my body against his broad shoulder as we round the street corner.

"Where are we going?"

"We need to get to the car," Nikita says. He doesn't stop moving.

"Wouldn't it just be safer to stay here and wait for backup? Or the cops?"

Nikita sighs impatiently and I realize it was a dumb question. Maybe a mob boss calling the cops and having them arrive at the safe house isn't the best idea. God only knows what Nikita has hidden in there, besides the guns spilling out of his pockets.

For the umpteenth time, I wonder what world I've fallen into, what crazy nightmare this has all been. I never even knew that this stuff—mob bosses and turf wars and sex slaves—existed in my city to this horrifying extent. It was right under my nose all along, just out of sight. And when I wasn't paying close enough attention, it reached out and dragged me down into its depths. I've tried to fight it every step of the way, but things have only gotten uglier. I thought being a powerful Bratva boss' prisoner was bad.

Being his hostage on the run is looking to be much, much worse.

Nikita must be able to tell I'm lost in worried thoughts, because he lowers me gently to the ground, draws a deep breath, and gives me the benefit of an explanation.

"They wouldn't be the only ones we would have to worry about if I called the police. Every other family would be after our heads. They all have contacts on the force, and they smell blood in the water. It'd be like sending up a flare to let everyone know where we are."

I furrow my brow. I was always taught to find a cop if you're in trouble. Coming to grips with the realization that they're as dirty as the mob is a struggle for me. I cross my arms across my chest, wincing once again at the pain in my feet. *Think, Annie, think,* I tell myself. I'm smart, and Nikita is the king of the city—or at least, he used to be. We can get out of this.

"Okay, so what's the plan then? You do have a plan, don't you?"

He rakes his fingers through his hair and closes his eyes. And just like that, my heart falls. This whole time—from the moment Nikita noticed that the music had stopped on the terrace—I thought that it would be just another test of Nikita's control over his world, a test he would pass with flying colors. He's been unstoppable since the second I first laid eyes on him in the club. Unyielding. Like a mountain against the storm.

But this look in his eyes is a sign of something different. It wouldn't be fair to call it fear. I don't think a man like Nikita even knows what fear truly is. But it's something similar, a cousin of fear—desperation, maybe. He wasn't ready for this. And he knows the stakes of the games he plays. It doesn't take much for me to understand them, either. We might very well die tonight. Because he doesn't have a plan. He doesn't know what to do or where to go.

And that's the scariest thing that's happened yet.

Seconds tick by and he doesn't say anything. Maybe I should just run. Maybe I'll have a better chance of surviving on my own. He's the target, after all; I'm just an innocent bystander. Right?

"Let's just get in the car," he finally says and gestures to a nondescript black sedan parallel parked a few spots down.

He helps me limp over to the passenger side and struggle into the seat. I throw my bag in the back as Nikita comes around the other side and clambers in.

"Seat belt," he says.

I almost laugh, but he isn't kidding. If things weren't so grim, I'd find this a lot funnier. He raises an eyebrow as he looks at me expectantly and waits for me to follow orders—almost like a dad with a feisty daughter. It's so unlike him and almost ... cute? Protective, caring. Not qualities I'm used to seeing in him. "Are you serious?" I ask.

"Better to die by the gun than flying through a windshield."

The moment of cuteness passes and I remember once again where we are and what we're fleeing from. I gulp and do as he says.

Satisfied, Nikita turns the key and the ignition starts. He pulls out his phone and thumbs through messages but doesn't make a call. When he's done, he powers it off and removes the battery. "They can track it," he says by way of explanation.

I shudder. These mob types have far more power than I ever realized before.

The neighborhood outside is dark and quiet. Nothing moves, nothing stirs. Nikita slides out of the parking spot, but before he can even straighten out, two cars screech around the corner, tires squealing, and stop in front of us.

They've found us.

Headlights shine in our direction, blinding us from seeing the driver or any other possible passengers. But the unmistakable click of doors cuts through the air. It sounds weirdly ominous.

For a moment, everything is silent. Then the world explodes.

"Get down!" Nikita shouts. He reaches across the console and shoves my head low just as bullets rain through the windshield. Glass splinters in a million directions, peppering my scalp like tiny needles. Nikita smashes the gas pedal and the tires screech against the asphalt. We careen into one of the enemy vehicles, but manage to slide through the gap and move down the street.

With one hand on the wheel, Nikita uses the other hand to grab a gun from his belt and fire out the broken driver's side window at the cars pursuing us. The shots come rapid-fire, one after the next. It's enough to keep the enemy shooters at bay, until I hear the metallic cough of the empty clip catching against the trigger.

"Fuck," he growls. "Annie, grab another clip from my bag."

I reach into the backpack on the floor in front of me and do as he says, handing over the metal sleeve with fresh bullets. He grabs it from me and reloads before sending another round of ammunition in the direction of the cars behind us. We're whipping around corners, clipping parked cars, swerving all over the road as Nikita alternates between looking ahead and aiming behind.

A hard right, a sharp left, we're flying now, doing sixty or seventy miles per hour in a crowded residential district. Thank God it's nighttime, or else we'd have a dozen dead pedestrians smeared across the front bumper already.

But no matter how fast we go, the men behind us stay close. Their bullets fly near, their whine like deadly bees zipping past my ears. Occasionally, one hits the frame of the car and lodges there. I try to stay low and keep my heart from bursting out of my rib cage.

We bowl through another intersection. Nikita is down to the last couple bullets of this clip. He fires one and manages to hit the tire of one of the cars behind us. I look over my shoulder and see the driver struggling to keep it aimed straight as he fishtails all over the breadth of the road.

But when I turn back around to face the front, I scream.

A man with a hot dog cart is idling his way across the crosswalk. Our headlights catch his face and reflect off the wide, terrified whites of his eyeballs.

"Nikita!"

He looks up, sees the cart, and cranks the steering wheel hard to the right. For a brief moment, it feels like we're flying. There are at least two wheels off the ground.

Then we smash down with a heavy crunch and an angry retort from the car's suspension. We're on the sidewalk now, tearing down branches of bushes and trees that drape over the low wall separating the apartment complexes from the street. Leaves and bits of wood fly in through the shattered windows, stinging my face. A loud bang on my side of the car sounds when we clip a mailbox.

Nikita sees an opening and twists us back onto the road, narrowly avoiding a pair of midnight dog walkers who look like they might've peed themselves at the unexpected sight of a sedan barreling down the city sidewalk with bullet holes in the windshield.

I look behind us. The pursuers aren't visible. Did we lose them? I'm cautiously optimistic. *Stay calm,* I remind myself. *This is just a bad dream.* I want to click my heels like Dorothy, *there's no place like home, there's no place like home.*

Nikita checks the mirrors repeatedly and continues to take as unpredictable a route as possible. Left, right, straight, down an alley and out again onto a main drag, lit by harsh streetlamps. "Stay low," he orders. He doesn't have to tell me twice.

I slink low in my seat and bring my knees up to my chest as if they're a shield that will protect me. This kind of thing just doesn't happen in real life. Shootouts and car chases are for action movies, not for the city where I grew up. And yet, here I am, with the bullet holes in the windshield and the terror coursing through my veins to prove that this is all far too real.

But for now, it seems like the worst has passed us. The night is quiet again, aside from the occasional groan from the beat-up metal exterior of the car. God only knows what we've run over or through in our mad dash from the safe house. I find myself thinking about how much it will cost to hammer out all the dents, and I have to catch myself and wonder why I'm focusing on such a ridiculous detail. I should be worried about surviving, not ding repair.

"Goddammit," Nikita snarls under his breath.

In the side mirror, a set of angry headlights has reappeared, not too close behind us but gaining speed fast. The sharp ping of a bullet slicing through metal and glass explodes inside the cabin once more.

Nikita presses down on the gas pedal. We lurch forward, back to top speed. We're approaching a Y-shaped intersection that I'm familiar with. The right-hand lane leads back into the grid of the city. The center takes us onto a highway, one that's sure to be busy, even at this time of night. And the far left is an exit ramp of traffic flowing in the opposite direction. Surely …

Nikita accelerates again and takes us into the left, oncoming lane.

I scream wordlessly, white-knuckling the center console, as the cacophony of pissed-off drivers erupts around us. Nikita growls through clenched teeth as we dodge left, right, left, into the bare shoulder of the road, back in the middle again. Headlights glare into our bullet-riddled cabin, with shouted curses flitting in from the cars we're barely missing as they stream past us.

The enemy car behind us keeps up, though thankfully the bullets have stopped for now. My head is on a swivel, looking ahead and behind. There's danger in every direction, but Nikita handles the wheel expertly, narrowly avoiding a collision every moment. Spying an opening, he cuts across three lanes. Our enemies are right behind us.

Time slows to a crawl. I see the semitruck coming from the left-hand side before Nikita does, but there's nothing either of us can do. We're committed now, helplessly in the hands of gravity and inertia. Either it hits us and we die, or it misses and we live. It's that simple.

I hold my breath as our vehicle glides through the gap. A space of no more than an inch or two separates us from getting clipped by the eighteen-wheeler.

We make it.

Our enemies are not so lucky.

The sound of the massive truck T-boning them is a scream of metal. Sparks fly through the smoke of destroyed engines and the stench of rubber melting on concrete. Watching over my shoulder, I see the momentum of the eighteen-wheeler drive the sedan into the concrete barrier separating lanes of the highway. There's another sickening crunch, and then everything stops.

But we keep going, swept away in the flow of traffic heading out of the city. The scene of terror recedes behind us, becoming smaller and smaller, until a bend in the highway hides it from sight. The only sounds now are the whispered wind streaming through bullet holes and the ragged pant of my own breath.

"Those poor people," I say.

"They were trying to kill us," Nikita says.

"Not them," I whisper. "The innocent ones."

Nikita re-grips the steering wheel. "No one is innocent," he says in a strange tone. I'm not sure if he's even talking to me, but it doesn't really matter. Instead, he continues to speed down the highway.

Neither of us talks for a long time.

∼

I can barely see the city lights in the distance behind us anymore. The traffic has dissipated for the most part, filtering out into the various veins of highway that lead into the heart of the suburbs. We keep going. Skyscrapers become strip malls become housing sub-developments and eventually are reduced to the scrubby forest lining the highway. The steady hum of the engine is like a lullaby. At some point, I'm not sure when, I fall asleep.

"Annie, wake up."

I open my eyes to find Nikita gently shaking my shoulder. We're stopped on the side of the road now. Outside the window, mountains stretch up to stab into the night sky. They dominate the dark horizon every which way I look. The range is high to the west and low to the east, curling at the end like a tail.

I blink the sleep out of my eyes. Silence fills the car like a heavy cloud. The fear that had gripped me from the moment the soldiers had appeared on the terrace is gone now. No more panic firing like a cluster of spark plugs in my abdomen. No more tension seizing hold of my limbs. My breathing is low and slow, and the only sensation in my body is an overwhelming ache, tinged at the edge by a hint of pain lingering in my feet.

Nikita remains silent so all I hear is my breath. He doesn't look at me, just stares straight out ahead into the night.

I turn to Nikita. "You think we made the news?" I ask.

He looks back at me, that familiar stern arrogance wrinkling his brow. He appears to consider my question seriously for a moment. Then, to my surprise, he bursts out laughing.

It catches me off-guard. Since the second I entered his company, he has been powerful, in control, deadly serious. But the last few hours have been the exact opposite—he's been a man running for his life, unsure of how this will all play out. And somehow, my question made him laugh.

I didn't mean it as a joke. Part of me is curious if our high-speed chase will end up on the TV. Maybe deep down, I'm hoping the cameras caught my image so that my friends and family know where I am. That they'll inform the cops of my identity and that I need help.

But Nikita is laughing, and soon, I am, too. It's the kind of laugh, half desperate and half overwhelmed, that starts suddenly and doesn't end soon. We're laughing and laughing and laughing, until we're clutching our sides and tears are pouring down our faces. The crickets in the night and the occasional whizz of a passing car fill in the gaps when we finally stop to draw breath.

A voice in the back of my head wonders what the hell has happened to my life. I'm in a bullet-ridden car, miles outside of the city, with a powerful Russian mob boss who says he owns me—and we're laughing like it's been a grand old adventure, a real knee-slapper of a time. What's wrong with me?

Eventually, we calm down again. I use the back of my hand to wipe the tear tracks from my face. Nikita coughs and composes himself again.

"Too late at night, I think," he says, answering my question. "Maybe there'll be something in the morning."

I nod. Then I realize suddenly how hungry I am. I reach into the back and grab the bag containing some food. Thank God the safe house had cookies. I grab the box and open them, shoving two into my mouth, not caring how bedraggled I look. I offer Nikita some but he just stares straight ahead. "You sure you don't want one?"

"I'm good."

I chew for a couple of moments, then swallow and pick out another cookie from the tray. "I've never been through anything like that before."

Nikita glances my way. "Did you check yourself? Did a bullet hit you?"

"I ... I don't think so."

He presses his lips tight together and does a quick scan of my body. "Check. With all the adrenaline, you might not feel it right away." There's a caring tone in his voice that I'm not used to.

I put the cookies down and run my hands up my legs, over my torso, and down my arms. Nothing. Only tiny beads of glass cover me. I gently wipe them off. "I'm good. What about you?"

"I'm fine."

I grab two bottles of water from the back and offer him one after I unscrew the top. He takes it and sucks down all the liquid without coming up for air and then tosses the empty bottle into the back. "Thank you."

I smile meekly and shove another cookie in my mouth. "If it wasn't for the bullets, I would almost say the car chase was kind of fun."

"Excuse me?"

I take a sip of my water before continuing. "When I was really young, I used to watch action movies with my dad. Anything with a car chase would do. We'd watch them, then go running around the backyard, him chasing me so I could pretend I was the one escaping." It's a memory I haven't thought of in a long time. Easy summer evenings, cicadas humming, my dad making *vrooming* noises as he chased me left and right, circling everywhere, until he'd finally snatch me up in his arms, squealing and giggling. I still remember what he smelled like. That was back before all the nightmares began.

"Who would've thought: the little bird is a closet speed demon."

I quirk my brow. "'Little bird'?"

Nikita looks uncomfortable suddenly, like he said something he didn't mean to let slip. "Never mind," he says gruffly. He looks down at the cookies in my hand. "I changed my mind. Can I have a cookie before you eat the entire package?"

His smile is infectious. I grin and place three in his hand. He chews thoughtfully. When he's finished, he nods like he's arrived at a decision.

"All right," he says. "Time to go."

"Where?"

He points. I follow his finger to the top of the mountain.

"You're kidding."

"Nope."

"Up there?"

"Yes."

"But ... why?"

He sighs with the exasperation of someone answering questions from a child. "The men following us will have radioed in a description of the car and the direction we were headed. It'll take them time to cover the distance, but make no mistake—they're coming to finish what they started."

I swallow hard. I shudder to think what will happen if we get caught. I hope I never have to find out. "Okay," I say. "So we walk?"

"Yes. Ditch the car, hide it, disappear until I can figure out what to do next."

I try to put on a brave face. What he's saying makes sense, but it's not exactly what I was hoping for. I look into the shadows of the trees clustered close together off to my right. That's where we're headed. Out of the frying pan and into the fire.

Nikita opens his door and gets out, grabbing his bags from the back seat as he does. I follow suit. But when my feet hit the dirt below, I wince, my body tensing from pain. I clutch the door in an attempt to alleviate the pressure from my feet. Nikita hears me hiss and comes around the front of the car. He wraps an arm around me and lowers me back into the seat.

"We need to walk, but I need to take a look at your feet first," he says as he gingerly removes the sneakers I threw on in our blind panic at the safe house.

The insoles are soaked in blood which has begun to dry, so when he peels them off it's as if he's also ripping new scabs away. I can't help but cry out. While he doesn't look up, I notice the way his face contorts and the way his thumb rubs gentle circles against my skin.

"I'm sorry," I say, unsure as to why I'm apologizing.

He sighs and stands. "Where's the bag with the supplies you took?"

"In the back."

He opens the rear door and searches through the bag, returning with peroxide and gauze. He swallows hard, his Adam's apple bobbing. "This isn't going to be pleasant."

I brace myself as he squirts the peroxide onto my feet. But nothing prepares me for the burning sting. There's hardly any skin left on my soles, and the peroxide is ruthless in seeking out every raw nerve ending and lighting it on fire. I whimper, squeezing my eyes shut to try to block out the pain as Nikita uses the gauze to pat at the cuts and pulls some pebbles from my wounds with a pair of tweezers.

When he's done, he wraps clean gauze over the tender skin and slips the shoes back onto my feet. I think of Cinderella at the ball and laugh inwardly. I'm no princess, this is no fairy tale, and the man kneeling before me is the farthest thing from Prince Charming that there is on this planet.

Except, maybe not.

There's a gentleness to his movements that I'd never noticed before, and the worry wrinkling his brow seems genuine. I think back to our frenzied romp on the table of the terrace and blush. Thankfully, he can't see me in the darkness. I force myself to think of something else—I'm not ready to process that particular memory yet.

"Thank you," I say as I gently lower myself to the ground.

The pain is still present, especially after the peroxide, but at least I won't have to worry about an infection anytime soon. He hands me a couple of painkillers to take.

"Where are we?" I ask, slinging one of the bags over my shoulder.

"I used to come here with my father. We should be safe here for the night, but I have to ditch the car. Gino's men will be looking for it."

"Won't they know to search here if we abandon the car?"

"Yes." Nikita empties all the bags and supplies from the car. "That's why I'm going to run it into there."

I turn to see where he's pointing and realize there's a small lake I hadn't noticed before. More of a retention pond, actually, just a man-made hole to collect water, but it seems deep enough to conceal the car, at least while it's still dark.

My jaw drops when I realize what he's intending to do, but Nikita is already swinging into action before I can even protest. He's behind the wheel again, with the driver's door swung open. He cranks the wheel around until the nose of the car is pointed at the lake, then guns it forward.

"Nikita!" I cry out involuntarily. I see a flash of movement. He dives out of the car moments before it crashes into the still surface of the water. He hits the ground and rolls in an elegant tumble.

By the time he's regained his feet, the car is filling with dark lake water and bubbling as it sinks. I stand in place, horrified. He comes up to me nonchalantly, brushing dirt from his clothes. When he's within reach, I slap him across the face.

"Don't do that again," I snap.

He looks stunned, and I don't blame him. I'm not entirely sure where that impulse came from. It's certainly not something I would've done even this morning. But right now, all I could think about was watching him drown, and for some reason that terrified me.

To my surprise, he looks embarrassed. "Sorry," he mutters. I can only sigh in response.

We watch as the car disappears below the surface. When it's gone, Nikita picks up his bag from where he set it on the ground before sinking the vehicle. "We need to get moving," he says. I follow his lead as we forge into the trees standing sentinel at the edge of the forest.

The path ahead is loose rock, each one washed smooth by the river that brought them down from the mountain peak. Thickly dark green boughs arch over the path from each side. It winds ahead smooth and level at first, but soon it becomes narrow, steep, and rocky. Each footfall costs me more strength. I try hard to ignore the pain throbbing in my feet.

"You came up here with your father?" I ask.

Nikita pulls himself up over a fallen stump then turns and offers me a hand to help me over as well. "Yes, it was our annual trip before he died."

We continue on. Nikita knows where to step as if he's traversed this exact path billions of times. He knows when to help me and guides me where to step. Even in the darkness, this is second nature to him. In some places, the path grows wide where the soil is soft and we quicken our pace to almost a jog, and then it narrows in the rocky passes. Sometimes the path is no more than a faint suggestion in the dirt.

It's one of these times when we stop that I notice Nikita is bleeding again from the bullet graze on his shoulder. I grab the bag from him and take out the peroxide and gauze.

"What are you doing?"

"You're bleeding," I say as I rip one of the holes in his shirt a bit wider.

"I'm fine."

I meet his gaze. "Don't care. You took care of me, so now I'm returning the favor, whether you like it or not."

He sits back and lets me tend to his wounds. But there isn't enough gauze to wrap around the deepest graze, so I grab the pocketknife from the bag and cut off a piece of the sweatpants I'm wearing to use as a makeshift bandage.

Nikita tracks my movements. I'm not sure if he's worried I might stab him or if he's impressed I'm taking care of him. That's one thing I'm starting to hate about him—that emotionless mask he wears. Every time I think I'm getting a glimpse of the man behind the walls, he throws them up again before I can be sure. He's a frustrating enigma.

I tuck the blade back into its sheath and return the multitool to the bag. Then I take the material I've cut and wrap it around his wound.

"Done," I say after securing the material around his arm.

Nikita nods and stands. "Let's go. We still have a long way to climb."

14

NIKITA

I sigh and my shoulders slouch as I stare off into the distance. This place ... it's so beautiful and serene. Just like I remembered. My eyes wander along the small hills to the valleys, following the dry creek beds my father and I used to camp next to. How many times did I stand on this very ledge with him? My father used to breathe in the fresh air, puffing out his chest as we gazed at the jagged peaks of the mountains. And something always stirred deep inside of me, a satisfied feeling I couldn't place or name.

Tonight, it's different. I exhale slowly, my breath clouding from the frigid temperature. I feel hollow, worn out, like a dishrag used too many times. I can't remember the last time I didn't feel this way. I can't remember the last time I felt anything at all, really.

Until Annie.

I'm aware of her in a way I've never felt with anyone else. Not just in tune with her feelings, with every sharp intake of breath or every awkward purse of her lips—though I feel those things as if they were happening to me. But I'm aware of her as I'm aware of myself. Her pain is my pain. Her exhaustion is my exhaustion. Her fear runs in me like it was my own, though it has been years since I was truly afraid of anything. I can't explain it and I don't like it, this sudden expansion of awareness that has taken me over.

I look over my shoulder to make sure she's okay. Sure enough, she's hoisting herself over a fallen tree and heading in my direction, grimacing with each step. What I wouldn't give to take her pain away.

"Nikita, wait up. It's dark and I don't know the area as well as you do. I don't want to get lost," Annie says from behind.

"Take your time. Just trying to figure out what direction to head in." I face forward and scan our surroundings. There was a place my father and I would camp out at when we came up this way: our secret hiding place, tucked away from the well-trodden main path, safe from all but those who already know where it is. I'm hoping it will keep Annie and me safe for the night.

"There should be a clearing to our left. It's hidden from the trail."

"Lead the way," Annie says as she climbs the rest of the way to meet me.

I stop and study her for a moment as she approaches. Her hair is long and ragged, strewn with sticks and leaves from the hike up. I've chosen the less-traveled route wherever I think she'll be able to handle it. Anything to hide our tracks from would-be pursuers. There is a weary slant to her shoulders and sweat is beaded on her upper lip despite the chill in the air. For a wild moment, I imagine kissing it away. Then the thought passes like a fever dream, and I remember once again where we are and what we are running from.

"You've handled yourself well tonight."

"Because I had a choice," she replies sarcastically.

"Few of us ever do."

Apparently, it was the wrong thing to say. I can see a sudden clench in her jaw, a tightness in her fists.

"*You* had a choice," she snaps. "*You* chose to drag me into this. And what's happened since? Nothing *I* chose, that's for sure. Bullets aimed for me, blood everywhere, the ambush on the terrace, a midnight car chase with our lives on the line, my feet scraped completely raw, and now this mad dash up a mountain in the godforsaken dark ... Would you like me to continue?"

"Earlier, you said it was thrilling."

"Please tell me you're joking," she says. "Please tell me that's a joke." It's dark, but I can still see the fire gleaming in her eyes, catching the moonlight and throwing it at me like a taunt, like a schoolyard dare.

"Would you prefer if I had left you on the terrace?"

"I'd prefer if you had left me to my old life, which I very much enjoyed, actually. Before I knew who you were or that any of this existed." She throws a hand in the air at "any of this" and I know exactly what she's referring to.

She means my life. My world. The empire my family has cultivated for generations, humming just under the surface of the city everyone thinks they know. But no one really knows it like I do. And once you learn what exists—how far it reaches, how ugly and depraved it is, run by dons like me and beasts like Gino—there is no going back. Annie knows that. Even if we make it out of here alive and Annie returns to her old life, it won't matter. The knowledge that I exist has changed her for good. She can never truly return.

And she hates me for it.

But I still can't shake the memory of her thrown across the dining table on the terrace, writhing and moaning. The soft swell of her lips against mine, the heat of her skin, the timbre of her begging whimpers. The thought alone gets me hard and makes my heart clench in an unexpected way.

I feel so many things attached to this woman, standing across from me with her hands on her hips, jutted out angrily. Responsibility and protectiveness and lust and fury at her constant insubordination. Why will she not just lie down and obey my orders, like everyone else in my life? Why will she not just do as I say? At every turn and in every way, she fights back, pushing at me, testing my limits. And yet, I can't find it in me to get angry and stay there. Over and over again, I come back to the same thought:

She is different than the rest.

Even now, in this moment, I'd kill her if she were someone else. No one talks to me the way she is doing and goes unpunished. I've spent my life building up a reputation as a ruthless mob boss, and all it takes is one petite accounting student to unravel all of it. So, as much as one voice in my head is screaming at me to make her pay for her sass, I can't bring myself to do it.

I'm responsible for her. And I have to make things right. Even if she still hates me when all is said and done. Even if I was wrong about the random tender moments I thought we were sharing—bandaging her feet, laughing in the car. I must protect her, even if we are to part ways later and never see each other again.

I try to tell her all that with one look, because the words running through my head don't seem to capture the weight of my remorse, of the responsibility I feel I'm bearing. So many things have changed in the last few days, but the walls I've erected around myself are still too tall to surmount. Sharing my thoughts out loud would mean turning my back on the legacy I've bled and sweated to create. So I can only look at her and hope she understands.

She crosses her arms and huffs. "Well? Anything to say for yourself?" Her words are angry, but her eyes are searching my face, trying to figure me out.

I cast my eyes down at the trail. "Let's keep moving," I say. "We're not safe yet."

The forest is dark and foreboding, but there is peace in its sullen ambience. I wonder how my father ever came to find the place where we're headed. My eyes flicker over the thick, dark trunks of the trees that rise steadily into the sky, branches interlocking with their neighbors like giants' arms linked together, protecting their home. The trees are densely packed together, leaving just enough space for Annie and me to maneuver through. I press my palm against the rough bark, and breathe in the scent of the forest. The musty scent of leaves after rainfall, the warm soil packed against the earth by scurrying animals, the scent of things in different stages of blooming and growth. The smell of life.

We round a crook in the path. Suddenly, behind me, I hear the tch-tch-tch of wood splintering. I whirl around, senses on high alert.

In an instant, I process everything, as if time had slowed to a crawl. Annie is on all fours, maneuvering up the steep, gravelly path. The heavy tree branch over her head is on its last few threads keeping it hoisted up against the trunk. There are mere seconds, maybe less, before it tumbles to the ground. It's at least twice as thick as her. She'll be pinned beneath it, probably hurt, possibly killed.

I react immediately, lunging forward and yanking her up by the arm. My momentum carries us back down the path. I pull her into my embrace as we tuck and roll. The loose rocks tear at my shirt and skin, and I roar in pain. I hear the branch give way as it crashes into the ground where Annie just was with a thunderous boom. The ground shakes, squirrels titter in fear, and birds caw as they flap away.

We roll to a stop at the base of another tree. I look back and shudder. To come this far and be killed by a tree ... fate would have to have a very cruel sense of humor.

My adrenaline subsides and I turn my attention to the girl in my arms. Her breath is rising and falling rapidly, heart beating like a hummingbird. She combs the hair back from her face and looks up at me. Neither of us says a word for a moment, but my chest throbs with an almost painful pang. She looks beautiful in the moonlight. Fragile and dirty and scared, yes. But beautiful. She's tucked against my chest, with my arms encircling her and keeping her close. The warmth of her body is intoxicating.

"You okay?" I whisper.

"Just peachy," she responds. I can see the war inside her. Gratitude for saving her, wonder at just what exactly is happening between us. Anger at what I've done to her, fear at what's being done to us. All of it brewing and bubbling and threatening to explode.

She disentangles herself from me abruptly and stands up, checking herself for any wounds suffered while I grabbed her and rolled. Finding nothing, she claps the dirt from her hands. "As you were," she says sarcastically.

I nod and get to my feet. Once again, the moment passes, and our respective masks settle back into place. "We should almost be there."

∼

Annie stays closer to me as we go back up, stepping carefully over the fallen branch and checking every few seconds to make sure no other trees are eager to drop a limb on our heads. At the edge of a cliff, I spot a rock with a stick figure carving. A smile tugs at my lips. I remember using my little pocketknife to chisel away at the rock, pretending I was some sort of explorer marking my territory. My father laughed and burst my bubble when he told me this was *his* secret hiding place.

But my father is dead. This is mine now.

I clamber up onto the cliff and look over the edge. A thin patina of crisscrossed branches hides whatever is below from sight. Given where we are on the mountain, it could just as easily be a thousand-foot drop into a shadowy chasm, though I know better.

I jump off the edge, crash through the branches, and land on the packed dirt a few feet below.

When the dust settles, Annie calls to me from above. "Nikita?" Her voice has a nervous warble.

"I'm down here. You'll have to jump."

"Umm." I can hear her above, though the branches hide her from sight. A few crumbs of dirt fall as she fusses around, hoping for a better way down. I remember doing the same with my father. The drop is scary for those who don't know what lies below. It's a truly blind fall.

Annie will just have to trust me.

"It's okay, Annie. I promise."

I hear her take a deep breath. "I don't know," she says nervously.

"I'll catch you."

"Okay ... are you sure?"

"I'm sure. Just jump."

A few quiet moments pass, filled only by the sounds of the nighttime forest. Rustling in the bushes, the occasional whoosh of a bat winging after insects.

Then I hear the scuffle of dirt. She's jumping. The branches part to give way to Annie as she slices down. I have just a split second to register the fear in her eyes before she lands in my arms. I bend my knees to absorb her impact. It takes everything I have, especially given the pain in my shoulder and knee, but I manage to keep my feet.

I set her down on her feet. But I hold her close, unwilling to let her go just yet. Heat and electricity course through my blood at having her body so close to mine. Her scent invades my nose. A mixture of sweat, lilac, and something wholly Annie. I hold onto her for longer than I should.

She's wincing. I look down and notice a thin trickle of blood between her toes. The wounds on her feet must have opened up again. "We're almost there. Can you keep walking?" I say.

"Yes."

She waits for me to lead, but she doesn't let go of my hand. My pace is slower as I guide her through the thicket. It's only a few dozen paces after the jump, but I'm moving carefully in the dark, placing every step just so in order to keep us safe in the night. Then I push aside a hanging curtain of moss and glide past.

"We're here."

I stop at the edge of the clearing and take it in. Everything is as I remember. The fallen stumps my father and I would sit on as we ate. The remnants of the firepit stones, arranged in a rough circle from our last visit. Even the old tin bucket I forgot to take back home still remains, though years have passed since it was last used.

The moonlight shines through the gap in the treetops, casting the whole place in a smooth, otherworldly glow. Beneath our feet, there is soft grass, like a blanket laid down in the middle of the forest.

"This place is beautiful," Annie says, releasing her fingers from mine and walking to the center of the clearing. I feel a soft tingle where I was holding her hand.

She stops in the middle, tilts her head up, and grins. Her smile shines like stars after dark, with no city lights to dim them. I admire her while she admires the night sky. These past two days, I couldn't wait to get home to her, to have her and taste her. And now that I have, I'm not so sure I'll be able to give her up.

I follow her gaze to the starry night above. It's a brilliant van Gogh, everything bigger and brighter, sharper and closer. It feels like the sky is pressing down on us. Like I could reach a hand up and touch it if I wanted to.

"You and your father came here a lot?"

I turn to look at Annie. She's looking back at me with a curious, unreadable emotion in her eyes. "Yes. This was our little hideaway. We'd camp here once a year."

"Do you miss him?"

The question surprises me, like a blow to the chest. "I've never thought about that before. I guess ... yes, I do." I haven't said that even once since the day he died. It feels uncomfortable and yet oddly relieving. "You should sit," I say, changing the subject. "I'm sure your feet need the rest."

She walks over to me. "Not before we take care of your wound. It's pretty deep."

"I'm out of luck if stitches are needed."

She shakes her head. "Luckily, I grabbed some butterfly closures from the medicine cabinet."

"Okay, little bird. Fix me up." I untie the makeshift bandage, then unbutton my shirt and take it off. The crisp air hits my skin and goose bumps spring to life. Though, I'm not sure if they're from the cold air or the way Annie's eyes run over my body. My cock twitches when her eyes rove down to my zipper.

Annie blushes when she notices I've caught her staring. Her eyes dart around as she tries to avoid me. She absently twirls a stray lock of hair between her fingers before she points to the left. "Um, let's sit over on the log so I can take care of that," she says and hurries away from me.

I sit down as Annie pulls supplies from the bag. She lays them out on the ground then looks me over once more. She grabs the peroxide and, with her other hand, spreads open my wound before she squirts the antiseptic liquid onto it. I flinch from the initial burn, my teeth sinking into my inner cheek. "Fuck, that hurts."

"Trust me, I know," she says, tilting her head down towards her feet.

I run my hand through my hair and sigh. Both of us could do with some serious medical care and rest. But it won't happen tonight.

She nods and continues cleaning out my wound. Then, she pats it down to dry the skin around it before placing the butterfly closures on it. Once she's done, she places a fresh gauze square over the wound and rewraps the piece of the sweatpants she cut up earlier to hold everything in place.

When she's finished, she slaps her palms down on her thighs, a proud smile plastered across her face. "All done."

I place a finger under Annie's chin and tip it up so that her eyes meet mine. "Thank you." The air around us is charged, vibrating. Again, I stare deeply into her eyes, wondering which side of her is winning the war in her mind and heart.

She snorts and pulls away from my grasp, busying herself by putting all of the supplies away. "Finally, the mob boss learns some manners."

I open my mouth to retort and then close it again. Annie smiles shyly, pats my arm, and then sits next to me on the ground, a slight shiver running through her body. I wrap my arm around her and pull her closer. The last thing either of us needs is to die from hypothermia. Up at this altitude, that's a very realistic threat. Annie rests her head on my shoulder and every one of my senses tingle. God, how I love having her this close to me.

"Thank you for keeping me safe," she whispers, her warm breath caressing my skin.

I run my fingers over her arms and press my nose into her scalp, inhaling. She presses closer to me and curls up, wrapping an arm around my waist. One day, when we aren't running for our lives, I'm going to bring Annie back here and we're going to camp out just like I used to do with my father.

"Where did you learn first aid?" I ask.

It's an innocent enough question, so I'm surprised when every muscle in Annie's body tenses and times passes before she speaks. "My father used to come home with wounds that my mom and I would have to tend to."

"Was he a cop?"

Annie sighs. "I wish. He was a scumbag. He worked for the mob."

Air rushes from my lungs. A thousand thoughts run through my head, all inadequate for the moment. I can see the hurt and anger in her eyes. There's a story there, an ugly one. I wrap my arms tighter when she begins to shiver again.

She starts speaking before I can figure out what I should say. "I wish I could forget a lot of it. Mom and I used to be afraid all the time. Bricks would be thrown through our windows and we even had body parts delivered to our house. I'll never forget the first time I opened a box and found a finger in it."

Her voice cracks and my heart aches at the thought of Annie—a young Annie, no less—finding a severed finger. That would never happen on my watch. Not that I haven't sent similar warnings. But I would never involve a young child.

On purpose, at least.

"Eventually my father got arrested. It was in the newspapers. The whole school found out and everyone turned on me. Not that they didn't already harass me for being poor, for wearing hand-me-down clothes, or for not having food. But my family did the best they could. Eventually, my mother and I moved and started over."

"Your mom sounds like a strong woman," I say.

"She is. She learned how to sew my father's wounds closed. She kept a brave face when our home was attacked. And she prayed with me every night. When we moved, she went and learned the skills she needed to get a job, and she worked hard. I get my work ethic from her. No shortcuts like my dad tried."

Out of nowhere, I think back to the old man who was dragged in front of me at the club the night I bought Annie. It wasn't so long ago, and yet the details are already hazy and indistinct. His eyes, begging for help. I could have let him go, fixed him up, solved his problems. All that was within my grasp. I had only to say the word.

I could have given him mercy. Instead, I gave him pain.

Did I send him home to young children with bloodstained clothes and crushing debt? Was his family afraid, the same way Annie was as a child?

"Are you okay?" Annie searches my face.

"Yes." I run my fingers through her hair absentmindedly. "I was just thinking about what you told me. What happened after you moved?"

She settles back down against me. "It all worked out in the end. Mom got us a house and I worked hard on my grades and ended up with a full ride to college." Her soft lips stretch into a smile that doesn't quite reach her eyes, which are lit with sadness.

Almost a happy ending. She almost made it. Maybe she would have.

If it weren't for me.

I took away her life. I ruined what her mother worked hard to give her. I dragged her back into the hell she escaped once before. I don't think I've ever hated myself as much as I do in this moment. I've never hated the life I live or the things I've done to secure my place in the underworld.

"Do you talk to your father?"

She bites the corner of her lower lip. "No. He's dead. Died in jail. But even if he was alive, I wouldn't have anything to say to him. I've moved on, made a good life for myself. And I don't want to remember what he represents. I don't want to live like that ever again."

Looking at Annie, I'm not so sure I want to continue living this life. Maybe there's another way. Maybe I can be like her and her mother and start over. Have a life where I'm not looking over my shoulder. A life where I can take my family camping and not worry about bullets flying through our windows.

Maybe it's time I consider leaving the business I was born into.

15

ANNIE

"Nikita?"

He's lost in thought, staring off into the distance. His facial muscles tense and his jaw ticks. I'm not sure where his mind is or if I can help him. Nor even if I should.

"I'm sorry you got dragged into this mess," Nikita says.

I look up at him and offer a weak smile. Then, I place a gentle kiss on his chest, just above his heart. A low growl vibrates from within him and I clench my knees together. Something about the sounds he makes stokes the fires within me.

Nikita pulls me closer and my hands slide up his arms. After our encounter on top of the table in the penthouse, and after everything else that followed, I want to feel him again. I want him to touch me again. He runs his fingertips down my spine, his touch sending sparks along my skin as he pushes my sweatshirt up and over my head. I unbutton his shirt and push it from his shoulders, the bloodied material falling to the ground.

"Jesus, Annie. You make me so hard from just looking at you." He pushes gently at my shoulders so I'm lying flush against the grass.

I wince when my bare skin connects with the cold ground, but Nikita is quick to clamp his mouth down on mine, and all thoughts of cold are forgotten as my skin flushes with heat. His hands roam over my bare skin and up into my hair. I hook my finger through the belt loop of his pants, pulling him forward and lifting my head to deepen our kiss.

"Nikita," I whisper, pressing my body into his, my legs winding around his hips. His erection nudges against my heated sex and I tilt my hips, grinding against him. I slide my hands around his hips, pushing his pants down until they bunch up about mid-thigh. "Take these off. Take everything off."

Nikita chuckles and swipes at my lower lip with his tongue before he climbs off me to shed the rest of his clothes. My gaze drops to between his legs and my eyes widen when he sheds his boxer briefs. His cock rises from its base, proud and fierce, thick and veiny. I swallow hard.

He leans over me and settles his mass on top of mine, so that I'm lying beneath him. Nikita Lavrin has a body like no other man I've been with before. All solid mass and smooth skin, defined muscles and broad chest and shoulders. He's all I can see and hear and smell and taste while he lies on top of me, his long fingers curled around my wrists, holding my arms captive above my head.

What we're doing is so completely unexpected, so unbelievably exciting, my entire body is shaking in anticipation. He's kissing me like he's a starving man and I'm the only thing he craves. I can feel his thick erection nudging between my legs, and I'm so wet for him it's almost embarrassing.

But I don't care. I'm drunk on the sensation of his body pressing into mine, his hungry mouth, his insistent tongue, those big, rough hands pinning me to the ground.

I had no idea being held down would arouse me so much, but oh my God, I'm so hot for him I feel like I'm going to burst. My center is dripping and I'm aching for relief. I need Nikita's tongue on me, sucking my clit like he did after dinner. I want to come on his mouth.

He whispers in my ear after breaking our kiss, "I'm not sure if I'll last very long. I might just come all over your hands the moment you touch me."

I want to laugh. I also want to moan. His blunt words turn me on. I'm dying to feel his member in my hands, in my mouth, and especially inside of me. I want him to fill me and stretch me again. I open my lips and tell him the truth: "I'm dying to taste you."

His eyes lock with mine. They're dark and full of smoldering heat. I want to stroke him, to make Nikita lose all control until he bursts in my grasp. Then I want to place my fingers into my mouth and suck them clean, tasting him.

Restlessly, I rub my legs against his. "Soon. But first, I want to touch you." His voice lowers as his fingers loosen gently around my wrists, until they're slipping away and he's nuzzling my neck with his face, his hands skimming along my sides. "I want to explore you properly this time. I want to take my time and savor you."

I'm not going to protest. That's exactly what I want him to do. All I can do is hold on for dear life. I sling my arms around his neck, my hands in his hair, gently guiding him down as he rains kisses across my collarbone, to my chest, to the tops of my breasts. My nipples ache for his mouth to wrap around them and his lips are everywhere but there. I don't know if I can stand this exquisite torture, his hands gripping my hips, his mouth all over my sensitive skin. I tighten my hold on his hair, tugging hard until he mutters a curse against my flesh before he licks one nipple, then the other.

The ragged moan that escapes me is nothing like the usual sounds I make in bed, and I clamp my lips shut, momentarily embarrassed. But then he does it again, his velvety damp tongue flicking back and forth over my nipple, driving me absolutely wild. Another shuddery moan leaves me, and I tangle my fingers in his hair, holding him to me as he licks and sucks and edges his teeth on my flesh, gently nipping.

It feels so good. I want more. Oh. God, I'm crazed with wanting his teeth on me, his hands all over me. "Harder," I whisper, my request shocking me, and he bites my nipple, hard.

Between my legs, I drip because I'm so wet and when he glides his fingers through my soaked folds, his thumb sweeping over my clit, I whimper and nearly come.

"Spread them for me," he directs into my ear. "Press your feet together. Let me see what a beautiful pussy you have."

I blush at his crudeness. If he were someone else, I might slap him. But coming from Nikita's mouth, those filthy words just spark another wave of heat racing below my skin. And, before I can think twice of it, I'm doing exactly what he ordered me to do.

"Good girl," he whispers. Again, the heat. I'm on fire. Burning up with need for him.

One strong finger works my needy pussy while his thumb strokes my swollen clit. A second finger enters me and Nikita fucks me with his hand until I'm writhing against his palm, chasing my release. He increases his speed and pressure until I'm moaning so loud I'm practically screaming.

"Do you want me inside you?" he whispers the heated words against my neck, and I crack open my eyes to find him watching me. His gaze is dark, full of forbidden promise, and I nod, a whimper falling from my lips. His answering smile is deliciously wicked. "Good. Because I can't fucking wait any longer. I've wanted to bury myself back into your pussy since the moment I pulled out at the penthouse."

I lean up on my elbows and press my mouth to the center of his chest. His scent surrounds me, the warmth of his skin, his salty taste. I'm licking a path down to his abs and he pulls away from me, hissing as if I've burned him.

"You're dangerous," he murmurs, tearing open the wrapper of the condom he pulls from his wallet and rolling it on. The sight of him entrances me and my heart rate accelerates, my mouth going dry when he catches me staring. He shakes his head with a slight smile curving his perfect, swollen lips. "I want to last, but you're going to make me come too soon, Annie. I want you too damn much; I'm aching."

Again, he stuns me, this time with his words. If I think about it too hard, the entire situation is mind-blowing. I'm naked in the middle of the mountains with a mob boss who purchased me for a quarter of a million dollars. We're about to have sex, and I want it more than I've wanted anything I can ever remember. If someone told me a month ago that I would be kidnapped, in a gunfight, and involved in a high-speed chase, only to want to have sex with the man who dragged me into the underworld, I would've laughed in their face.

I'm not laughing now, though. Instead, I'm grabbing for Nikita, bringing him down on top of me, his big body pushing me into the compact dirt. I wrap my legs around his hips, curling my arms around him so I can stroke down his smooth back, damp with sweat despite the chill of the night, as our mouths find each other, lazily kissing, nipping at each other's lips, tangling our tongues.

He tastes amazing. I love the sounds he makes, the way he holds me. And when he slowly slides inside my body, inch by excruciating inch, a shudder sweeps over me, my eyes shutting against the intensity of emotions swirling within. He doesn't move, doesn't so much as breathe, and I'm breathless too. I've never felt so connected to another person before.

"Christ, you feel so good," he whispers close to my ear as he slowly begins to move. I shift with him, lifting my hips, tightening my legs around him. He starts thrusting faster, almost as if he can't help himself. I rock against him, sending his cock deeper inside my body, and he's groaning, straining above me. I can see it in the tension in his face, across his shoulders.

I'm close too, though we've barely begun. I've been on edge since he made me come on the terrace. There was no relief with that orgasm. All it did was create the need for more.

"Tell me you're going to come," he whispers, his ragged voice sending a shiver over my skin. He reaches between us, his fingers slipping over my clit, rubbing circles around it, driving me straight out of my mind. "Say it."

"Yes," I moan. "So close. I'm going to come, Nikita."

Nikita rears up on his knees and grasps hold of my waist, pulling me closer as he pounds into me. I close my eyes, breathless at the brutal way he's handling me, truly fucking me. The men of my past always handled me gently, as if I were made of glass and might shatter at any moment. Not Nikita. He's all predator, primal fierceness, his hands gripping me, his cock pounding inside of me, his mouth brutalizing mine. It's as if he's completely overcome.

I love it. I crave it. I'm going to explode.

Closing my eyes, the familiar sensations threaten to wash over me, and I try to hold them off. But my sex clenches around Nikita and whimpering, I shake my head, panting his name, and then I can't hold back any longer. I'm coming. Lost in the deliciously warm, pulsating sensation as the second orgasm of the night takes me completely over the edge.

I could curl into a little ball now and die happy, but we're not yet finished. Nikita continues to pound into me, grunting and groaning, his eyes closed and every muscle in his body flexing. He fucks me through my orgasm and soon his thrusts grow erratic, his breathing shallow, and the words coming from his mouth turn into panted gibberish.

"Oh fuck. Oh fuck. Annie, I'm coming."

He collapses on top of me seconds later, his warm weight comforting, yet making it all feel far too real. His mouth presses to my neck, wet and hot as he whispers unintelligible words. I smooth my fingers down his back, feel the shivers still trembling through him, and I kiss his cheek.

Nikita grabs my sweatshirt and slips it over my head. Once my pants are back on, he pulls me tight into his chest and nuzzles my hair. "You're beautiful."

"Thank you," I say, scooting tighter into him. "Is your arm okay? Do you want me to take a look at it?"

"I'm fine, Annie." He places a tender kiss on my shoulder.

What I wouldn't give to be in a warm bed right now. I'll even take the big comfy bed in Nikita's penthouse so I can curl up under the blanket, plaster my face into the oversized pillow, and drift off into a blissful sleep. Not that the mountain isn't beautiful.

I run my fingers over Nikita's arm, trying not to think of the wild animals lurking in the trees, the violent men on our trail, or any of the other million and one things likely to try and kill us in the night.

Moments later, a faint snore tickles my ear. Nikita's grip isn't as tight and I twist to face him and see he's asleep. He seems peaceful. Calm. His features are much softer in sleep; the lines that usually crease his brow have vanished. I run my hand over his cheek and kiss his nose before burying my face into the nook between his arm and chest.

A part of me feels hidden from the world, from the dangers that lurk around us. It feels like, by hiding against Nikita, I'll be safe. Truth is, I guess I'm still a kid that way. Like somehow hiding under the covers makes me invisible to my enemies. And, in just two short days, Nikita has become my blanket.

Nikita twists and groans in his sleep. I pull away the slightest bit and look at him. He mumbles and grimaces, tossing around again, mumbles again. I run my hand over his arm, hoping my touch will soothe him.

What is he dreaming about?

I lie awake, watching him until he settles in and his breath slows until it becomes rhythmic. I turn and put my back to him, pulling his arm around me, and exhale, hoping sleep will take over soon.

Instead, my brain stutters for a moment and my eyes take in more light than I expect, every part of me going on pause while my thoughts catch up. How am I lying in Nikita Lavrin's arms without being scared?

Not one inkling of fear.

The man is a monster. He had me kidnapped. I was at the auction and saw the other girls he abducted and sold as sex slaves. He's a killer, too. Granted, the men he killed in front of me were trying to kill us, but from what I've learned over the past forty-eight hours, Nikita is hardly an innocent. He's a powerful don, with a city in the palm of his hands.

He's the same kind of ruthless psycho as the men who drew my father into a downward spiral. He's the type of person who would order someone to trash my childhood home, to send body parts in the mail.

And yet... he's more than that.

He kept me safe. He took care of me, when he could have left me to die. He made love to me.

How could a man who's supposed to be a monster care about those things? Monsters don't care. So, Nikita must be different.

But how different? Enough to matter? Enough for me to stay?

The question turns in my mind for a couple of minutes. I could try to run. I remember where the road is and the trail back down the mountain would be easy to follow. Even if the car is submerged in the lake, there was a ranger station we passed a couple of miles down the road. I could make it there, or hitchhike back to the city.

I sigh and close my eyes.

It would never work. The mercenary men might intercept me. They might not be as kind as Nikita. And with the way the Italian mobster drooled over me at the auction, I'm sure he'd rape me before he ended my life. He wouldn't take care of me—of my needs—the way Nikita has done.

So my choice is no choice, really. For now, I'll stay. Hopefully, the universe will present me with an opportunity to escape in the future. I just have to be patient and wait.

I try to quiet my mind from all the questions racing through it. Questions I don't have answers to. And others that just make me more confused. Soon, a blackness comes over me. I scoot closer to Nikita, seeking his warmth. My eyes begin to feel heavier and heavier until I can no longer keep them open and they flutter closed as I drift into a dreamless sleep.

16

NIKITA

My dream ends abruptly as I'm shaken back into reality. As I wake, I'm first aware of the coolness of the air and its loamy fragrance. My clothes feel damp in the dew of the dawn. I half wonder if I'm still dreaming as my eyes open, blinking the sleep away. I feel weak and worn thin, and my shoulder and knee are still throbbing, though the pain has lessened somewhat since yesterday.

What time is it? How long have I been asleep? And most pressing of all ... what do we do now?

Annie presses against me, soft breathing emanating from her small lips. It's so innocent and unguarded. My fingers gently rake through her tangled hair, not wanting to wake her. She's been through so much. Between the terror of the auction and the attack by Gino's men, her body and mind must be exhausted.

The first orange-hued rays appear over the treetops. A warm breeze chases away the previous night's chill. I see a bird perched on a branch across the clearing. It's pecking away the dew from its feathers and chirping into the morning air. I watch as it hears something in an adjacent tree. Its head swivels immediately in that direction, cocked to the side, fearful and ready to take flight.

Just like Annie at the auction.

It spins left and right, left and right, but no threat emerges. Cautiously, it settles back on its haunches. Then, with a soft chirp and a flap of its wings, it takes to the sky and disappears from view.

I sigh. If only we could fly away so easily.

My gut twists as bile creeps up the back of my throat. What have I done to this poor girl? Her feet are slashed up, her life fucked up ever since my men kidnapped her. Not to mention the target I put on her back the moment I outbid Gino. If he gets his hands on her, the Italian will certainly kill her, if only to spite me.

One thought rings through my head over and over again like a funeral dirge: I should have set Annie free.

Annie stirs in my arms and my gaze drops to her. She nuzzles against my chest and sighs, completely comfortable, which I don't understand. Why didn't she leave? She could've found her way back to the main road. She could've run away as I slept. Hell, she could've slept on the other side of the clearing as far away from me as possible, at the very least.

So why is she curled up against me as if I haven't done anything wrong to her?

And why the hell did I sleep with her? That was wrong of me. The thrill of the escape played a role, but it was still a choice I made. I should have been more levelheaded, more in charge. I should've protected her not only from the soldiers, but from myself as well.

I'm a fucking fool.

Annie groans and stirs once more in my arms. Waking, she stretches and then looks up at me, blinking, strands of hair covering her eyes.

Suddenly, she bites her lower lip and scurries out of my arms until she's sitting on her knees a couple of feet away.

I miss the warmth of her body against mine instantly. I want to pull her back down and hold her, and lie here all day. But she looks uncomfortable, uncertain even, and that makes me uneasy.

She tucks a loose lock of hair behind her ears, her eyes focused on her knees. "Good morning."

"Good morning." The air between us is tense and awkward. "How do your feet feel this morning?"

She looks down and wiggles her toes and grimaces. "They hurt. More than they did yesterday."

I sit up and move her legs into my lap, taking off the socks, and examining her soles. Fucking Christ. The cuts are deeper than I remember, and it looks like they cracked open even more from all the hiking. She definitely needs stitches. "I think they need to be cleaned out again. Do you want me to do it?"

She nods, her teeth sinking into her plump bottom lip. I reach across and grab the bag, my arm brushing Annie's soft skin. A low groan escapes my lips and I quickly look away. Annie needs medical attention, not a fucking, though I want to give her both.

"I didn't mean to fall asleep on you," she says, almost as if distracting herself from the impending sting as I hold the bottle just above the cuts on her feet.

"I understand. I'm sure you must've thought I was your boyfriend," I say and she flinches, though I'm not sure if from the peroxide or the mention of a boyfriend.

Something deep inside me rears its ugly head and the thought of my little bird with another man causes my blood to boil.

"I don't have a boyfriend. Not that it's any of your business."

My lip lifts on one side in a lopsided grin and I turn away so she doesn't see my amusement. I rewrap her feet and put back on the socks. "We should get up." I rise, stretching out the weariness in my limbs.

"Nikita, look!" Annie exclaims.

I whirl around and see her pointing to the far side of the clearing. From behind a thin screen of bushes, a pair of bucks gaze at us through the brush. Two racks of broad, velvety antlers spread above their heads. They stop and look at us, ears twitching. For a moment, we stare at each other, neither side moving. Then they snort and retreat back into the forest.

I turn back to Annie, who smiles wide. She turns to look at me. "I've never seen anything so beautiful."

Though her smile is warm, I feel like I'm in the wrong place, as if such comfort is only meant for others. I could lose myself in her words and the depth of her eyes; I could feel at home.

"Why did you stay?"

Annie jerks her head up so her gaze meets mine. I can tell it's an unexpected question. To be honest, I didn't expect to ask it myself. But now that I have, I need to know what she will say. Why didn't she run when she had the chance?

She chooses her words carefully. "I ... I'm not sure. I thought you were a monster. If you were, I should have run. But I didn't. So ... maybe you're not." It sounds as if she's reasoning it to herself out loud, like she isn't so sure of her own motivations.

Moments pass without either of us speaking, and then she sighs but holds her head high. "But understand that I stayed because I wanted to, not because I'm your slave."

I walk over and grab the bags, slinging them over my shoulder, and then head back over to her and hold my hand out to help her to her feet. When she's standing, I grip her chin and make her meet my eyes. "Don't think too much."

Without letting her respond, I kiss her gently. Her lips are soft against mine.

But then I break the kiss off. "Come with me," I whisper. "There's something I want to show you."

Taking her hand, I lead her through across the clearing and through the woods, close to where the deer went. We trudge silently for a few minutes, picking our way through the dry needles and leaves underfoot. I keep her hand clasped in mine for reasons I don't fully understand myself.

"Where are we heading?"

"You'll see," I say.

When we get to the cliff, I sit. Annie hesitates, then settles against me, like she did last night. We look out over the horizon, where the sun rises. Mellow blues and pinks blur together as the sun's rays chase away a silver mist from the valley below us.

Annie grabs my hand and squeezes it tight as she takes in the view. Then she ducks her chin and turns to look at me over her shoulder.

My dick hardens at the sight of her lips so close to mine. My chest expands and my heart thumps faster. Annie's lips part and she shifts in my lap, rubbing against my erection. My eyes close and I groan.

"I want to see you." The rasp in her voice makes me shiver.

Wrapping my arms around her, I claim her mouth with my tongue. She leans down and licks my neck, stopping at the pulse point before capturing the lobe of my ear.

Within seconds, our clothes are pooled around our feet, and she's standing in front of me in only tiny lace panties, a slight blush creeping from her chest to her cheeks. "Beautiful."

Her lips cover mine again. I open for her, welcoming her tongue, greeting it with mine. My lips seek and search, punish and soothe, all at once. I lower her and climb on top of her body, licking my way up her legs and belly, stopping to circle each breast before again finding her mouth. I kiss her hard. "Tell me what you want."

She licks her lips. "I want to taste you."

I growl and slide the rest of the way up her body until I'm planting a knee on each side of her head. I stroke myself just inches from her face. "You want this?"

She nods.

"Tell me."

"I want your cock, Nikita."

I guide my length into her waiting mouth. When I press the tip to her lips, she opens, eager to accept. She grabs my ass, pulling me harder into her. Already, her velvety tongue is threatening to make me explode any second.

I pull away and she whimpers, so I bend down and kiss her lips. "You're driving me crazy and I don't want to come yet."

My hand travels to her breast to play with a nipple, squeezing just hard enough for Annie to feel it. When she groans, I squeeze again. My fingers travel down her body, pulling her underwear off, and settle between her thighs, flicking my tongue over her engorged clit. "God, you taste so good. So wet for me already."

"Nikita," she cries out as my tongue plunges inside her, my teeth scraping her outer lips. "Yes. Please." Her words come out in pants.

The flat of my tongue washes over her clit as one finger, then two invade her, pumping hard and deep.

"Oh, Nikita. Oh my God. Please don't stop." Annie writhes for a minute before her sex squeezes me and she explodes, twitching on my fingertips.

Fuck. I damn near blow my load, but I want to be inside her. I *need* to be inside her. And now.

"Open your eyes, Annie."

She stares up into my eyes as the tip of my cock spears into her until I bottom out. My thrusts are hard and powerful as our bodies pound together. I'm on fire. I snap my hips, withdrawing just enough, and slam back into her, violent need driving my body as I chase my own release.

Without warning, I pull out and flip her over, pulling her hips up until she's on her knees, before thrusting inside her again. Gripping her by the back of the neck, I push down until her cheek is against the dirt and grind into her over and over. "Your pussy feels so good. So wet and tight."

I fuck her mercilessly. It's insane. Wild. Primitive.

My sweat drips down on her, and she pushes up onto her hands until her back is connected with my body. My arms encircle her waist and hold her still as I thrust up, my mouth sucking her neck.

Then I shift her again, lowering myself to the ground so that she's on top of me, grinding her clit into my pelvis hard. My fingers pinch her nipples as she drives down over and over.

I tell her to lean back and she obeys instantly, changing the angle and giving me better access to her clit. I rub her furiously, pushing her over the edge one last time. And when her sex clenches around my aching cock, I grab her hips and slam home one last time, exploding deep inside of her.

Annie collapses on top of me and I wrap my arms around her, holding her trembling body. Basking in the sun and satiated, we lie there in silence. Something is brewing between us. Too soon to be love.

Love? No, I don't love. I fuck. I use. I dispose.

Perhaps the time has come for that last part.

17

NIKITA

Annie shifts and slides to the side of me, my body missing the warmth of her skin. She sits up just as a cool breeze washes over us and goose bumps cover her skin. I grab her sweatshirt and hand it to her. "You should put this on before you catch a cold."

She takes the shirt from me and slips it on before standing to collect the rest of her clothes. I prop myself up on an elbow and my gaze runs over what the piece of clothing doesn't cover. Those long legs, that plump ass, and her still-wet pussy. My dick begins to swell again and when she glances over her shoulder, her mouth dropping a little when her eyes land on my dick, I'm fully erect once more.

"Annie, if you keep staring at me like that, you're going to have to do something about my current situation."

Her tongue swipes her top lip and I groan, wanting to be inside her mouth. She puts on the sweatpants and starts to make her way over to me when something rattles from one of the bags. I swing my head over to listen. A vibration like an annoyed rattlesnake sounds again. I spring to my feet and grab a stick before heading over to the offending backpack with Annie at my side.

"Stay back," I say to her, my arm pushing her behind me. "Might be a snake."

"Um, Nikita, snakes that make that type of noise don't live in this part of the country."

I turn and glare at her. But the sound goes off again and I inch closer, pushing the bag over with the stick. No animals. I throw the stick off to the side and grab the back, unzipping it and emptying the contents onto the ground.

"You had a phone the entire time?" Annie asks as she scoops the phone off the floor.

My brain stutters for a moment and my eyes take in more light than I expected, every part of me going on pause while my thoughts catch up. "I honestly forgot I threw the burner phone in the bag. Hell, I even forgot I turned it on."

I grab the phone from her and check the screen.

Eitan.

I let the call ring out without answering and grab my clothes, my erection gone and my pulse rate skyrocketing. "We need to pack up and move."

"Why?"

"I'm not sure who to trust and if they're tracking us through the phone we could be in danger." I shove my legs into my pants, button them, and put on my shoes as fast as I can as Annie stuffs all the contents on the ground back into the bag. No matter how hard I try to control my breathing, dread won't release its grip over me.

The phone rings again. Eitan's name flashes on the screen once more. I snarl and swallow past the growing lump in my throat as my finger hovers over the answer button for a second before touching the screen. I don't say a word in case it's not Eitan but someone who has his phone.

"Nikita? Nikita, are you there?" my advisor's voice comes through the speaker.

"Yes."

"Are you okay? Where are you?"

He sounds genuinely concerned but I'm not ready to give him any answers. "I'm safe. What happened?"

"Augustin. He betrayed us." The venom in Eitan's tone tells me all I need to know. I can trust him. I remain silent and listen as he continues speaking. "He was with the men who were tracking Gino but then communication went dead. When I sent Jimmy to check things out, he called and reported all the men were killed. But he couldn't find Augustin's body."

I rake my hands through my hair, cursing under my breath. This is too familiar. Just like what happened to my father. My heart begins to pound until my head aches from the building pressure. "How did they find me?"

"Augustin must've given him your address and the security code to the penthouse. When we raided his apartment, we found pictures and notes. He'd been tracking you."

Annie's pacing in front of me like a caged tiger, her skin paling with each passing second. "And the weapons shipment?"

"Gone. Augustin sabotaged it. Gave everything to Gino." Eitan sighs on the other end and I know there's more. "Nikita, Gino launched an attack on all our soldiers and businesses across the city."

"Fuck. Fucking fuck."

How could I have been so fucking stupid? How could I have been so blind and weak? How could I have been *just like my father*?

God fucking damn it. I swore never to be like him. Anger boils deep in my system, as hot as lava. It churns within, hungry for destruction, and I know it's too much for me to handle. The pressure of this raging sea of anger is the force I need to exact revenge and I allow it to fuel my darkest desires.

I allow the darkness to swallow me whole.

"Eitan, we're at the site my father and I used to camp at. Get to the base of the mountain as fast as you can and tell no one."

"We?"

I snort. "Yeah, Annie's with me."

Eitan doesn't say a word other than to let me know he's on his way and then hangs up. I tuck the phone into my back pocket and button my shirt, not wanting to waste another second.

Revenge is the only thing I want right now. And I *will* get it.

Annie timidly walks over to me and places her hand on my arm. I stare daggers at her and keep moving. She should've had everything put together already. She should know better than to waste time on stupid things like sympathy. We're in a war right now.

"Nikita, what's going on?"

"I found out who betrayed me. Now, it's time for payback," I sneer.

Annie's brows furrow as she looks at me, standing there like a fucking helpless deer. I'm halfway across the clifftop before I realize she isn't behind me. I whirl around to stare at her. "Annie, what the fuck are you doing? I told you to get everything ready."

Her fingers curl into small fists, red coloring her cheeks. "Excuse me?"

"I don't have time for this. Eitan is meeting us at the base of the mountain. We have to hike back down. So: let's go." I'm impatient, fists clenching and unclenching, running my hands through my hair over and over again. I want blood spilled and I want it now. Why can't she understand that? Why can't she see that it's time to strike back?

She looks at me with an unreadable expression. Something akin to fear, sorrow, confusion, all of those and none of them. Part of me wants to hold her and make her understand. *Look at what's happened!*

But I can't—because in so many ways, she did this to me. I became too enthralled with Annie and now many of my men are dead. Others will be soon, too, if I don't hurry. Lives were wasted because I was paying attention to the wrong thing. My businesses can be rebuilt. My soldiers can't be brought back from the grave.

"I told you—we need to go. Now."

Annie flings the backpack in her hands at my feet. "I understand you're angry, but don't take it out on me. I was shot at too, remember?"

I reach down, grab the pack, and sling it over my shoulder before grabbing the second pack and doing the same. If she's going to throw a temper tantrum, then I won't waste the energy on getting her to understand what's happening. Is she sad? Hurt? I don't give a fuck. There's no time for sadness or pain.

She was never meant for this world; that much is obvious to me, now. I can hardly believe I didn't see it before. My men are paying for it. *I'm* paying for it.

Time to turn that around.

"Are you ready or not?"

"Yeah," she says and brushes past me without a second glance, charging ahead toward the path.

No matter how much I try to convince myself I don't care, I hate the way she looks at me. Hate the brush-off and how wet her eyes are. But this is my life. I'm where I am because of how I handle myself. Why change when I've been successful, especially after the mutiny erupting at my feet?

I close my eyes and picture how the conversation would go, if I could even figure out where to begin:

"Last night was a mistake. My world is different than yours. You wouldn't understand and you can't understand. And as for the sex, it was great. But that's all it was. Just sex. Nothing more."

Would she cry? Hit me? Curse at me or spit in my face? I can't say for sure.

And then another thought occurs to me: *have I made an enemy?* We're making our way down the path, faster than last night, and though I can see Annie wincing at every step on her tender feet, she doesn't stop or slow down. Fury emanates from her.

What if I had left her behind and Gino had gotten ahold of her?

Fuck.

She's a weakness. Not just a mistake of the past. Not just a temporary flight of fancy, easily fixed and forgotten. She's seen my home. Heard about my past. She knows me in a way that few do.

And Gino is just the man who would exploit that.

I grind my molars when she turns around a bend and disappears into the trees. The bag on my shoulder shifts when I stomp to follow her. I stoop to readjust the strap, and the burner cell tumbles to the forest floor.

My eyes go wide. Annie found the cell phone so quickly when I dumped the bag out. And she wasn't afraid the noise could've been a snake. Not to mention I don't remember turning the phone on.

Fuck. Fuck. Fuck.

It must have been her. She turned it on when I was sleeping. She's been playing me from the very beginning.

I rip the phone from my pocket and scroll through the call history and text messages. Nothing. But she could've erased them. She must've betrayed me when I was sleeping. My gaze lifts to search for her but she's gone. How could I have been so stupid to expose myself so badly?

I race off toward the path. God only knows what awaits me at the bottom of the mountain. Maybe a squad of police. Maybe Gino. This whole 'innocent abductee' routine could've been an act. Gino could've orchestrated the whole thing. And Augustin. He was the person who grabbed her, wasn't he? Or at least, that's what was reported to me. Was this all a lie?

The bags are weighing me down and catching on every overhang and bush. Every hang-up is costing me time, as Annie hurtles down the mountain ahead of me. She's getting further and further away.

I growl and continue to race on until I spot her. "Annie!"

She doesn't stop or turn around. When I'm within arm's reach, she releases a branch she had been holding out of the way. It arcs back like a whip and smacks me in the cheek, splitting open my skin.

"Fucking hell!" I curse. I can feel the blood trickling down my jaw.

Rage blinds me. I lunge towards Annie. One hand flies up to her throat and lifts her into the air, pinning her against the rock ledge that runs along one side of this flat part of the trail. Dust floats around our feet.

"Did you betray me?" I roar. "Was it you?"

My voice echoes in the empty woods. The only other noise is Annie struggling to breathe. "Nik ... Nikita ... stop! Please ..." Her words are hoarse and faint.

Suddenly, her dancing feet lash out and connect with my groin. I curse again and drop her. She falls into a puddle on the ground, wheezing.

The woods are silent.

"I didn't do anything," she says after a while. She isn't looking at me, or at anything, really. Her eyes a vacant, thousand-yard stare. She's rubbing her throat. I can see the red imprints of my fingers on her soft skin. "I didn't know you had a phone. And if I wanted to betray you, I would've hiked down the mountain while you were sleeping instead of waiting for you to wake up, you fucking beast."

I'm still breathing hard. Anger? Shame? It's hard to say why.

She glares up at me with pure hatred in her eyes. I almost stumble backwards at the sheer force of her gaze. I've never seen anyone with such venom in their stare. It's haunting in a girl like her. She was innocent when I met her. Now ... I've made her into something else.

"I just want to go home. I want to graduate and get a job like a normal fucking person," she says. "I want to forget you ever exist."

She pushes herself back up to her feet. Her hands ball into fists at her side and her lips press so tight they're a thin line. "What, you have nothing to say now? After you accused me of betraying you? Like I want to be part of whatever Augustin did. You do know the man smacked me around and kidnapped me, right? I told you that. Oh, but I must be lying because everybody is a liar to you."

"Shut up," I whisper.

"Just take me home. I want to go home."

I'm at a loss for words. She takes one more look at me, then shoves past and continues down the path.

I don't want to believe her, but I know deep in my bones that she's telling the truth. She isn't the type of girl to play the high-stakes game I've accused her of. She doesn't know this world. She doesn't want to be a part of it. Again and again in her life, she's been dragged in. Just when she was almost free, I did it to her once more.

Only a moron would've stayed until morning if they'd been the cause of this. And Gino's men did try to kill her, too.

I turn and follow her down the trail again. The woodland seems ominously quiet. The sound of our own footfalls is silent and all that can be heard is the whisper of the leaves.

18

ANNIE

I picture Nikita's face the rest of the way down the mountain.

Skin flushed with rage, his eyes black and lifeless. Nostrils flared. Jaw clenched. I've seen that face before. Or rather, one just like it. The face of a monster.

My father used to look at me just like that.

There are so many things I remember from those years. The bricks through the window, that bloody stump of a finger in the cardboard box. I will never forget the dirty boots of the mob men propped up on our coffee table—not as long as I live.

But what I remember more than any of that, more than any of the other horrors that haunted my mother and me through the worst stage of my life before now, are the eyes of my father. Mere inches away from my face, the whites nearly gone, the pupils so dark that they seemed bottomless, I remember how he looked at me. He wasn't my father anymore in that moment. He was just a beast.

He wasn't like that at first, of course. It started with anxiety. After the men left, he would hold my mother and me in his arms and just apologize, over and over again.

I'm sorry. I'm sorry. I'm sorry.

He meant it, too, I think. At least, part of him did. But the part of a man that cares about what he does to the women in his life? That part can't last long, if he's to survive in that world.

The anxiety never left, but it did change. It became frustration. It became anger. It became furious outbursts over the randomest things—the TV on too loud? He'd scream himself hoarse. A pair of dirty shoes left in the front hallway? He'd punch walls, so close I could feel the dust from the drywall.

And soon, walls weren't enough. Then the only thing left to hit was us.

He told me once that he wished I'd never been born. "If it weren't for you, we would've been fine. We woulda been just fine." His voice was so weird when he said that. I didn't even know what he meant. I mean, I did, but I didn't. I just remember how weird his voice was when he said it. It was just him and me, sitting in the kitchen. I was doing math homework, I think. He was drinking whiskey, like he always did on the rare nights when he was home. And he just looked at me out of nowhere and said that, with that weird tone in his voice, like he was strangling or drowning.

We woulda been just fine.

I didn't know what to say. How could I? I was a child, a little girl. I didn't know anything about the world, or why he'd chosen to do the things he did. I was a good girl. I got good grades, I stayed out of trouble, I kept my room clean. But that didn't matter. I was just a mouth to feed, in his eyes. I was a burden.

My mother came home soon after that. She had shopping bags full of groceries.

"Where did you get that shit?" my father asked her.

She hesitated before she answered. When she did, I knew right away that something bad was going to happen. She did, too, I think. But neither of us could really stop it. We were powerless, or at least we felt that way, and that meant basically the same thing. "There was a … a market," she said. Both my father and I knew she was lying.

"What kind of 'market'?" he questioned acidly.

"At the … at the food bank." She swallowed hard.

"The food bank. The fucking food bank." He plunged the tip of his cigarette into the whiskey as he repeated what she had said in a soft, numb voice. I could hear the sizzle as the flame died.

Then, in one sudden motion, he stood, turned, and hurled the glass tumbler at my mother's head. She ducked—thank God she ducked—and it smashed against the kitchen wall behind her. I screamed. She screamed, and fell into a sobbing puddle on top of the bags of food. Apples rolled across the tile floor.

But my father wasn't done with her. He marched over and hauled her to her feet.

Whap. Whap. Two quick backhanded slaps on either side of her face.

I hadn't moved since the moment my mother walked in the door. I remember the sound of the hit, the way my mother stumbled and reached out to the counter for balance. I remember the way my father stood over her, greasy bangs falling across his forehead, rage purpling his cheeks. I remember the way he slammed his hand down on the counter over her head and said the next time he'd really light her up for talking back.

Then he turned to me.

I don't remember what he said but I remember his eyes. Dark and lifeless. I sat there shaking. And he walked up to me, put his face right in mine, and called me a little cunt, and that I should take notes and learn how to be respectful. I was so scared I peed.

Then he walked out the door, and slammed it shut behind him.

∽

I'm sitting on a rock at the foot of the mountain when Nikita approaches. He fell behind me, weighed down by the bags full of supplies and weapons. I'm just finishing tightening the bandages on my feet, which are crusty with last night's blood, when he comes to stand in front of me.

I stare at him, unable to speak. Even if I could speak, I don't know what I would say.

"Annie?"

Nikita gazes back at me. He says nothing either. The woods around us are silent.

I don't have the energy to fight with him anymore. I don't have the energy for any of this, really. So why does it keep finding its way to me? Why can't I escape it? I make myself a promise: I'm going to get Nikita to take me home, by any means necessary. Then I'm going to pack my things, and I'm going to leave this city, and I'm never, ever going to come back.

I look up at him. "You know, I was just thinking about my father."

Still, he says nothing.

"The first time I saw him hit my mother."

Silence. Staring.

"After he slapped her, he came up to me. Do you know what he said to me, Nikita?"

The soft whine of car engines, far in the distance, where the highway slices through the park, is the only thing I can hear.

"He called me a little cunt. And he said I should take notes, so that the same thing didn't happen to me. It scared me. A lot. I peed myself, you know. I was just a little girl. What kind of man says that to an innocent little girl?"

I break our gaze. I don't want to look at him anymore. I don't want to see the blackness again.

I keep my eyes fixed on the ground while I continue talking. "And do you know what reminded me of him, Nikita? You. You're a fucking monster. I want you to take me home right now. And then I hope to God I never see you again. Because if I do … well, I don't know, actually. I'm not like you. I don't plan for that kind of thing. But whatever I choose to do, I won't regret it. Because I will know one thing more than anything: whatever I decide … you'll deserve it."

Nikita steps back. And then steps back once more. His fingers rake through his hair and his face contorts in a way I haven't seen before. Not one of anger but of hurt. His mouth opens and closes a couple of times as if he's searching for something to say.

But there's nothing.

A car pulls up just then. It's an older model Nissan Rogue. You wouldn't think twice if you saw it drive past you, which I guess is the whole point. An older man exits the driver's side and walks over to Nikita.

I stay seated on the boulder and watch as the driver and Nikita embrace. That must be Eitan. After the two men separate, Eitan looks at me. Nikita does not. They have a quick, whispered conversation, then Eitan comes over and gives me a polite nod.

Without a word, he takes my bag from me and guides me to the vehicle. Nikita is already in the passenger's seat. Eitan opens the door, and I climb into the back.

No one says anything for a long time. I close my eyes and rest my forehead against the window, cool to the touch. I feel an urge to cry, and an urge to sleep, but mostly I just feel numb. That's fine, I suppose. Better than any of the alternatives I can think of.

The closer we get to the city lights, the slower traffic moves. The familiar cacophony of car horns and impatient taxis takes over the silence. I should be grateful—I've grown up with that as a constant background noise—but part of me actually misses the stillness of the mountain as we wind through the city streets

"Where do you live?" Nikita's voice comes out gruff and scratchy.

"Me?" What a stupid question. He must know where Eitan lives. "Near the college on the north side."

"What's the cross street?"

"Just drop me off at the campus and I can walk the rest of the way."

Eitan looks at Nikita, who nods. I straighten up just as I notice that my palms have begun sweating. I bite my nails the rest of the way, unsure of what to expect.

Within the hour, Eitan pulls the SUV into visitor parking. Nikita gets out of the car and opens my door. I step out tentatively, watching his every movement. I look around, half expecting to see his bodyguards, but the only people around are other college students walking to and from class.

"How far are you from here?" Nikita looks off into the distance over my head, refusing to meet my gaze.

I point. "The building down the street. The brick one with the yellow flowers."

Nikita follows where my finger indicates, as if taking in features so he can identify the building at a later date. He shoves his hands in his pockets, still staring at my crummy student housing.

"You're free to go."

I can think of a million things I want to say. "Fuck you" is extremely high at the top of my list. "Why?" is up there too, for so many reasons. But what I settle on is the same thing I told him the first night at dinner on his terrace. Was that really only a few days ago? It seems like a lifetime.

I look Nikita in the eyes and say, "My freedom was never yours to give or take away."

Nikita opens his mouth to respond, but I don't wait for an answer. I turn and walk away. I want so badly to look back at him, but I refuse to give the man the satisfaction. As I put distance between him and me, I hear the car door open and slam, then the rev of the engine as Eitan ushers them away.

Away from here. Away from me. Away from my life for good—I hope.

I'm not sure what I expected. Maybe a goodbye. Or good luck. Something other than the stoic, stony silence. I went through hell with that man. I slept with him. But like he said, the sex meant nothing. So why does it hurt so much? Why do I want him to care? To say goodbye like it means something to him?

I wipe my eyes and adjust my ponytail. I won't cry for him. I say that out loud, like a promise to myself. "I won't cry for him."

My feet take me in the direction of the apartment, my brain on autopilot. After everything I've been through in the past couple of days, I'm not exactly sure how I feel. Confused. Angry. Scared. Alive. All the emotions are jumbled and not one wins.

"Mizz Thornton?" a familiar voice calls out when I cross the street.

Henry.

I turn to find my old friend huddled in the corner. His face is bruised and his lips are cracked from the cold weather. "Henry? What happened to you?"

"I could ask you da same thing? Haven't seen ya around. Ya okay?"

I offer him a sheepish smile. If he only knew what I have gone through. "Henry, are you okay?"

"Yes, ma'am. Went to the shelter, like ya said to do. Wasn't very friendly. Won't go back." Henry glances at a passerby and holds up his cup. "Mizz Thornton, ya wouldn't happen to have any spare change?"

"I'm sorry, Henry. I lost my bag."

"No worries. Ya go head on home before ya catch a chill."

I nod and head off down the road. When I get to the building, I head to the bush on the side, hoping the spare key is still there. Nikita never gave me back my stuff. I doubt I'll ever see those things again.

I find the key, steady my shaky hands, and put the key in the door. Before I open it, I offer up a quick prayer: *please let the house be empty.* If I see my friends, I'm going to sob like a baby. I'm not ready for that, or for any human contact, really. I just want a hot shower and a cold, dark room, and maybe to sleep for the rest of my life. If I can get that, I'll be okay. Now if I can just make it to my room before—

"Annie!"

"Where have you been?"

My roommates rush at me, hugging the bejesus out of me, and I groan, not from the contact, but because my body aches and they're squeezing way too tight. I should've taken a minute to come up with a cover story before I came home.

The two drag me over to the couch and the three of us collapse onto the soft cushions. Jenna and Wendy stare at me expectantly. And when I don't respond, Wendy purses her lips. "Annie, we were so worried. Jenna planned on calling the cops if you hadn't come home today. We were going to file a missing person's report."

"Yeah, especially when we couldn't reach you. We looked all over the club for you. And then I found your phone on the floor. We haven't really slept since that night. You better have a good explanation," Jenna says.

I bite my lip. It would be so easy to tell them. I could just start at the beginning and tell them about being kidnapped and sold and screwed and shot at and chased and about sprinting up a mountain and falling asleep in Nikita's arms. Wouldn't that be easy? Wouldn't that make me feel better? And once I'd told them, we could go to the police together and I could turn Nikita and his whole crew in, and they'd all be arrested and rot in jail for the rest of their lives.

Don't they deserve that fate? Don't I deserve that closure?

They do. I do.

But I can't.

I open my mouth to tell the story, starting with Augustin at the club, and it's like my voice gets stuck in my throat. I can't tell them, no matter how much I should.

Because there's a man in Nikita worth saving.

He's a coldhearted bastard and a cold-blooded killer—I know that.

He's a ruthless mob boss and a seller of women—I know that, too.

He's a thief and a crook and a monster and the right thing to do is throw him behind bars so he can never hurt anyone else the way he did me. But beneath all that, there is a good man. A man who is loyal and smart, caring and kind, and who looked at me in a way that I've never been looked at before.

I felt something when he kissed me. Something special. The thing they tell little girls to seek out—the kiss that feels right. There isn't much that's made sense since the moment I was dragged into the back hallway at the club, but that's the only thing I can hang onto, the only truth that fits into my reality.

I say it to myself for the first time, and I know it to be true: *I'm in love with the mob boss.*

I suck in a deep breath and glance between my roommates. "Well, remember that guy I was dancing with?"

"Yeah, so?"

"I ... went home with him."

Both of my roommates gasp.

"Actually, I shouldn't say home. He had a little cabin we went to a little outside the city. It was very romantic. A nice little getaway. I realized I lost my phone and when I asked to borrow his, we found the reception was out up in the mountains. Must've been some interference." I roll my eyes dramatically and sigh, hoping they buy the crap I'm feeding them. "And, as luck would have it, when we decided to head back into the city, his stupid tire ended up getting stuck in the mud and we had to push the car out. Common sense should've dictated not to bring a sports car into a rural area, but what're you gonna do?"

Jenna grabs my hand as Wendy giggles. I offer up a tired smile.

"So yeah, that's pretty much it."

Jenna sucks in a big breath and my two friends look at each other. "All right, time for the big question ..." Jenna says.

They chime in at the same time.

"Are you going to see him again?"

19

NIKITA

Three weeks. Three fucking weeks.

My fist crashes into the table. No matter how hard I've tried, I can't figure out a way to wage this war against Gino. Three weeks since I've come back to reclaim what's mine, and I'm still hiding like a fawn in the bushes. How did this fucking happen?

I stand up and drop my plate into the sink, half-eaten food flopping into the basin. I sneer. This is my life now. This little fucking safe house on the edge of the city and suburbs in a poor middle-class section, so as to be as inconspicuous as possible. My family fought hard for power and wealth. I had it all, and now I'm walking across a fucking linoleum floor in a room with water stains on the ceiling and rats scurrying in the walls.

I walk back into the living room and drop onto a hideous, decrepit couch. It wheezes under my weight, like it's every bit as exhausted as I am. Eitan glances up at me from a map spread over the rickety kitchen table.

"We don't have a lot of men left. I think whoever's here already is all we're going to get." His jaw clenches, his fingers drumming against the arm of the velvet chair. "Nikita, I'm not sure how we're going to get out of this. Even the council has turned its back."

The frustration builds and I think I might explode. I want to shout, have a tantrum, and beat my hands on the ground like a toddler. I want to vent, let it out. Above all, I want to wring the life from Gino's throat.

Instead I take a deep breath. Acting like a child will get me nowhere. Once, I was on top. All- powerful. I need to become that cruel and calculated person once again, and take back what is mine.

"Run me through the list of what's left," I order, closing my eyes. I need to think.

"Now that the laundromat on 5th has been burned out, we're down to the electronics shop on Haven Boulevard, a stolen goods fence working out of the back of his van on Columbus and Rio, and two street gangs on corners in Los Arcos neighborhood, who are moving what little molly and cocaine they manage to scrounge up. We're running out of resources, Nikita."

"Tell me something I don't know," I sigh.

"And even the ones we have left aren't going to last. The corner kids are getting jumped every other day. They know we can't protect them anymore. I wouldn't be surprised if they cut and run soon. One of Gino's lieutenants even killed a runner yesterday. A little kid. Nine years old."

Fuck.

I did everything right—everything—and still this place is a goddamn mess. My father must be rolling in his grave. I lost everything he built, everything he sacrificed for. All because I let my guard down. I should've seen it coming. Shouldn't have gotten so comfortable. My palms rub up and down my face as if I can make the failure disappear. "What about the men? The soldiers, I mean."

"Whoever is here are the only ones confirmed alive. A few reports of others who are holed up or left the city, but nothing for certain, and they aren't likely to come out of their holes anytime soon. You can't blame them, sir."

"What about the other families? Has anything changed there?"

Eitan leans back and laces his fingers behind his head, exhaling in a slow, soft whistle. I know he's tired; we've been working all hours of the day and night since the moment he picked me up from the mountain. The bags under his eyes are growing. "Most are staying out of it. We just got word today that the Mendoninos took over some territory of ours near the docks, so they've made their choice, apparently. The East Side Boys have passed along some useful information, but they're not going to cross Gino, especially not now that he's equipped with the remainder of our weapons import left over after he sold the bulk of it to the cartel. We need to face the reality, Nikita: we're outnumbered, out-armed, and outmaneuvered. I just don't see a way out, try as I might. You need to consider fleeing."

"Don't ever say that word to me again, Eitan. I'm not running from my city like a fucking coward."

Eitan sighs and nods solemnly. "I know, Nikita. I just wish you would."

I stand and go over to him. He's been working his fingers to the bone, all for the sake of my family. "I'm sorry, my friend," I rasp. "I owe you better than my anger."

He looks up at me, dog-tired but eternally loyal. "I swore to your father that I'd protect you, Nikita. It seems I'm failing."

I slump into the seat across from him and scan the map of the city for the umpteenth time. It is littered with red Xs and outposts circled and then crossed off. Death and destruction at every intersection, every depot I once controlled. The last remaining territory is where we are now. Enemy arrows are aimed at us from all directions.

We're sitting ducks.

I wonder what my father would say if he saw me right now. He's dead, buried six feet under the ground, and yet I can almost feel the weight of his sadness. I've stumbled so far from the course my father set. And what bothers me most is that I don't know how far I'm destined still to fall.

"We have scouts on the college campus keeping an eye on movements near Gino's headquarters. The school, at least, seems safe enough for now. If anything happens there, the police and government will be on it. They're keyed up as well. Too many bodies in the news lately," Eitan says.

The moment he mentions the college, my thoughts go to Annie. Who am I kidding? One of the reasons I haven't been sleeping well is because I can't stop thinking about her. Wondering if she's safe. Wondering what she's doing. And wondering if she's even thinking about me.

"Nikita?" Eitan's voice cuts into his thoughts.

"Just thinking about ... nothing, actually. I want those men to stay posted there. At the very least, we can keep our watch trained on Gino himself. Better pray that there's an opportunity to cut off the head of the snake. Otherwise, our options are limited, and dwindling in number."

"Do you want to send someone to keep an eye on her?" Eitan asks. I know who he's talking about, of course, just like he knows what thoughts are running through my head. Neither of us has said Annie's name out loud in three weeks. It's like she's cursed us.

Do I want her to be protected? Yes. Should I send guards to watch over her? Probably. But I'm hesitant. She already thinks of me as a monster. Sending someone to watch over her might make her think I'm trying to own her again. That I don't care about her, when nothing could be farther from the truth. I don't want to suck her back into this war, into this world. But my enemies are all around and it's only a matter of time before they figure out where she is. What she means to me.

And if that happens, she will truly be in danger from which she can't escape.

I swallow past the lump in my throat. "No," I whisper. "No."

Eitan eyes me kindly. "Nikita, I've been with the Lavrins since your father first took over. I've seen a lot, been through a lot myself." He shakes his head. "I've had a good life, a wonderful wife, may she rest in peace, and children, all grown with lives and families of their own."

"I'm not in a mood to be lectured, my friend."

He leans forward onto his elbows. The bare bulb overhead flickers once. "But not all have benefited from this world. Would you bring children of your own into it? Knowing what you know? Knowing the risks you've taken?"

My own children? I've never thought about having a family. Never thought about bringing a life into this world. But if it happened, I'm also not sure if I'd want them to take over the family business or get as far away as possible. I sigh and my shoulders slump forward.

"Let me tell you a story."

"I've heard all of your stories, Eitan."

"Not this one," he says. "Listen: a long time ago, when I first met your father, I was with a woman—my high school sweetheart. We were in love. Planned on getting married once she graduated college." Eitan looks away, taking a deep breath in. "She meant the world to me. Made my heart beat faster the moment she walked into the room."

My tension evaporates. I've never known Eitan to be with anyone outside of Maria. I lean back in my wooden chair and fold my arms across my chest.

"I remember her voice still. She was an amazing singer, unlike me. I can't carry a tune if my life depended on it. Yet, she'd always want me to sing along with her. One day, she was on her way home from college. I had set up a grand romantic gesture where I'd ask her to marry me. I wanted to give her the world."

Fuck. She left him. Cheated on him. Had to be. Why else wouldn't he have married her?

"The bus never made it. Some freak accident, engine trouble. It exploded. Everyone on board died."

Neither of us talks for a minute. I can see the pain etched in his face, like it happened yesterday. Maybe, in his mind's eye, it's always happening, again and again, like Chinese water torture. Drip. Drip. Drip.

"Nikita, I've seen the way you look at Annie. I see the torture in your face any time you think about her. It's the same look I had with Emily. She was my world, the love of my life," Eitan says.

I shake myself. "I don't love her. She's just an innocent person who got caught up."

Eitan snorts. "No one is perfectly innocent, Nikita. Just as no one is perfectly guilty. We are, all of us, a mix of everything."

Before I can respond, a soldier bursts into the room from down the hall. "Just got word that the guys in East Los Arcos got hit, hard. The rest of the stash, all the week's take—gone."

Gino.

I'm up on my feet immediately. My fingers clench and unclench as I spring toward the front closet to grab a jacket and my holster. I'll kill whoever's there. Once my jacket is on, I grab the keys from the hook in the foyer and head out the door, part of me relieved to leave Eitan and the whole conversation behind.

Soft rain paints the car windows as I drive onwards. Lavrin soldiers—what's left of them—follow closely in two Jeeps. The skies are overhung with a blanket of gray, so much so that I can barely tell the difference between the sky and clouds. I watch raindrops race down to the windshield as I fly down the road, hoping for a distraction so I can get my mind straight.

But the drive to the office only brings thoughts of Annie to the forefront. I can't deny how perfectly she fit into my arms. Or how many times I've jerked off to thinking of her. Multiple times throughout the night on some occasions, like my dick just couldn't be satisfied.

I make a right turn and pull into the empty lot, my foot on the brake and my fingers wrapped tightly around the steering wheel as I scope out the scene. This could be a setup.

But there aren't any other cars, no lingering shadows, no lights that are out. I kill the ignition and step out into the rain. Removing my gun from its holster, I walk the perimeter of the building, my eyes scanning every blind spot, every tree, and even the roof above until I get to the front door of the corner bodega where the crew sets up shop.

It's wedged open.

I wait, peeking in through the crack. No sounds. No movements. The alarm is off and no one knows the keycode except my men. I snarl as I wonder if I've been betrayed again.

I push the door open slowly, keeping my body against the wall as I move through the small office. The store is empty, but the computer and cabinets in the back office are all trashed. Files are strewn about, chairs overturned. What the hell were they looking for?

I don't keep anything sensitive in here. Not when some cop with a hard-on for justice can kick down the door at any point in time. Not when the feds can raid the place if they want, looking for something to pin on Lavrins.

Just as I turn the corner into the main part of the bodega, my shoe squelches. I look down to see a dark puddle. Blood. The metallic scent stings my nose. Someone was here. My gut churns. Who was killed?

Slumped in the candy aisle is one of my men. Dead. Skizzo ran the crew moving drugs out of here. He also kept an eye on things for me. He had the code to the place. He knew I didn't keep anything of value here.

Shit.

I can hardly stand to look at him. He's strapped to a chair, his fingers jutting at gross angles and a bloody stump where his tongue once was. The motherfuckers even ruptured his eyeballs. Gino is one sick fuck, I'll give him that. And ruthless. Blood is sprayed against the rows of candy across from him and spread like a carpet around his feet. It looks like he tried to crawl away while bleeding out. They made him suffer.

I lean against the desk, unable to look at him and unable to look away. Tears form in my eyes, both from sadness for my loyal soldier and from anger at Gino. None of the families are safe from him, yet none of them have stood against the Italian. Instead, they sided with him.

Meanwhile, I've made them rich. I've kept them safe. But they're greedy and opportunistic. And they only respond to cruelty. Well, they seem to have forgotten the person I am. The person who seized power and controlled this damn city. They made an enemy out of the one person they should've kept happy. Gino might be crazy, but there's nothing more dangerous than a Lavrin.

It's time the underworld remembered that fact.

20

ANNIE

Nothing is the same anymore.

The things that once entertained me are now lifeless. The things that once seemed routine are now terrifying. If I'm not looking over my shoulder to make sure I'm not being followed, I'm bored out of my mind. I can't focus enough even to watch something stupid on TV, and I can't walk to the grocery store without my heartbeat jumping up to two hundred beats per minute and making me break out in hives. I don't want to go out and I don't want to stay in. I just want things to be the way they used to be.

But I know damn well that that's not going to happen anytime soon. Mostly because, every time I close my eyes, I see him.

Nikita.

Staring at me, with those black coal pits for irises. Is it rage that I'm seeing in his face, or lust? I can never tell. Truth be told, I'm not sure I want to know. There's no telling what lies down the tracks of *that* particular train of thought, and I have no interest in finding out. I won't. I shouldn't. I can't.

I pull out the stack of papers the professor handed to me to grade. Being a TA is just oh so much fun. But it helps pay the bills as I search for a job. In these last couple of weeks, the majority of lecturers just finish out the senior-heavy classes. They want the semester to end as badly as any of the students do, so unless someone does something to really get on a teacher's bad side, everyone is graduating.

The TA job is mindless and easy. Mostly, it involves red pen scribbles with a coffee close at hand. But the simplicity is dangerous, because it lets my mind wander. I try to keep it focused on the here and now, and above all, things that are in my control. Things like: what the hell am I going to do with my life? All the dreams I had about being an accountant, working with numbers, and being able to go home at the end of the day—like a normal person, to a normal family—have all mutated into something ugly and repulsive. I don't want safety or certainty, at least not in the way that I used to crave those things. The monotony is no longer appealing. Maybe it never was. I don't know. I don't know much of anything anymore.

I know pretty much this and only this: I have to finish grading or I'll lose my TA position. And, though so much else has vanished from my life, the bills I need to pay have not.

My phone rings and I glance at the screen before answering. My stomach plummets. It's Griffin & Sons, Incorporated. I interviewed with them last week. Everything went so well. I knew the job was mine; they more or less told me as much in the interview. But as I walked around the office afterwards, staring at the cubicles and the fluorescent lights and the hideous carpet, I just wasn't sure I wanted the job anymore. It didn't feel right.

Even thinking that is crazy. A month ago, I would've been jumping with joy in the streets to get this call. Griffin & Sons is a massive, powerful accounting firm with offices nationwide and a roster of clients to die for. Good benefits, lots of opportunity for upward mobility, competitive pay, and … blah blah blah. I can't even bear to think about it. The checklist for why I should pick up this call and give an enthusiastic *yes* to the job offer is a mile long.

Which is why one little voice in my head is screaming bloody murder at me when I let it go to voicemail.

I pick up my mug and gulp down lukewarm coffee as I watch the rings die down. Yuck. No amount of sugar makes this crap taste any better. The bitterness is too reminiscent of my own life. Grabbing my pen, I open the first test and start grading.

Time passes, one page at a time. How the hell do teachers do this every day? After the twentieth test, I'm convinced the students in Accounting 101 are all stupid. None of them have passed so far. It's just one wrong answer after another. I glare over at the rest of the thirty tests I still have to mark. Ugh. Why the hell did they ever get rid of Scantron tests? It would be so much easier to run this through a machine.

"Hey there, girlfriend." Jenna strolls in, dropping her purse on the table and nearly knocking over my stack of already graded exams. "Uh-oh. I know that face. What's eating you today?"

"Got stuck grading again."

"You sure that's the only reason?" Jenna raises an eyebrow as she stares at me.

My roommates have been all over my case, asking questions about the guy I "left the club" with, wondering why he hasn't called. I try to deflect and demur—anything to change the subject. But if Jenna and Wendy are anything, they're persistent. It's the same conversation over and over again: *a weekend getaway in the mountains with a handsome mystery man? How can you NOT be dying for a call back?* Every time they bring it up, I just smile and look away, hoping they'll get the hint soon and let it go. Fat chance of that, though.

"Annie, talk to me."

I open my mouth to say something, then close it again. What is there even to say? No matter how hard I try, I can't stop thinking about him. Most days I wonder if he's alive. I scan the internet, the newspapers, and even the local news broadcast. I'm pretending that it's a newly sparked interest in the comings and goings of the city where I've lived my whole life, but I'm not kidding anybody. I know I'm looking for him, to see if his name pops up. It never does, though. I don't know if he's alive or dead, in the city or gone for good. He's a ghost.

Until the moment I go to sleep. Then, he haunts my dreams.

But not in the dangerous way. Not in the threat-to-my-life way. No, it's worse. They're sex dreams. And every time I wake up my body craves him. Some days I even find it hard to eat I miss his touch so much.

"I'm just tired, Jen. Accounting is putting me to sleep these days, that's all. I'd better take a nap before I ruin some kid's future by accident." I force a lopsided grin and hope that it doesn't look as fake as it feels.

She reaches out and pats my hand with an all-knowing smile on her face. She's sweet, and her heart is in the right place. It always has been, since the day we met, two giggly, nervous girls at freshman orientation. We clicked right away, and then Wendy came along a few weeks into our first semester at school, and it was like we'd known each other all our lives. Jenna is as kind as they come.

But she doesn't know what I'm wrestling with. The thoughts by day, the dreams by night, the memories all the time. It's not her fault—I'm the one who is keeping secrets, after all, and I know without a doubt in the world that she would be the first one to listen and give me a shoulder to cry on, if I asked.

I just can't let myself do that. I don't know why, but every time I try to tell Jenna or Wendy about what happened to me—what *really* happened to me—it's like my lungs stop working and my throat closes up.

"All right, yeah, you deserve it, girl. Go lie down. I'll be quiet out here; you won't hear a peep." She smiles again and searches my face. I wonder if she knows I'm hiding something or if she's just being kind. Either way, a nap sounds really good right about now, before I face-plant on this towering stack of exams.

I sigh and stand, cracking my neck in each direction, before tossing my pen on the table and shuffling back to my bedroom.

I'm half asleep by the time I reach the door. And when I hit the pillow, I'm out like a light.

∽

Nikita appears. He's not wearing a shirt. The ripple of his muscles through his chest and shoulders looks like wires held in tension. He's angry that I didn't answer my phone earlier. "Isn't that what you wanted?" he asked. "A job? Security? A normal life? You should have answered that call, kitten." He pulls off his belt as he tells me what a bad girl I've been.

My teeth sink into my bottom lip.

I slide my hand under the waistband of my shorts, and down across my panty-covered sex. My fingers do a slow and steady dance along the folds of my labia, gently rubbing toward my clit and when my fingers make contact, I close my eyes and let out a huge sigh. My hand keeps stroking my pussy through my panties, while my left hand slides below my shirt to caress my breasts. I alternate from one nipple to the other, pinching each one and twirling it between my fingers as the hand on my sex picks up its pace. I'm hot and wet, each image of Nikita pushing me closer to the edge.

I rub faster circles over my clit, causing my knees to come together. Two fingers bury inside me and I begin driving them faster into my sex. My back arches and my legs shake as my sex tenses around my fingers. My body begins to jerk in spasms as my orgasm washes over me and I fall back against the pillows, satiated.

While the orgasm was good, it's not the same as the ones Nikita gave me. My touch doesn't compare to the way he works my body over. I groan and turn onto my side, closing my eyes and wishing my brain would just shut down. The confusion and frustration make me so tired and, every day, I pray the two emotions will stop haunting me. But tonight, they're stronger than ever. At least the orgasm tired me out enough and my breathing starts to slow as I drift off.

∼

The sun in my face wakes me up. Slowly and reluctantly, I uncover my face. I blink, close my eyes, and blink again. Sunbeams sneak through the gaps between the slats in my blinds, aimed straight at my face, like Mother Nature poking me in the eyeballs and telling me to get my ass out of bed.

I groan, roll over, and look at my alarm clock. *Holy shit.* I slept for way too long. It's already late in the morning. I can't even remember the last time I slept fourteen hours straight. I think about the dream and shiver before I sit up, drag my feet off the bed, and rub my knuckles onto my eyes.

The aroma of sweet and salty foods invades my room and I head toward the kitchen where Wendy and Jenna are preparing breakfast. My mouth instantly waters when I spot my favorite treat sitting on the counter. Decadent cinnamon buns from the corner bakery, each one as large as a side plate with gooey cinnamon filling. Cream-cheese icing covers the golden tops so heavily that it's tough to take a bite without getting an icing moustache. They're my soul food, and I'd club a baby seal to get my hands on them right now. My stomach rumbles.

"Look who's finally awake," Jenna says as she spreads avocado over toast and sprinkles tomato on top. "Your breakfast awaits, Sleeping Beauty."

"Ha. Ha. Gimme that," I say with a laugh as I swipe a cinnamon bun from the box and sit down at the table.

Bacon sits on the plate in crispy waves, the fat glistening in the sunlight streaming through the dining room window. I grab a piece and stuff it into my mouth. The salt mixed with the lingering sugar from the bakery bun is perfection.

Jenna and Wendy join me. Both swipe through their phones as they make faces and shove food in their mouths. I snort. Nothing like being so disconnected from human interaction. "You guys gonna put down the phones anytime soon?"

"Sorry, Annie. Just checking my bank account. My dad still hasn't transferred over the money I asked for," Wendy says.

"And I'm waiting to see if I got the internship at the publishing house in the fall," Jenna says.

"You better bring home some new releases before they hit the shelves. I'm dying to read a new fantasy," I say.

Jenna sticks her tongue out at me. "Not before I read it first."

Wendy rolls her eyes. She's not big on reading, and she never misses a chance to call Jenna and me four-eyed bookworms—which, to be fair, we are. She's more of a cheesy rom-com movie chick. I tried to introduce her to audiobooks, but I think she made it halfway through the first one I gave her before passing out. I remember finding her on the couch, snoring with her mouth wide open, as a baritone-voiced man narrated love scenes into her earbuds loud enough that the sound leaked out and I could hear him. The memory still makes me laugh.

"Ugh, my dad isn't giving me money until next Tuesday. Supposedly, he's only sending money once a month—on the fifteenth, like I'm on welfare or something. The man will never use all his money by the time he dies, even if he tries. But nooo. He has to torture me."

"Woe is you," Jenna says, laughing. "I mean–"

"Wait." I hold up a hand, cutting her off. "Next Tuesday is the fifteenth?" *Please let her be wrong. Please let her be wrong.*

"Yeah, Ms. Sleepyhead. You've slept away so many days this week you're losing track of time," Jenna says.

No. This can't be happening. No. No. No.

My period is late.

I stand up so fast my chair scrapes against the tile floor. I toss my plate in the sink and head to my room to grab my purse and bolt out the door. I'm not about to explain to my roommates that I might be pregnant. After all, this might just be the stress from everything I went through. I mean, all the events have given me nightmares and affected my sleeping patterns. Yes, no need to freak out. It's just stress.

I take the long way to the pharmacy to avoid Henry. Time is of the essence—for my sanity, if nothing else—but avoiding people is even more important. If anyone so much as makes eye contact with me right now, I might break into hysterical tears. My feet pound the pavement. I round the corner and see the big red letters of the pharmacy come into view.

I burst through the doors. Racing down the aisle, I grab a handful of pregnancy tests—the more, the better, right? My cheeks are hot and red. I have no idea why I'm embarrassed. I'm not a young teenager. I'm an adult.

An unwed adult who may be carrying a mob boss's child.

But no one knows that. I make my way to the register, put my items down, and the clerk rings them up. After paying, I grab the bag and race out the door. But instead of heading home, I walk to the campus library. There are numerous bathrooms there and I won't have to explain to Wendy and Jenna why I suddenly ran out. They'll be all too curious about what I have in the pharmacy shopping bag.

Luckily, the library isn't that far, or maybe I'm just walking that quickly. But I bound up the stairs to the second-floor restroom and hurry into a stall, slamming the door as soon as I walk in. I rip open the first box, do my thing on the stick, and wait, shaking it to hurry up whatever voodoo takes place inside these things. I feel as if hours are passing by instead of seconds. I keep my eyes closed for as long as I can. Finally, after a couple minutes have passed, I take a deep breath. I'm not ready to see the results, but I allow my eyes to drift open.

Positive.

No. No. No. I rip open the second box, repeat the process. Pee, close my eyes, wait.

Positive.

The third. Same thing.

Positive.

What the actual fuck? Why? Why is this happening to me? The universe has thrown some of the worst crap at me and instead of picking on someone else, it chooses to deal me another shit hand at life. I sink to the floor and bury my face in my hands and cry. I don't know what to do or who to turn to.

I just want my mom.

I need my mom.

I want to go home. To my real home.

I'm not sure how long I sit there, crying until there are no more tears left. I feel numb, like I'm in a dream of a dream. Eventually, I make myself get up.

I wipe my eyes and throw the tests into the trash can. After washing my hands and straightening my hair, I head up to the third floor and sit at one of the empty computers. Pulling up one of the discount travel websites, I book a flight home. I definitely need my mom. She'll know what to do.

Luckily, there's a flight for later today. I pull my credit card from my wallet and pay for my ticket, wincing when I get the confirmation email notification on my phone. Looks like grading more tests is in my future, because that bill is going to hurt.

I forward the flight info to my mom and tell her I'm making a surprise trip home for a few days.

<Everything all right, baby?>

<Ya. Just need some mom love. I miss u.>

<Ok hun. I'll make chicken parm tonight. Ur fave. See u soon! Love u.>

<I love u too, mom.>

No need to let her know about the pregnancy via text. That information requires a face-to-face conversation, and a stiff drink before, during, and afterwards.

I log out, gather my things, and head home. My eyes are swollen and red-rimmed from crying. I brace as I open the door to the apartment, wondering what Jenna and Wendy are going to say and how I can weasel my way out of that conversation.

But to my surprise the apartment is empty. Thank God for small favors amidst this shitstorm of bad luck. I hurry to my room and pull my suitcase from the closet. As soon as I'm done packing, I pull a check from my purse and fill it out so that my roommates have my part of this month's rent. I leave it on the counter in the kitchen along with a note saying I needed to go home and that I'll give them a call tomorrow.

Then I head back into my room, grab my suitcase, and lock up before I head downstairs. Checking the clock on my phone, I realize the train won't get me to the airport in time, which means I'm going to have to hail a cab. Great, another bill to add to my growing collection.

The best place to get a taxi is a few blocks west. At least the weather is nice enough that I don't have to worry about standing and waiting in the rain. I really don't need any more obstacles thrown at me right now. What I can use is actually a one-way ticket to an endless spa vacation.

But lugging a suitcase four blocks is no fun, especially when the pavement is all cracked and overgrown. I kick a twig in front of me and launch it into the street.

A few taxis drive down the street. Lights are off, though, so they must already have customers. But I only have one more block to go. I hope the traffic isn't bad, otherwise I'll really be cutting it close. At least my suitcase is small enough to carry on so I can just go right to the security line.

I huff and blow a strand of hair from my eyes just as I hear tires skid. I whip my head around, expecting to see a near accident. But what I find is a sickeningly familiar face exiting the passenger side of the car.

He's got dark hair slicked back, olive skin, and gold jewelry dripping from every possible place —rings, necklaces, an extremely expensive-looking watch. His cheesy shirt is two buttons undone, revealing a broad chest full of curly hair. He looks every bit the part of the Italian gangster.

Which he is.

"Hello, *dolce*," Gino snarls. "Been lookin' for ya."

I drop my suitcase and start running. But a hulking brute in a designer suit rounds the corner and grabs me in a bear hug. Two more come and take hold of my arms and legs.

I start screaming. And screaming.

But no one comes out of their houses. No one steps up to protect me. No one grabs my hand and leads me to safety. Nikita isn't here this time. I'm alone. *Where is he?* I wonder crazily as the men toss me into the trunk of the luxury sedan. I land with a painful thud.

When I look up. Gino flashes me a cruel, toothy grin.

Then he slams the trunk shut, and all I can see is darkness.

21

NIKITA

I know it's early morning because my heart is pounding right out of my chest. That's how I wake up every day now, like someone just fired a gun next to my eardrum. Only, there is no gun. At least, not yet.

I open my eyes and look at the ceiling over my cot. Cracks spiderweb through every inch of the plaster, and water stains are spreading out from one corner like a plague. This place is crumbling around me, like my world. And there's not a damn thing I can do about either one.

Hopeless week after hopeless week is taking its toll on me. I'm weary —deeply bone-tired, soul-tired—in a way that I can't remember ever feeling before. Even when I first came up to take the reins of my father's business, I didn't feel this unending exhaustion.

Nor the desperation. I feel like I'm on the losing end of a brutal chess beatdown, watching one by one as my pawns are taken from me and dumped into the river, bloodied and bruised. Rooks, bishops, knights —all are stripped away and tossed into a dumpster like anonymous bags of trash. My men. They were loyal to me. They had families.

And now they're dead, for the sake of the side they chose. There's only me left. A lonely king, with little but himself to rely on.

I shake off the morbid thoughts and stagger to the kitchen, rubbing sleep from my eyes. Breakfast is meager, these days. A few bites of some fruit, if I'm lucky. Not that I have much stomach for eating.

"Didn't sleep well again?" Eitan enters the kitchen and pours himself a cup of coffee.

"None. Spent half the night counting bodies, the other half counting sheep. Surprisingly, neither helped."

Eitan snorts, then lifts his ceramic mug to his mouth. "You never know where inspiration strikes."

I eye the coffee table as Eitan and I enter into the living room together. It's old-fashioned and wooden, not one of those mass-produced items with veneers over compressed fiber boards, but actual, real wood. My father purchased it from an antiques auction years ago.

I shudder as my eyes scan the surface, strewn with notes and drawings from the meetings I've had with Eitan and the rest of the men as we try to come up with a way to take down our enemies. But none of those pieces of paper contain anything remotely useful. And in an hour, we'll be at it again, talking through every possible angle and brainstorming, only to come up empty-handed.

"Should I call the men in?"

"Not yet." I need some time to get my thoughts in order, to prepare myself for the inevitable dead-end we'll meet at the end of the day. My head throbs already, like someone has taken a knife to the inside of my skull. I lean back into the couch. Squeezing my eyes shut, I try to will the pain to go away. "Fuck, this headache is killing me."

"Do you need something for it?"

I open my eyes and look up at my advisor. "Only a miracle, Eitan. Only a miracle."

He gives a hollow laugh and settles down into the dusty armchair on the other side of the table. His eyes roam over the map spread out on the table. "Where will it be today?" he mutters, as much to himself as to me. He lets a wandering finger trace over the contours of the city. "Downtown? By the docks? Los Arcos?" He points at each in turn, and I know exactly what he's picturing:

Blood. Bodies. The taunts of Gino smeared across city sidewalks like hideous graffiti. Men, women, and children—none have been spared.

"Not yet, Eitan," I say. "For just a few minutes, let me enjoy the silence of the morning and a simple cup of fucking coffee. Then we can face the day."

I can feel his gaze on me. He's a good man. He deserves better than this: boarded up in a rat hole, waiting to die. "As you wish, Nikita."

I let my mind wander. Unsurprisingly, it doesn't take long before she appears in my thoughts. *Annie Thornton. The girl who got away.* It's a funny thought, in a morbid sort of way. I picture her doing the most mundane things. Laundry, cooking, studying. I don't know exactly why, but it's comforting to think of Annie living a normal life, when mine has been anything but since the moment she entered it. My little bird, winging in and then out of my life ... and leaving utter carnage in her wake.

"Thinking about her, sir?"

I huff. "Am I so obvious?"

"Your face scrunches up every time you do."

I raise my head slowly and look at him. "She probably went home to her mother by now. I think graduation took place last week. 'Tis the season, you know?"

Before Eitan can respond, the front door swings open and one of our men stumbles inside and collapses in the foyer. Blood seeps onto the carpet beneath him. Eitan and I spring up and race over to his side.

Eitan closes the door and locks it as I drag the man into the living room. Already, the man's eyes are swollen shut and bloody spit drools from his slack, broken jaw. His face is soaked with congealed blood, and more of it leaks from cuts beneath tears in his clothing. When he tries to speak, his cracked lips fail at the first syllable. He's messed up in a bad, bad way.

Hearing the commotion, a few of the other soldiers from bedrooms down the hallway come running in and together, we lift him onto the couch. The man is mumbling incoherently. I lean closer to put my ear by his lips, hoping to make out what he's saying.

But it's just gibberish. I sigh, frustrated, and lean back. "Clean him up," I order the soldiers. "We need to figure out what he's telling us." I start to stand and walk away, when suddenly, the man grabs my forearm. His grip is surprisingly strong, given his condition, and there's a new fire and clarity in his eyes.

I watch his lips work as he forces out the words. "Gino ... has ... a ... message."

Fuck.

The Italian won't stop until we're all dead. My headache comes back full force and I rub my temples. "What did he say?"

"He ... has her."

Panic begins like a cluster of spark plugs in my abdomen. Tension grows in my face and limbs, and my breathing becomes rapid and shallow. "Repeat that."

"He has her," the man sputters again. The burst of strength that gave him the energy to speak is fading quickly now. I can see the lights in his eyes dimming. He just took too much damage; his body can't sustain him much longer. Slowly, his grip on my forearm eases and falls away.

And just like that, he's dead.

I stand and scream. "Fuck!" Lashing out, I kick over the coffee table and send its contents flying all over the room.

Eitan hands the bandages and alcohol to one of the other men and walks over to me, placing a hand on my shoulder. But I angrily shake it off and punch the wall. Over and over until my knuckles are bloody. Drywall splinters and the room fills with the dust of the plaster, but I don't stop. I need the pain, I need the blood, I need to know I'm fucking alive.

"Nikita," says Eitan. "This isn't helping her."

I whirl to face him, fists raised. My first instinct is to strike him. Eitan closes his eyes, ready for the blow. Then, the fight just disappears from my body. My shoulders slump.

He's right. Punching a wall won't save Annie. Screaming and flipping tables won't stop Gino. There is only one thing left to do.

I look at the blood dripping down my fingertips, then up at Eitan. "I'm going after her," I rasp. "And I'm going to kill him for touching her."

Eitan nods, and we begin to prepare.

Before we leave, I gather the men around me. The last remnants of the Lavrin Bratva. Good men, loyal men, fierce men, all of them. Some served my father and his father before him. Now, they have only me to lead them.

"I'm going to say this one time and one time only," I begin in a solemn voice. I look around the dingy room at each of them in turn.

"Any man who joins me on this mission will likely die. The odds are poor. The Italians have more men, more guns, and they will be on their home territory. They're vicious dogs, every last one of them, and they will not hesitate to make your death long and painful." I swallow hard. "So, if any one of you wants to walk away now, I will never blame you for that choice. Go, take your families, and run. And live. You deserve that much. I would give you more if I could, but this is all I have left. You're forgiven already, and no matter what you decide, the Lavrins will remember your name and your loyalty."

I pause and wait.

Not a man moves.

"So be it," I say, nodding. "Then we're leaving now. To face death."

The ride to Gino's headquarters is long and quiet. Most of us are mentally preparing, making sure our gear is ready. Everyone carries numerous magazines filled with ammunition.

Eitan and one of the men go ahead of the rest of us to find a spot to set off the explosion. We need a diversion to force our way in, and the grenades we'll be using are the last resource we have left.

Our watches are timed so that no other form of communication is needed. Once we're in place, I eye the watch on my wrist, adrenaline flooding my system. I haven't yet let myself think about what Annie is experiencing right now. Has he laid a finger on her? Is she alone? Both thoughts make me ill. I shudder and check my gun once again.

For the last few moments of silence we have left, I close my eyes.

I wonder what my father would say to me right now, if he could. Would he be proud? All I can picture is the little bird in his hand, testing its wings. So pure. So small. So fierce.

Then the beeping from my wristwatch cuts through the air and we exit the van just as an enormous explosion goes off. Windows shatter.

Smoke and fire rush out. Thousands of shards of glass and steel shower all around. That's our cue.

We race along the hidden route to the main complex. But we don't get too far. Gunshots begin to crack into the air as loud as thunder. Gunshots in movies and video games are merely an annoyance, a tinny pop and crackle. But out here, they're as good as a hypodermic to the heart. Each one isn't just loud, it booms and echoes, seeking to deliver death.

We fan out, ducking and dodging, returning fire when we're able, hiding as we must. It's a dogged, bloody fight, but we make our way around each corner. Each foot of ground is hard-gained. Already, I can see my men—what's left of them—sporting bleeding wounds.

We pass the first layer of security, and soon enough, the gunshots come thick again as more of Gino's soldiers arrive. The industrial complex is a hell zone of zipping bullets and groaning, dying soldiers. Metal shrieks and concrete shatters.

I pop up from behind a concrete pillar, take quick aim, and fire my weapon in rapid succession, killing three men as I move closer and closer toward the blast site. No matter what, I need to get inside. When I tuck into an alcove in the wall of the building, I turn to check my men. No one is dead, but many are wounded. That's the best we could have hoped for, for now.

I spy an Italian creeping up across the empty lot, knife drawn, ready to slice the throat of one of my soldiers who is focused in another direction. I drop to a knee, brace, and fire. Through my scope, I see a bullet hole bloom in his forehead. He hits the ground in a sickening tumble.

I'm reloading and looking for my next target when I spot a familiar weapon. A weapon that came in on the shipment Gino stole from me and which would end our attack in a matter of minutes.

A machine gun.

"Fall back!" I rush out, throwing my hand out to command my men to move back just as the distinctive rat-tat-tat of the ammunition cuts through the air. One of the men to my right erupts in a mushroom cloud of blood. He's torn to pieces instantly as I jump over a couple of empty drums and duck for cover, cursing under my breath.

Fuck. There's got to be another way in.

I see a door to my right, rusted over. When I hear the machine gun pause for a moment, I take to my feet and sprint that way as my men return fire behind me. I make it to the door, yank it open.

I'm almost inside when I feel a hand seize my ankle. The unexpected touch sends me tumbling to the floor in the dark hallway within. The man who grabbed me falls in. I spot the glistening edge of a knife blade before the door slams shut, trapping us in the pitch black.

I deliver two quick heel strikes to the man's face. His nose crunches under my boot, but it's not enough to stop him. His knife bites into my calf in one long slice. I roar as pain explodes in my lower leg. The hot rush of blood starts to fill my boot.

I need to move quickly, or this bastard will slit my throat in the dark and leave me here to die. Swinging my injured leg around his throat, I pull him into a chokehold with my shin cutting off his airway. I use my free hand to grab his knife-hand wrist and twist hard. Bones crack beneath my grasp. I hear the knife clatter to the floor.

The man is thrashing in my grasp, but when he reaches up and punches blindly into my groin, I let go with a pained grunt. The sickening lurch of his blow makes my stomach churn, but I don't have time to think before he's on top of me, raining punches down. Half of them miss, but enough land on my face and shoulders to disorient me.

I throw a blind punch back and get lucky, connecting with his jaw. The man falls to my left and I roll on top of him immediately.

Time to end this.

My hands find his throat and begin to squeeze all the air from his body. I can feel his fingers scrabbling over my face, looking for my eyes. I bite down hard on his thumb and taste the coppery tang of blood. He screams hoarsely; I don't let go.

Only when his thrashing has stopped and the man is strangled beneath me do I finally relinquish my grip and slump to the side. My breath comes in ragged gasps. The pain in my calf where he knifed me is a bitter throb, sharp and relentless.

I'm running out of time. I don't even know for sure if Gino is here, or if Annie is. And if he catches word of our suicidal assault on his headquarters, there is no telling where he might take her away to. This is my last—and only—chance to save her.

I stagger down the dark hallway, trailing blood. There's a dim light at the end of the tunnel, streaming down weakly from overhead. I reach out and find the cold metal rungs of a ladder. *Don't think; climb.* I mount it and make my way up.

At the top, I push aside a manhole cover and find myself in an empty hallway. It's silent, aside from the occasional pop of gunfire from far away, muffled by the walls. But I stay on guard. Down the hall, a light is on in one of the rooms. Someone is talking and shadows dance across the floor. I take a breath and narrow my eyes as I inch my way closer.

"It's got to be Nikita?"

Augustin's voice, I realize.

"Of course it's him. We have his little girlfriend. Did you think the Lavrin hothead wouldn't try to come and rescue her?" Gino laughs. "He'll die trying and I'll get what I've been waiting for."

"Go to hell," Annie spits at them.

My heartbeat races the moment I hear her voice. She's alive. I swallow and push on. Failure isn't an option. Not when it comes to protecting Annie. But I don't know the layout of the room or where she is. Or if they have a gun pulled on her.

Please, Dad, if you can hear me, watch over Annie and keep her safe.

I inhale and exhale a couple of times, then charge toward the door, throwing my body into it. As I crash into the room, I take quick count of everyone. Augustin and Gino are unguarded. Annie is held down to a table by Augustin gripping her arms, while Gino wrenches her legs apart. The Italian's pants are unzipped and unbuttoned. I can see the ugly head of his cock protruding from his boxers.

I hurl myself at him. No fucking way is the bastard going to rape my little bird.

22

ANNIE

An hour earlier

Not again.

Not again. This can't be happening to me again.

"Why so glum, princess?" The Italian's thick accent wrenches me back to reality.

He reaches across and pats my leg, his touch lingering longer than I care for, his face moving a little too slowly as he takes in the sight of me. Then he grins, and as he does so the temperature in the car falls a little. It's a Cheshire grin of sorts, the kind that's so wide it's more as if he wants to eat everyone than say hello.

"Don't worry, little girl. We're going to have so much fun, and soon the memory of Nikita will disappear from your mind, no?"

I sneer and quickly wish I hadn't. Gino tenses and his eyes are unblinking. No way will he make me forget Nikita, not when I'm carrying the man's baby. And not when my heart belongs to him. No, the only way Gino could ever make me forget about Nikita would be if he kills me.

Goose bumps pepper my skin at the last thought. Gino will most likely kill me—and my baby. I just pray it's quick. No torture, no slow death. Just put a bullet in my brain.

"Nikita won't be coming to save you this time. He's got no army, no allies. And I don't think he'll waste whatever he does have coming to rescue a slave." Gino taps his chin with his index finger. "Tell me, darling: why did he let you go?"

My eyes widen at the question. Gino must suspect that I mean something to Nikita. Why else would he have kidnapped me. But maybe, just maybe, he doesn't know that. So, I shrug and look out the window. "Said I was a bad lay."

The Italian's high, cold cackle makes my skin crawl and my body tremble.

"Nikita fucks so much I'm sure every pussy feels the same to him," Gino says as he flips his wrist in the air. "The man didn't need another slave. You were just another power play, another way for him to rub in everyone's face the money he has, the control he has. Or rather, *thought* he had. The Lavrin accounts are looking rather bare these days, though. And that's why the council didn't care when I made my move against him. Because Nikita Lavrin is finished in this city."

I swallow past the lump in my throat and stare out the window, worrying about Nikita.

The car drives through the city and toward the water. I know my journey is coming to an end when the warehouse is in front of me. I should have expected it. The houses gave way to barren industrial territory a full twenty minutes ago. Old machinery lines the road, covered in dirt, like metallic skeletons of huge, ugly beasts from thousands of years ago.

A warehouse beckons in the distance. It has the curved roof of an aircraft hangar and the walls are corrugated tin surrounded by a chain-link fence.

The driver pulls up to the west end of the lot and two men push open a gate to let us through. The car pulls up to the side of the warehouse and stops. A couple of men come out and open the door, helping Gino out. I follow and when I look up, I spot a familiar face standing next to Gino. A face I had prayed I would never see again.

Augustin.

"So happy to see you again. But from the look on your face, I'm going to guess the feeling isn't mutual," Augustin says. He smiles, and for a moment, I'm transported back to the nightclub. This smile was where it all began. *Take a shot with me,* he said. If only I'd thrown it in his face instead. Maybe this would all be different.

The men surround us and cut off any hopes I had of running away. Not that I would get far, but a girl can always hope. I watch everyone without turning my head. My heart is hammering but I keep my gait casual with no hint of hesitation. No sense in showing my fear. I won't let them get the best of me twice.

Augustin and Gino instruct most of the men to stand guard at different places and then head up a flight of metallic stairs. Two guards escort us to the top of the staircase, then take up stations there. Only Augustin and Gino continue inside with me. Augustin stands behind me. I straighten my spine in an effort to pretend I'm not afraid of him. Gino opens the door to the room.

I pause on the threshold. If I go in here, I might not make it out. Chances are pretty good that I'll die in this godforsaken dump.

But Augustin doesn't give me the time to reflect. He shoves me in the back and I stumble inside into Gino's arms. The men laugh cruelly as Augustin pulls the door closed behind me.

"You must've had a lot of fun with Nikita. How many times did he fuck you?" Augustin crosses his arms and waits for me to respond.

"According to the girl, she's a bad fuck. That's why Nikita let her go," Gino sneers.

Augustin shakes his head. "No way. Not for a quarter of a million dollars."

Gino takes his jacket off and sets it down on a chair. "You don't really think I bought her story? My men told me that he went out of his way to protect her on the rooftop of his penthouse. That told me everything I needed to know. The girl means something to him. Why do you think she's here?"

Augustin and Gino grin. I'm the bait they're using to lure Nikita into a trap.

I have to find a way to let him know. He can't die because of me.

Gino steps into my space and I back up until I bump into a table. When I turn around to try to maneuver around it, Augustin is there. He grabs my wrists and pulls so that I fall flat against the table. Oh God.

"That's right, Annie. When I said I'd make sure Nikita was a distant memory, what I meant to say was that I'm going to fuck you until you don't remember what he feels like," Gino says.

"And I think I'll fuck that pretty little mouth of yours so you forget what he tastes like, too" Augustin says as he yanks my hair.

Please, dear God, please make it stop. Maybe if I tell them I'm pregnant, they'll stop, I think. Then I look at Gino's scowling face and realize that it might just make him punish me more.

Gino kicks my legs apart and I scream. But his hands hold my hips in place. I can't go anywhere. I bite the inside of my cheek and prepare for the worst. I hear the metal sound of a zipper being undone and the rustle of clothing moved aside.

"Look at me, darling," Gino barks. Augustin forces my head up to see Gino waggling his cock between my legs like some hideous snake. He starts to stroke himself harder and harder. I gulp against a knot in my throat.

Then I close my eyes and pray that it will be over quickly.

∽

Suddenly, a bang rips through the air. The door swings wildly and crashes into the wall. And Nikita stands in the doorway with his gun pointed at Gino.

"Annie, get down!"

Augustin releases me as he fumbles for the gun at his hip. I scream, roll to one side, and drop to the ground just as the crack of gunfire cuts through the air. Gino is a couple of feet in front of me and pulls his own gun out, firing at Nikita, who has tucked and rolled to the far side of the room. I crawl on my hands and knees to a desk at my right and duck behind it as I try to keep safe from the bullets screaming through the room.

"Missed you, boss!" Augustin shouts from the opposite corner of the room as a couple of more bullets crack through the air.

Nikita growls and says nothing. More bullets slam into the walls and ceiling.

I have no idea who's firing anymore. I just lean against the desk, my knees to my chest, waiting for the gunfire to stop. I hear two more pops and then a pained groan.

And then ... silence.

Gino's sinister laugh fills the room and my heart plummets. Did they kill Nikita?

I peek around the corner just in time to see Nikita and Augustin tumbling head over heels on the dusty floor. Fists fly back and forth. Off to the side, I see Gino, bleeding profusely from a wound in his leg, sliding away, leaving a trail of blood behind him like a slug.

I don't know where to look. Nikita's fist slams into Augustin's face while Augustin sinks his own fist into Nikita's stomach. They struggle to their feet, stumble apart for a brief second to catch their breath, and then dive back at each other with twin roars, eyes narrowed.

Nikita dodges Augustin's swinging fist and comes up with his own uppercut. It dazes him for just a brief instant. Then Augustin's rears his head back and slams it into Nikita's face. They separate again, bloody and dusty, before Nikita shakes it off and blindly throws a sloppy kick

Augustin steps back, easily evading the kick. "You shouldn't have come here, Nikita," he taunts through a mouth full of broken teeth. I can see blood droplets spatter against the wall from a gruesome gash in Nikita's leg. He lands heavily and barely keeps his feet, favoring the injured leg. It looks bad. My heart is pounding against my ribcage.

"I came to get something of mine," Nikita retorts. He charges once again at Augustin, this time throwing his elbow into the other man's face. The sickening crunch makes my stomach churn and I gag. Blood spurts from Augustin's face and he falls backward into a shelf. Nikita sends two more quick punches into his face and the man slumps aside, unconscious.

Off to my right, I see Gino tearing off his shirt and fashioning a tourniquet around his bleeding leg. His face is pale and drawn, but the evil gleam in his eyes is as bright as it was the moment he first snatched me from the sidewalk.

Slowly, Nikita extracts himself from Augustin's limp limbs and stands straight. He turns painfully to look at Gino, who is still half lying on the ground, panting.

"So much fire in you, Lavrin. Too bad your father didn't have such fight in him," Gino hisses.

"Enough from you, Gino. You've made your last mistake."

"Care to wager who's going to die?" Gino smiles, his eyes briefly glancing over Nikita's shoulder.

I follow the look only to find Augustin standing above me, a gun pointed at my head. Everyone in the room freezes, until Augustin reaches down and hauls me to my feet by the roots of my hair. I scream, not that he gives a damn. Hell, he probably enjoys my fear.

"Get up, you cunt," he bellows. "And you!" he adds, whirling around to point his gun at Nikita. "Hands up. Don't make a fucking move."

My terrified gaze darts between Nikita and the other men. I try to find a weak point, something none of them are paying attention to, a way out. But there is none. Augustin's gun prods me in my lower back.

"Over here, bitch," he snarls, pushing me away from the corner of the room. "I want you to look at him while I put a bullet in his head. Then I'm going to fuck you till I've had my fill."

When we reach the middle of the open space, Augustin kicks me in the back of my legs, sending me to my knees with a thump. I'm a few feet away from Nikita. His gaze is fixed on mine, unreadable, as Augustin comes to my side, gun pressed against my temple.

"I'm sorry, Annie," Nikita whispers. "I tried."

Above me, Augustin's eyes are dark, as if he's lost his soul. They're darker than my father's. Darker than Nikita's.

"Kill her!" Gino screams.

Augustin's gun cocks with a metallic *click*.

For the second time in the last five minutes, I close my eyes and wait for the horrible fate that awaits me and the baby in my womb.

And for the second time, I'm saved.

Everything happens fast. The door flies open. Augustin spins around. Two shots fire in quick succession. I open my eyes and try to comprehend what just happened.

Eitan is slumped in the doorway, gushing blood from a bullet hole in the dead center of his chest. And next to me, Augustin's body is sprawled out on the ground. His face is a hideous, exploded mess of blood and brain. I fall to my hands and knees and retch.

No one needs to tell me Augustin is dead. I know it in my gut. Shoes scuffle across the floor and I swing my head toward Gino. He's scrambling to the desk I was hiding behind moments ago.

Nikita jumps towards Gino. He gets a hand wrapped around the Italian's ankle and drags him back to the middle of the room.

"Fucking Lavrin! I will end you," Gino screeches. "Get the fuck off me!" He's fumbling in his pocket for something as Nikita reaches for his gun where it clattered to the floor earlier. I'm frozen with fear. I can hear Eitan gurgling in pain behind me.

Gino withdraws a knife from his pocket, unfurls it, and starts to drive it towards Nikita's turned back.

Nikita grabs the gun and starts to spin back.

For a long beat, it's like time stops. Gino's knife, speeding up with deadly intent, freezes in the air. Nikita's gun is rising to level with Gino's face.

But it's too slow. He's not going to make it.

No. No. No. I can't let this happen.

I reach out blindly to my side. My fingers close on a steel pipe, fallen from the ceiling during the shootout. I raise it over my head, then bring it down with a bone-shattering crunch on Gino's face.

Then time kicks back in, and the room is filled with screams and the smell of blood. Gino's knife falls to the floor and skitters away. Nikita stands and looks at me with wide eyes. Gino moans and groans and remains on the floor clutching the back of his head.

Nikita runs over to me and grabs me in his arms. "Are you okay?"

"I think so," I say, running my hands over my body to make sure I haven't been hit by a stray bullet.

I sigh and my shoulders slump. I'm okay. I survived. My baby and I survived. My body tenses once again and I avoid Nikita's gaze. Not really the best time to tell him I'm pregnant. God only knows what we may have to fight against outside to get out of here.

23

NIKITA

Having Annie in my arms safe and sound is all that I wanted. I squeeze her tight, unwilling to let go. She buries her face in my shirt and cries softly. She was brave today. She saved my life. I fully expected her to run the first opportunity she got, but she didn't. And her face when I was shot told me all I needed to know. She cares about me.

"I'm so sorry I pushed you away," I say as I kiss the top of her head. "I don't know what I would've done if they'd hurt you. Or worse."

"I'm okay," she mumbles, but squeezes me tighter.

"Are you sure you're okay?" I pull away slightly and push the hair from her eyes.

She looks up at me and nods. Her expression softens as she looks over me to make sure I'm all right as well. How have I survived without her these past weeks?

"Annie, I love you. And I know I'm an idiot for running away scared because of how I felt. But I swear I won't do that again." I place my hand under her chin and tilt it up so that she looks at me as I say my next words. "I love you with all my heart. That means I will defend you with my life even if the odds are insurmountable. It means I will comfort you in the difficult and painful times. It means I will rejoice with you when times are good. It means I will never betray you, never give up on you. I'm yours into eternity and I will never abandon you."

I bend down and kiss her lips. She tastes so sweet, like honey and apricots, her skin soft and smooth. I bask in our kiss, hungry for more.

"Did you memorize that speech?" she asks me.

I grin; I can't help it. "I've been working on it for a while," I confess sheepishly.

Annie reaches up and her hand caresses the side of my face. She searches my eyes and takes a deep breath. My nerves fire and butterflies swarm in my stomach because I'm unsure if she'll return my affection or reject me. And her rejection would shatter my soul.

"I love you too. It's confusing because of the way we met. But our night together in the mountains, the way you protected me, the way you held me. Somewhere along the way I fell in love with you. I know you're different than my father, that you would never hurt me. You've proven that."

Annie pushes to her tiptoes and plants a kiss on my cheek. It's the best feeling in the world. My chest expands and there's a weightlessness washing over me as if all the chains, fears, and turmoil have evaporated, allowing me to finally be happy.

"Fuck!" I curse suddenly, remembering abruptly. Annie and I both turn to face the doorway. Eitan has lost consciousness. Blood pools on the tile beneath him. I rush over and take his head in my hands.

"Eitan, Eitan! Wake the fuck up! Don't you dare fucking die on me," I bark.

He wavers in and out, eyes fluttering. His hand grabs mine weakly. I look up at Annie. "We need to get him out of here."

Just then, I hear two sets of footsteps pounding towards us. Two of our soldiers appear in the doorway. "We found a secret way in and barricaded ourselves in here, sir. The rest of the men are holding off Antonio's troops," one of them reports. "But I don't think we have long."

Annie grips my shoulder in fear. "What are we going to do, Nikita?" she whispers.

"We wait," I say. "Some friends of mine are coming."

Everyone looks at me in confusion. But moments later, a cascade of sparks comes lancing into the barricaded door at the end of the hallway. The blades of a power saw poke through the metal, and soon, the whole door comes crashing inwards.

In the space opened up, a man steps in. He's got a braided beard, a dozen piercings, and a leather vest on that reads "East Side Boys MC" across the back. When he sees me, he grins.

"Not a moment too soon, eh, Nikita?" he growls.

Behind him, his men come pouring in, armed as they check the area for any remaining enemy troops. A club doctor follows them, and when he notices Eitan bleeding in my arms, he sprints towards us. "He needs a hospital immediately," the doctor says. I nod, and two East Side Boys come up with a makeshift stretcher and hustle him outside, the doctor running alongside them.

We've won. My enemies are conquered. My woman is safe. But my advisor is at death's door.

Everything has come at such a cost.

The hospital is noisy. Patients whine, machines beep, a TV overhead mumbles staticky nonsense at an irresponsibly high volume. I'm in an uncomfortable chair outside of one of the rooms.

Someone opens the door and emerges into the hallway. "Mr. Lavrin?" says a nurse with a clipboard. I stand immediately and then fall back in my seat. I've already been tended to and bandaged. The wound on my leg is going to keep me limping around for months, but it's better than most of the alternatives.

"Is Eitan okay?" I demand immediately.

The nurse shakes her head. "Your friend is still recovering from surgery. We don't know anything yet. But your, uh …"

My heart stops. I push inside without waiting for her to finish.

Annie is propped up on a hospital bed. She smiles at me nervously when I enter. "Are you okay?" I ask. My voice comes out in a whispered rasp.

She bites her lower lip and dips her head. Her face is marked by furrowed brows and a clenched jaw. My heart stutters again and breathing becomes difficult. Something must have happened. Did she get shot? Stabbed? Raped? The possibilities horrify me.

"There's something I need to tell you and I'm scared," she says.

My heart beats a mile a minute. Was I too late? Did Gino hurt her? A hurricane builds inside me, one of anger and confusion and sorrow. "This is my fault."

"Um, sort of, yeah."

My mouth opens and closes but words don't come out. Her response isn't what I expected. I mean, yes, it's my fault she was put in danger. And Annie hasn't lied to me yet, so I'm not sure what I expected her to say. I sigh. I know what I wanted her to say—that it wasn't my fault. That somehow whatever she's worried about telling me has nothing to do with me or the life that I lead.

Annie hesitates, then says, "Nikita, I'm ... uh ... I'm pregnant."

Words leave me. I stare into those bright, wide eyes, burning with insecurity, and my heart falls silent. But I can't will my lips to move.

"Do you have nothing to say? Please tell me what you're thinking," she begs, her eyes desperately searching mine ... waiting.

Instead of answering her with words, my lips slam down on hers as I press my tongue to the seam of her lips and when she opens for me, I delve inside her mouth. The kiss is hot, fiery, passionate, and demanding. Her arms reach up and tangle around my neck, moaning as she presses her body against mine.

She pulls away and clasps her hands on either side of my face. "I take it you're happy?"

I nod and place my hand on her belly. I'm going to be a father. I'm going to have a family. I smile from ear to ear. Finally, a chance to be a role model like my father once was to me. "Yes. Yes, I'm very happy."

I lace my fingers through Annie's. We're going to be parents. "I swear that I'll protect both of you for the rest of my life."

A knock catches my attention and both Annie and I swing our heads toward the doorway.

Eitan.

He's holding onto an IV stand, dressed in a hospital gown, and he looks like absolute hell. His eyes are bloodshot, his skin is pale, and he's barely managing to keep his feet. But the smile on his face is pure and genuine. I'm guessing he overheard our conversation. Part of me expects him to shoot me one of those 'I-told-you-so' looks but he doesn't. He just walks over and hugs Annie and congratulates her, kissing her cheeks.

He turns to face me. I want to tell him something—thank you, I suppose—but instead I just embrace him. He was my father's advisor, and then mine. But he has become so much more than that. My best friend. My brother.

I open my mouth to tell him that I owe him my life, but before I can speak, two nurses come bounding into the room after him, furious. "You aren't supposed to be out of your room for days, sir!" they screech. He sighs and says nothing as they load him into a wheelchair and whisk him away.

***

One Week Later

I turn and look to the chair. Gino is strapped to it. His face is still bloodied and swollen. Every breath he takes rattles through the shattered bones of his nostrils.

I run my hands through my hair three times in quick succession and fix Gino in a stare that could have frozen the Atlantic. What the hell to do? The Italian bastard threatened my family, my unborn child. He wanted to kill me, to end the Lavrin reign. So many of my men are dead.

All because of him.

"Nikita, this matter needs to be addressed," Eitan says and holds out a gun. He's still in a wheelchair, but he's recovered enough of his color and energy to be discharged from the hospital. This will be his last act before a well-deserved retirement.

I grab the gun and growl. I stalk over to Gino and put the muzzle of the gun to his temple. The man deserves to die for all he's done. If I hadn't arrived when I did, he would've raped Annie. My arm shakes and my finger brushes the trigger. Gino deserves to be killed. No one will ever be safe with him alive.

I swallow and turn my head to see Annie. She demanded to be here for this. She wanted to see the end of him, she told me. To watch a monster finally get what he has long deserved.

But when I look at her, I don't see the woman I love. I see instead the stories she told of the man whom she considered a beast: her father. It's a look I never want to see again, especially not from the mother of my child. And I never want my child to tell the same stories of me. To think of me as a monster.

Because I refuse to be that. Maybe I was once. But not anymore.

Annie's father destroyed everything that should've been held sacred: family, his own flesh and blood. Maybe that's why my father showed mercy. He wanted to hold onto his humanity. All those times I thought of him as weak, he was actually being strong. He was fighting back against the darkness, fighting to keep himself from becoming what he hated most.

I turn back to Gino. His face is blank and his pupils dilated. He probably can't even comprehend exactly what is going on. The strike of Annie's pipe back in the warehouse did a serious number on his mind. But there's enough of him left to know what's about to happen.

This is the end of him.

Or is it?

I take a deep breath and pull the gun away from Gino's head, tucking it into the waistband of my pants. "Contrary to what you think of my father and me, we aren't weak. We just aren't the soulless monsters that you are."

A soul.

"What you waiting for Lavrin?" Gino grumbles.

"I'm not going to kill you," I say.

Eitan wheels forward so he's at my side. "Nikita, what are you thinking? He's a danger to us all. He'll try again. You know this."

I nod. "He will, I'm sure. But he'll try with everyone. And if he does ... we'll be ready."

Gino's eyes narrow and his lip curls up.

I kick his legs. "I'm not going to shoot you, but I'm banishing you from the city. If you ever step foot here again, you'll die. The families that patrol the city will kill you."

I turn to one of my soldiers, waiting at the door. "Untie him." The man hurries to do as I said.

When he's freed, Gino staggers to his feet and steps into my space. Everyone in the room immediately raises a gun at him, but I wave them off. He's no threat to me now.

"You think I'm going to run like a chicken with its head cut off, Lavrin?"

"If you know what's good for you ... yes."

I take one last look at his ruined face. He's here, in front of me, completely at my mercy—the man who tried to take everything from me.

And then ... I forgive him.

I pivot and walk over to Annie. Grabbing her hand in mine, I guide her towards the exit. Before I leave, I pause and look at the soldier standing guard.

"Escort Gino outside the city limits," I say to them. "And spread the word: if anyone ever sees him here again ... kill him."

The men grab Gino under the arms and drag him from the room. I'm not sure if he'll make it that far. While I can control my men, I can't control the other families who have put a price on his head. With Gino gone, I return my attention to Annie.

She smiles at me and my heart warms. Gone is the look of fear from her face. All I see is love. For me. I pick her up, turning in circles. She is beautiful and she's chosen to be mine.

A part of me is sad for my father not being here. He would've loved Annie and I regret they will never get to meet, that my child will never get to meet his or her grandfather. Plus, I want him to see the man I've become since meeting Annie. And the man I will become once my child is here. I hope I'll be just like him. Ruthlessness and violence will not enter my home. It will be a place of love and safety.

And if I falter, I know Annie will set me back on the right path. That she'll stick by my side and guide me back toward the right path. I pull her down and kiss her once more. I don't think I'll ever get enough of the taste of her lips.

It's been a journey, a hard one. But in the end I'm king of the city once again. And this time, I'll rule differently. This time, I intend to be a king that's loved, not feared. This time, I intend to do it the right way.

The Lavrin way.

24

ANNIE

Months have passed and everything has gotten better. Wendy and Jenna finally met Nikita, and learned the truth about what happened. They weren't thrilled at first. In fact, they gave him major attitude for weeks. And I had to spend those weeks playing referee to keep the peace. Nikita understood and dealt with their wrath. More so because my mother was in their corner as well.

But everyone finally got past their emotions and moved forward for me and the baby. Well, not completely, as Jenna and Wendy then began arguing over which one of them would be the baby's godmother. I still haven't made that decision. How can I choose between my two best friends?

"Did you get lost in there?"

I giggle. "I'm fine. Hold your horses. I'll be out in a bit."

Moving in with Nikita is one of the best decisions I've made. Of course, the gigantic walk-in closet helped. Jenna and Wendy asked if they could move in, too, and then followed up by asking Nikita if he had any brothers he'd like to introduce them to. Nikita just shook his head, laughed, and walked out the room.

"Just making sure you and the baby are fine."

I roll my eyes. While Nikita is very sweet—and calmer than when I first met him—he's taken to hovering and being a tad overprotective, which tends to grate on my nerves especially when my hormones fluctuate. But he deals with my attitude, and completely ignores what I say because he continues to hover.

"Are we still going to my mother's house for the holidays?"

"Yes, but I don't understand why she just won't come here," Nikita answers.

"Because she wants to feel like she's got family. She wants to get the house ready and cook and decorate." I don't know how to explain it to him, but my mom worked so hard for what she has, and now she finally feels like she has a family to fill her home. A grandchild to come and visit her.

I walk over to the lingerie drawer in the closet. Nikita is in for a surprise. It's funny to think how closed off I use to be, how my roommates had to drag me out to a club, and force me to get dressed up. And now, I have an entire freaking dresser full of the sexiest lingerie that I love wearing. Maybe I just love showing off my baby bump to the man I love. But somehow, I've become more comfortable in my own skin.

"Annie?"

"What did I say about hovering? Calm down and give me a second."

His growl reverberates into the closet. There's something sexy about the way he gets mad at me when he doesn't get what he wants the very damn second he wants it. And there are times I hold out until he begs because I find that sexy as well.

I grab the powder-blue thong and lace baby doll and slip it on. Then I walk over to the full-length mirror and fluff my hair. Everything needs to be perfect. After applying some vanilla bean lip balm, I grab the collar from its hook and clip it on.

Nikita doesn't own me, he never has, but now I choose to be his slave. It's something he enjoys—and enjoys only with me, that's one rule I made—and I want him to be happy. Plus, it's been an eye-opening experience. To completely surrender to another, to trust that person wholly, is something I never thought I'd be able to do. But here I am, doing just that with Nikita.

I sashay out of the closet and pose against the door frame, accentuating my larger breasts—*thank you, future son or daughter*—and twirl a lock of my hair around my finger. Nikita sits up in bed, eyes wide and mouth hanging open. When I bite my lower lip, his Adam's apple bobs visibly as he swallows. But that isn't the only thing visible. The way the sheets pitch over his crotch makes my skin flush.

He's hard as a rock for me.

"So, do you like?" I take a step forward and turn in a slow circle so he can view all sides of me.

He doesn't say a word and just nods.

I laugh. Never has Nikita been at a loss for words. I quirk a brow as I make my way towards the bed. "Worth the wait, huh?"

"It always is."

I crawl onto the mattress and over to him. I brush my lips over the tip of his cock, still hidden under the sheets, and his body jerks as a low groan passes through his lips. "Someone's sure worked up."

"Little bird, you have no idea what you do to me. How sexy you are." His baritone voice cracks, telling me just how needy my baby's daddy is.

I straddle him and gently press my lips to his. Our kiss is tender. Nikita cups my face with his hands and pulls away, lifting my face so our eyes meet. We stare at one another in silence and then his fingers fall to the collar around my neck.

"It means the world to me that you would surrender yourself to me. That you'd be mine. My property. My woman." His fingers trace the pink bejeweled leather until they're on the buckle in the back. He clicks it and the collar falls from my neck. "But I want to know you're here because you want to be, not because I paid for you."

"Nikita," I say, taking his hand in mine and placing it on my belly. "We're going to be a family. I want to be with my child's father, with the man who risked his life to save me and protect me. I love you. And I choose to be here."

Nikita smiles at me and my heart melts. There are times he becomes insecure in our love, and the emotion conflicts with the tough man he is when it comes to the business, but it just shows he's also tender and cares for those around him.

I lean in and kiss him again. His hands remain on my belly and his lips remain closed. For a moment, I wonder what's caught his attention since he's not really into the kiss, but then I feel it. That pressure. That annoyance. Our child is kicking me yet again. And Nikita is in heaven.

I roll my eyes and slap his shoulder. "I'm here trying to be sexy, to get my needs met. And now you're poking my belly in an attempt to play with the baby."

Nikita looks up at me, his face contorted into an expression that reminds me of a child being reprimanded after being caught eating a snack before dinner. I pull his hand away from my belly and place it on my ass, pushing my breasts into his chest. "Now, can I have your full attention?"

Nikita smiles and scoots me up higher on his hips so he can shimmy his briefs off. I kiss him, gently at first, my hands in his hair, and then deepen the sweet kiss, tangling our tongues. His hands lift my ass and he pulls back, his eyes on mine as he flips us over.

I wrap my arms around him and run my hands up and down his back, from his ass to his thick hair, and back down again, while I rub his thighs with the soles of my feet. I can't stop touching him, rubbing myself against him. "You feel so good."

"Let me make love to you, little bird." He nibbles my lips, along my jawline, and over to my left ear. I tilt my head, giving him easier access to this sensitive spot, and he licks under my ear where he knows his touch makes me crazy. "I love how you smell, Annie. So soft and clean and sweet. Like apricots and honey." His teeth clench gently onto my earlobe and I squirm under him. "You feel so damn good, sweetheart. So smooth and firm and small."

His words are intoxicating me, making love to me as thoroughly as his body is, and my heart rate speeds up and my breathing quickens.

"Nikita," I whisper.

"I can't get enough of you." His hips start to move in a slow circle, rubbing his hard, thick cock along my folds, and I arch my back, pushing against him.

"Nikita, I need you." I grip his firm ass in my hands and pull him against me, almost coming undone at the sensation of his long shaft rubbing my lips and the head of his cock making my clit pulsate, an orgasm working its way through me.

"So beautiful," he whispers against my neck, and pushes his forearms under my shoulders so he's cradling me, his hands cupping my neck and fingers pushed up into my hair. He holds on and pushes harder, faster, rubbing himself against me. "I love making you come like this."

"Oh God," I whisper. Our voices are soft; we're panting quietly, making love almost reverently. I feel tears pool in my eyes and I close them, the tears spilling down my temples.

"Little bird, don't cry." He settles his lips on mine again, rubs them back and forth, caressing me and then kissing me sweetly, softly. "Come for me."

I come apart, my body quaking and pushing against him. He deepens his kiss and pulls his hips down, finding my opening with the tip of his cock and pushing into me, so, so slowly until he fills me completely. He sinks into me to the root of his cock and stops.

"Open your eyes."

His eyes are on fire, looking down at me with such love, and more tears leak out of my eyes.

"Your eyes are the most brilliant I've ever seen, and they sparkle even more since you've become pregnant." He moans and his gaze never falters. "I love it when you look at me like this."

"How am I looking at you?" I whisper and push my fingers into his thick hair, loving how it feels to have my head and shoulders cradled in his arms and his body draped over mine, filled up with him.

"Like I'm all you see," he whispers back to me.

I run my fingers down his face and cup his cheeks in my hands, looking him square in the eye, not paying any attention to the tears on my face. "You are all I see."

He growls softly and kisses me desperately. His pelvis begins to move, slowly pulling in and out of me. I grip his ass in my hands again and I feel another orgasm building up in me. He must feel it too, because he moves faster, and pushes into me a bit harder with each thrust.

"Let go, Annie," he murmurs.

"Come with me," I whisper.

He groans and pins me with his raw eyes, and he pushes into me twice, three times, and then grinds himself against my clit as he spills into me, and I come apart beneath him, not taking my gaze from his, as my body shudders around him.

"Oh my God," I whisper as my body calms.

He collapses onto me and buries his face in my neck. "God, I love you, Annie."

∽

I awake to soft sheets, and the morning light trickled in through the blinds. Shedding the remaining glimpses of a dream, I soak in the warmth of my covers. My arm reaches to the space next to me only to find Nikita's not in bed. But his smell still lingers and I inhale and smile.

Down the hall, there are pots banging and I'm sure the staff is preparing breakfast. Nikita must've gone to work early, letting me sleep in. These days, I need my rest, even taking a couple of naps throughout the day. The baby is growing rapidly and my body drains of energy quicker than usual.

But I'm hungry, so I hoist myself from my comfy place and throw on a robe before heading downstairs. The cool tile on my feet is soothing. But I'm not prepared for the scene before me. Out on the terrace is the most beautiful setup I've ever seen, better than the first dinner I ever had with Nikita.

Jasmine flowers line the terrace; nothing is more perfect to me. Five white petals with sunshine yellow in the middle. Their fragrance is like a drug. It gives me a high, my brain buzzing—happy, serene.

The entire place looks like a fairy-tale garden, complete with teacups and large candles. Even the powder-pink tablecloth adds to the fantasy feel. An empty, rustic birdcage sits in the corner like the ones people use at weddings to place the cards they receive in. When did Nikita have time to set this all up?

There are also flowers on the table. They're fresh, some open and others in bud. I love to watch how the sunlight brings a brightness to each petal it touches and a shine upon the deep green foliage.

"I was hoping you'd like them," Nikita comes up behind me and wraps his arms around my waist, his hands settling on my belly. He kisses my cheek and escorts me to the table.

"What's the occasion?"

"Just a breakfast date with my woman." Nikita takes my hand and pulls out my chair, helping me sit since my belly is big and getting in and out of chairs isn't the easiest act anymore.

The servers bring us plates of eggs and toast. A bowl of cut fresh fruit is placed in the middle of the table full of strawberries, blueberries, melons, and grapes. A glass of orange juice and water are set next to me.

"Did you sleep well?" Nikita asks before taking a bite of his food.

My cheeks burn and I nod as I drink some of the orange juice, praying I don't choke on it. I slept as well as I could, given that he insisted on having sex with me three other times throughout the night.

After placing my napkin in my lap, I dig into my food, barely chewing it. I'm not sure if it's myself or the baby or both of us that are starving, but I can't get the food into my stomach fast enough. I barely chew my scrambled eggs, opting to just swallow them as they're so soft and fluffy. Nikita chuckles from across the table.

"You better slow down before you choke."

I snort. "Tell that to the little one. He or she is just as hungry, and your plate has just become my next target."

I reach across and stick my fork into a piece of his bacon and shove it into my mouth before he has a chance to say anything.

"If you keep stuffing yourself, you'll miss the best part."

I quirk my eyebrow and stare at him. The best part? What has this man been up to as I was sleeping? I narrow my eyes at him and he breaks out into a series of snorting chuckles. So sexy ... *not*. But before I can ask him what his little secret is, a familiar scent floods my nose.

Cinnamon, freshly baked bread, and sweet icing.

One of the men places a box down and I tear it open to find my favorite meal of all time, and the one thing I have been craving all month. I pull the large cinnamon bun from its confines and bring it to my mouth, biting a chunk out of it. When I lower it to my plate, Nikita reaches over with his fork and I smack his hand away as I lick the frosting from my lips.

"Mine!" I growl playfully.

He stands and walks toward me. "Maybe you should eat that thing more slowly." He sounds kind of weird. Nervous, almost.

"Why, so you can try to steal some? Nuh-uh, mister. Back off." I take another mouthful and chew.

Nikita rolls his eyes and swipes at some of the frosting piling up on the side of my lips. "Annie, take smaller bites. Please!"

"Whatever." I bite into heaven once again and this time as I chew my teeth hit something rough. Fuck. I grab my napkin and spit the chewed bun out. "What the hell is this?"

I pick through my chewed food to find the culprit that nearly cracked my tooth when a shiny stone sparkles in the sunlight. The air rushes from my lungs and I just hold my palm open. Nikita takes the item from my hand and cleans it off with his napkin.

"You know, I meant this to be romantic, hiding an engagement ring in something your eyes glaze over for. But I never expected you to eat like it's going out of style." He shakes his head and chuckles. Then he drops to one knee. "I want us to be a family—officially. I want to spend the rest of my life with you and raise our children in a loving home. I want to wake up to you every morning and fall asleep next to you every evening. You make me whole in every way. Annie Thornton, will you marry me?"

I spring out of my chair and it tips over and hits the terrace floor with a bang. I launch myself into Nikita's arms and he stumbles backwards as I wrap my arms around his neck and kiss him. "Yes!"

THE END

~

Thanks for reading! But don't stop now – there's more. Click the link below to receive the FREE extended epilogue to <u>SOLD TO THE MOB BOSS</u>.

So what are you waiting for? Click below!
https://dl.bookfunnel.com/eefzxgxp2b

SNEAK PREVIEW (BROKEN VOWS)

Keep reading for a sneak preview of BROKEN VOWS by Nicole Fox!

She's my fake wife, my property… and my last chance at redemption.

She's beautiful. An angel.

I'm dangerous. A killer.

She's my fake bride for a single reason – so I can crush her father's resistance.

But marrying Eve brings me far more than I bargained for.

She's fiery. Feisty. Won't take no for an answer.

She makes me believe that I might be worth redemption.

Until I discover a past she's been hiding from me.

One that threatens everything.

Now, I know that our wedding vows are not enough.

I need to make sure she's mine for good.

A baby in her belly is the only way to seal the deal.

In the end, the Bratva always gets what it wants.

∼

Luka

Their fear tingles against my skin like a whisper. As my leather-soled shoes tap against the concrete floor, I can sense it in the way their eyes dart towards and away from me. In the way they scurry around the production floor like mice, meek and unseen in the shadows. I enjoy it.

Even before I rose through the ranks of my family, I could inspire fear. Being a large man made that simple. But now, with brawn and power behind me, people cower. These people—the employees at the soda factory—don't even know why they fear me. Other than me being the owner's son, they have no real reason to be afraid of me, and yet, like prey in the grasslands, they sense the lion is near. I observe each of them as I weave my way around conveyors filled with plastic bottles and aluminum cans, carbonated soda being pumped into them, filling the room with a syrupy sweet smell.

I recognize their faces, though not their names. The people upstairs don't concern me. Or, at least, they shouldn't. The soda factory is a cover for the real operation downstairs, which must be protected at all costs. It's why I'm here on a Friday evening sniffing around for rats. For anyone who looks unfamiliar or out of place.

The floor manager—a Hispanic woman with a severe braid running down her back—calls out orders to the employees on the floor below in both English and Spanish, directing attention where necessary. She doesn't look at me once.

Noise permeates the metal shell of the building. The whirr of conveyor belts and grinding of gears makes the concrete floors feel like they are vibrating from the sheer power of the sound waves. A lot of people find the sights and smells overwhelming, but I've never minded. You don't become a mob underboss by shrinking in the face of chaos.

A group of employees in blue polos gather around a conveyor belt, smoothing out some kink in the production line. They pull a few aluminum cans from the line and drop them in a recycling bin, jockeying the rest of the cans back into a smooth line. The larger of the three men—a bald man with a doughy face and no obvious chin—flips a red switch. An alarm sounds and the cans begin moving again. He gives the floor manager a thumbs up and then turns to me, his hand flattening into a small wave. I raise an eyebrow in response. His face reddens, and he turns back to his work.

I don't recognize him, but he can't be in law enforcement. Undercover cops are more fit than he could ever dream to be. Plus, he wouldn't have drawn attention to himself. Likely, he is just a new hire, unaware of my position in the company. I resolve to go over new hires with the site manager and find out the man's name.

When I make it to the back of the production floor, the lights are dimmed—the back half of the factory not being utilized overnight—and I fumble with my keys for a moment before finding the right one to unlock the basement door. The stairway down is dark, and as soon as the metal door slams shut behind me, I'm left in blackness, my other senses heightening. The sounds of the production floor are but a whisper behind me, but the most pressing difference is the smell. Rather than the syrupy sweetness of the factory, there is an ether, chemical-like smell that makes my nose itch.

"That you, Luka?" Simon Oakley, the main chemist, doesn't wait for me to answer. "I've got a line here for you. We've perfected the chemistry. Best coke you'll ever try."

I pull back a thick curtain at the base of the stairs and step into the bright white light of the real production floor. I blink as my eyes adjust, and see Simon alone at the first metal table, three other men working in the back of the room. Like the employees upstairs, they don't look up as I enter. Simon, however, smiles and points to the line.

"I don't need to try it," I say flatly. "I'll know whether it's good or not when I see how much our profits increase."

"Well," Simon balks. "It can take time for word to spread. We may not see a rise in income until—"

"I'm not here to chat." I walk around the end of the table and stand next to Simon. He is an entire head shorter than me, his skin pale from spending so much time in the basement. "There have been nasty rumors going around among my men."

His bushy brows furrow in concern. "Rumors about what? You know we basement dwellers are often the last to hear just about everything." He tries to chuckle, but it dies as soon as he sees that I'm not here to fuck around.

"Disloyalty." I purse my lips and run my tongue over my top teeth. "The rumbling is that someone has turned their back on the family."

Fear dilates his pupils, and his fingers drum against the metal tabletop. "See? That is what I'm saying. I haven't heard a single thing about any of that."

"You haven't?" I hum in thought, taking a step closer. I can tell Simon wants to back away, but he stays put. I commend him for his bravery even as I loath him for it. "That is interesting."

His Adam's apple bobs in his throat. "Why is that interesting?"

Before he can even finish the sentence, my hand is around his neck. I strike like a snake, squeezing his windpipe in my hand and walking him back towards the stone wall. I hear the men in the back of the room jump and murmur, but they make no move to help their boss. Because I outrank Simon by a mile.

"It's interesting, Simon, because I have reliable information that says you met with members of the Furino mafia." I slam his head against the wall once, twice. "Is it true?"

His face is turning red, eyeballs beginning to bulge out, and he claws at my hand for air. I don't give him any.

"Why would you go behind my back and meet with another family? Have I not welcomed you into our fold? Have I not made your life here comfortable?"

Simon's eyes are rolling back in his head, his fingers becoming limp noodles on my wrist, weak and ineffective. Just before his body can sag into unconsciousness, I release him. He drops to the floor, falling onto his hands and knees and gasping for air. I let him get two breaths before I kick him in the ribs.

"I didn't meet with them," he rasps. When he looks up at me, I can already see the beginnings of bruises wrapping around his neck.

I kick him again. The force knocks the air out of him, and he collapses on his face, forehead pressed to the cement floor.

"Okay," he says, voice muffled. "I talked with them. Once."

I pressed the sole of my shoe into his ribs, rolling him onto his back. "Speak up."

"I met with them once," he admits, tears streaming down his face from the pain. "They reached out to me."

"Yet you did not tell me?"

"I didn't know what they wanted," he says, sitting up and leaning against the wall.

"All the more reason you should have told me." I reach down and grab his shirt, hauling him to his feet and pinning him against the wall. "Men who are loyal to me do not meet with my enemies."

"They offered me money," he says, wincing in preparation for the next blow. "They offered me a larger cut of the profits. I shouldn't have gone, but I have a family, and—"

I was raised to be an observer of people. To spot their weaknesses and know when I am being deceived. So, I know immediately Simon is not telling me the entire story. The Furinos would not reach out to our chemist and offer him more money unless there had been communication between them prior, unless they had some connection Simon is not telling me about. He thinks I am a fool. He thinks I will forgive him because of his wife and child, but he does not know the depths of my apathy. Simon thinks he can appeal to my humanity, but he does not realize I do not have any.

I press my hand into the bruises around his neck. Simon grabs my wrist, trying to pull me away, but I squeeze again, enjoying the feeling of his life in my hands. I like knowing that with one blow to the neck, I could break his trachea and watch him suffocate on the floor. I am in complete control.

"And your family will be dead before dawn unless you tell me why you met with the Furinos," I spit. I want nothing more than to kill Simon for being disloyal. I can figure out the truth without him. But it is not why I was sent here. Killing indiscriminately does not create the kind of controlled fear we need to keep our family standing. It only creates anarchy. So, reluctantly, I let Simon go. Once again, he falls to the floor, gasping, and I step away so I won't be tempted to beat him.

"I'll tell you," he says, his voice high-pitched, like the words are being released slowly from a balloon. "I'll tell you anything, just don't hurt my family."

I nod for him to continue. This is his only chance to come clean. If he lies to me again, I'll kill him.

Simon opens his mouth, but before he can say anything, I hear a loud bang upstairs and a scream. Just as I turn around, the door at the top of the stairs opens, and I know immediately something is wrong. Forgetting all about Simon, I grab the nearest table and tip it over, not worrying about the potential lost profits. Footsteps pound down the stairs and no sooner have I crouched down, the room erupts in bullets.

I see one of the men in the back of the room drop, clutching his stomach. The other two follow my lead and dive behind tables. Simon crawls over to lay on the floor next to me, his lips purple.

The room is filled with the pounding of footsteps, the ring of bullets, and the moans of the fallen man. It is chaos, but I am steady. My heart rate is even as I grab my phone, turn on the front facing camera, and lift it over the table. There are eight shoulders spread out around the room, guns at the ready. Two of them are at the base of the stairs, the other six are spread out in three-foot increments, forming a barrier in front of the stairs. No one here is supposed to get out alive.

But they do not know who is hiding behind the table. If they did, they'd be running.

I look over at one of the chemists. They are not our family's soldiers, but they are trained like anyone else. He has his gun at the ready, waiting for my order. I nod my head once, twice, and on three, we both turn and fire.

One man falls immediately, my bullet striking him in the neck, blood spraying against the wall like splattered paint. It is a kind of artwork, shooting a man. Years of training, placing the bullet just so. Art is meant to incite a reaction and a bullet certainly does that. The man drops his weapon, his hand flying to his neck. Before he can experience too much pain, I place another bullet in his forehead. He drops to his knees, but before he falls flat on his face, I shoot his friend.

The men expected this ambush to be simple, so they are still in shock, still scrambling to collect themselves. It makes it easy for my men to knock them off. Another two men drop as I chase my second target around the room, firing shot after shot at him. He ducks behind a table, and I wait, gun aimed. It is a deadly game of Whack-a-mole, and it requires patience. His gun pops up first, followed shortly by his head, which I blow off with one shot. His scream dies on his lips as he bleeds out, red seeping out from under the table and spreading across the floor.

There are three men left, and I'm out of bullets. I stash my gun in my pocket and pull out my KA-BAR knife. The blade feels like an old friend in my hand. I crawl past a shivering Simon, wishing I'd killed him just so I wouldn't have to see him looking so pathetic, and out from behind the table. I slide my feet under me, moving into a crouch. The remaining men are wounded, and they are focused on the back corner where shots are still coming from my men. They do not see me approaching from the side.

I lunge at the first man—a young kid with golden brown hair and a tattoo on his neck. It is half-hidden under the collar of his shirt, so I cannot make it out. When my knife cuts into his side, he spins to fight me off, but I knock his gun from his hand with my left arm and then drive the knife in under his ribs and upward. He freezes for a moment before blood leaks from his mouth.

The man next to him falls from multiple bullets in the chest and stomach. I kick his gun away from him as he falls to the floor, and advance on the last attacker. He is hiding behind a metal table, palm pressing into a wound on his shoulder. He scrambles to lift his gun as I approach, but I drop to my knees and slide next to him, knife pressed to his neck. His eyes go wide, and then they squeeze shut as he drops his weapon.

The blade of my knife is biting into his skin, and I see the same tattoo creeping up from beneath his collar. I slide the blade down, pushing his shirt aside, and I recognize it at once.

"You are with the Furinos?" I ask.

The man answers by squeezing his eyes shut even tighter.

"You should know who is in a room before you attack," I hiss. "I am Luka Volkov, and I could slit your throat right now."

His entire body is trembling, blood from his shoulder wound leaking through his clothes and onto the floor. Every ounce of me wants this kill. I feel like a dog who has not been fed, desperate for a hunk of flesh, but warfare is not endless bloodshed. It is tactical.

"But I will not," I say, pulling the blade back. The man blinks, unbelieving. "Get out of here and tell your boss what happened. Tell him this attack is a declaration of war, and the Volkov family will live up to our merciless reputation."

He hesitates, and I slash the blade across his cheek, drawing a thin line of blood from the corner of his mouth to his ear. "Go!" I roar.

The man scrambles to his feet and towards the stairs, blood dripping in his wake. As soon as he is gone, I clean my knife with the hem of my shirt and slide it back into place on my hip.

This will not end well.

Eve

I hold up a bag of raisins and a bag of prunes a few inches from the cook's face.

"Do you see the difference?" I ask. The question is rhetorical. Anyone with eyes could see the difference. And a cook—a properly trained cook—should be able to smell, feel, and sense the difference, as well.

Still, Felix wrinkles his forehead and studies the bags like it is a pop quiz.

"Raisins are small, Felix!" My shouting makes him jump, but I'm far too stressed out to care. "Prunes are huge. As big as a baby's fist. Raisins are tiny. They taste very different because they start out as different fruits. Do you see the problem?"

He stares at me blankly, and I wonder if being sous chef gives me the authority to fire someone. Because this man has got to go.

"You've ruined an entire roast duck, Felix." I drop the bags on the counter and run a hand down my sweaty face. I grab the towel from my back pocket and towel off. "Throw it out and start again, but use *prunes* this time."

He smiles and nods, and I wonder how many times he must have hit his head to be so slow. I motion for another cook to come talk to me. He moves quickly, hands folded behind his back, waiting for my order.

"Chop up the duck and make a confit salad. We can toss it with more raisins, fennel—that kind of thing—and make it work."

He nods and shuffles away, and I mop my forehead again.

At the start of my shift, I strode into the kitchen like I owned the place. I was finally sous chef to Cal Higgs, genius chef in charge at The Floating Crown. After graduating culinary school, I didn't know where I'd get a job or where I'd be on the totem pole, and I certainly never imagined I'd be a sous chef so soon, but here I am. And now that I'm here, I can't help but wonder if it wasn't some sort of trick. Did Cal give into my father's wishes easily and give me this job because he needed a break from the insanity?

I've been assured by several members of staff that the dishwasher, whose name I can't remember, has been working at the kitchen for over a year, but he seems to be stuck on slow motion tonight. He is washing and drying plates seconds before the cooks are plating them up and sending them back out to the dining room. And two of the cooks, who were apparently dating, decided that the middle of dinner rush would be the perfect time to discuss their relationship, and they broke up. Dylan stormed out without a word, and Sarah, who should be okay since she was the dumper, not the dumpee, is hiding in the bathroom bawling her eyes out. I've knocked on the door once every ten minutes for an hour, but she refuses to let me in. Cal has a key, but he has been shut away in his office all night, and I don't want to go explain what a shitshow the kitchen is, so we are making do. Barely.

"Sarah?" I knock on the door. "If you don't come out in five minutes, you're fired."

For the first time, there is a break in the crying. "You can't do that."

"Yes, I can," I lie. "You'll leave here tonight without your apron. Single and jobless. Just imagine that shame."

I feel bad rubbing salt in her wound, threatening her, but I'm out of options. I tried comforting her and offering her some of the dark chocolate from the dessert pantry, but she refused to budge. Threats are my last recourse.

There is a long pause, and I wonder if I'm going to have to admit that I actually can't fire her—I don't think—and tell the staff to start using the bathrooms on the customer side, when finally, Sarah emerges. Mascara is smeared down her cheeks, and her eyes are red and puffy from crying, but she is out of the bathroom. As soon as she steps through the doorway, one of the waitresses darts in after her and slams the door shut.

"I'm sorry, Eve," she blubbers, covering her face with her hands.

I grab her wrists and pry her palms from her eyes. When she looks up, her eyes are still closed, tears leaking from the corners.

"Go to the sinks and help with the dishes," I say firmly. "You're in no state to cook right now. Just focus on cleaning plates, okay?"

Sarah nods, her lower lip wobbling.

"Everything is fine," I say, speaking to her like she is a wild animal who might attack. "You won't lose your job. Cal never needs to know, okay? Just go wash dishes. Now."

She turns away from me in a daze and heads back to help the dishwasher whose name I can't for the life of me remember, and I take a deep breath. I've finally put out all the fires, and I lean against the counter and watch the kitchen move around me. It is like a living, breathing machine. Each person has to play their part or everything falls apart. And tonight, I'm barely holding them together.

When the kitchen door swings open, I hope it is Makayla. She has been a waitress at The Floating Crown for five years, and while she has no formal culinary training, she knows this kitchen better than anyone. I've asked her for help tonight more times than I'm comfortable with, but at this point, just seeing one, capable, smiling face would be enough to keep me from crying. But when I turn and instead see a man in a suit, the tie loose and askew around his neck, and his eyes glassy, I almost sag to the floor.

"You can't be back here, sir," I say, moving forward to block his access to the rest of the kitchen. "We have hot stoves and fire and sharp knives, and you are already unstable on your feet."

Makayla told me a businessman at the bar had been demanding macaroni and cheese all night between shots. Apparently, he would not take 'no' for an answer.

"Macaroni and cheese," he mutters, falling against my palms, his feet sliding out from underneath him. "I need macaroni and cheese to soak up the alcohol."

I turn to the nearest person for help, but Felix is still looking at the bags of raisins and prunes like he might seriously still be confused which is which, and I don't want to distract him lest he ruin another duck. I could call out for help from someone else or call the police, but I don't want to cause a scene. Cal is just in the next room. He may have hired me because my father is Don of the Furino family, but even my father can't be angry if Cal fires me for sheer incompetence. I have to prove that I'm capable.

"Sir, we don't have macaroni and cheese, but may I recommend our scoglio?"

"What is that?" he asks, top lip curled back.

"A delicious seafood pasta. Mussels, clams, shrimp, and scallops in a tomato sauce with herbs and spices. Truly delicious. One of my favorite meals on the menu."

"No cheese?"

I sigh. "No. No cheese."

He shakes his head and pushes past me, running his hands along the counters like he might stumble upon a prepared bowl of cheesy pasta.

"Sir, you can't be back here."

"I can be wherever I like," he shouts. "This is America, isn't it?"

"It is, but this is a private restaurant and our insurance does not cover diners being back in the kitchen, so I have to ask you—"

"Oh, say can you see by the dawn's early light!"

"Is that 'The Star-Spangled Banner'?" I ask, looking around to see whether anyone else can see this man or whether I'm having some sort of exhausted fever dream.

"What so proudly we hailed at the twilight's last gleaming?"

This is absurd. Truly absurd. Beyond calling the police, the easiest thing to do seems to be to give in to his demands, so I lay a hand on his shoulder and lead him to the corner of the kitchen. I pat the counter, and he jumps up like he is a child.

I listen to the National Anthem six times before I hand the man a bowl of whole grain linguini with a sharp cheddar cheese sauce on top. "Can you please take this back to the bar and leave me alone?"

He grabs the bowl from my hands, takes a bite, and then breaks into yet another rousing rendition of "The Star-Spangled Banner." This time in falsetto with accompanying dance moves.

I sigh and push him towards the door. "Come on, man."

The dining room is loud enough that no one pays the man too much attention. Plus, he has been drunk out here for an hour before ambushing the kitchen. A few guests shake their heads at the man and then smile at me, giving me the understanding and recognition I sought from the kitchen staff. I lead the man back to the bar, tell the bartender to get rid of him as soon as the pasta is gone, and then make my way back through the dining room.

"She isn't the chef," says a deep voice at normal volume. "Chefs don't look like *that*."

I don't turn towards the table because I don't want to give them the satisfaction of knowing I heard them, of knowing they had any kind of power over me.

"Whatever she makes, it can't taste half as good as her muffin," another man says to raucous laughter.

I roll my eyes and speed up. I'm used to the comments and the cat calls. I've been dealing with it since I sprouted boobs. Even my father's men would whisper things about me. It is part of the reason I chose a path outside the scope of the family business. I couldn't imagine working with the kind of men my father employed. They were crass and mean and treated women like possessions. Unfortunately, the more I learn of the world beyond the Bratva, the more I realize men everywhere are like that. It is the reason I'll never get married. I won't belong to anyone.

I hear the men's deep voices as I walk back towards the kitchen, but I don't listen. I let the words roll off of me like water on a windowpane and step back into the safe chaos of the kitchen.

The kitchen seems to calm down as dinner service goes on, and I'm able to take a step back from micro-managing everything to work on an order of chicken tikka masala. While letting the tomato puree and spices simmer, I realize my stomach is growling. I was too nervous before shift to eat anything, and now that things have finally settled into an easy rhythm, my body is about to absorb itself. So, I casually walk over to where two giant stock pots are simmering with the starter soups for the day and scoop myself out a hearty ladle of lobster and bacon soup. Cal doesn't like for anyone to eat while on service, but he has been in his office all evening, and based on the smell slipping out from under his door, he will be far too stoned to notice or care.

The soup is warm and filling, and I close my eyes as I eat, enjoying the blissful moment of peace before more chaos ensues.

The kitchen door opens, and this time it really is Makayla. I wave her over, eager to see how everyone is enjoying the food and whether the drunk patriot finally left the restaurant, but she doesn't see me and walks with purpose through the kitchen and straight to Cal's office door. She opens it and steps inside, and I wonder what she needed Cal for and why she couldn't come to me. Lord knows I've handled every other situation that arose all night.

I'm just finished the last bite of my soup when Cal's office door slams open, bouncing off the wall, and he stomps his way across the kitchen.

"Eve!"

I shove the bowl to the back of the counter, throwing a dish towel over top to hide the evidence, and then wipe my mouth quickly.

"Yes, chef?"

"Front and center," he barks like we are in the military rather than a kitchen.

Despite the offense I take with his tone—especially after everything I've done to keep the place running all night—I move quickly to follow his order. Because that is what a good sous chef does. I follow the chef's orders, no matter how demeaning.

Cal Higgs is a large man in every sense of the word. He is tall, round, and thick. His head sits on top of his shoulders with no neck in sight, and just walking across the room looks like a chore. I imagine being in his body would be like wearing a winter coat and scarf all the time.

"What is the problem, Chef?"

He hitches a thumb over his shoulder, and Makayla gives me an apologetic wince. "Someone complained about the food, and they want to see the chef."

I wrinkled my forehead. I'd personally tasted every dish that went out. Unless Felix managed to slide another dish past me with raisins in it instead of prunes, I'm not sure what the complaint could be. "Was there something wrong with the dish or did they simply not like it?"

"Does it matter?" he snaps. His eyes are bloodshot and glassy, yet his temper is as sharp as ever. "I don't like unhappy customers, and you need to fix it."

"But you're the chef," I say, realizing too late I should have stayed quiet.

Cal steps forward, and I swear I can feel the floor quake under his weight. "But you made the food. Should I go out there and apologize on your behalf? No, this is your mess, and you will take care of it."

"Of course," I say, looking down at the ground. "You're right. I'll go out there and make this right."

Before Cal can find another reason to yell at me, I retie my apron around my waist, straighten my white jacket, and march through the swinging kitchen doors.

The dining room is quieter than before. The drunk man is no longer singing the National Anthem at the bar and several of the tables are empty, the bussers clearing away empty plates. Happy plates, I might add. Clearly, they didn't have an issue with the food.

I didn't ask Makayla who complained about the food, but as soon as I walk into the main dining area, it is obvious. There is a small gathering at the corner booth, and a salt and pepper-haired man in his late fifties or early sixties raising a hand in the air and waves me over without looking directly at me. I haven't even spoken to the man yet, and I already hate him.

I'm standing at their table, staring at the man, but he doesn't speak to me until I announce my presence.

"I heard someone wanted to speak with the chef," I say.

He turns to me, one eyebrow raised. "You are the chef?"

I recognize a Russian accent when I hear one, and this man is Russian without a doubt. I wonder if I know him. Or if my father does. Would he be complaining to me if he knew my father was head of the Furino family? I would never throw my family name around in order to scare people, but for just a second, I have the inclination.

"Sous chef," I say with as much confidence as I can muster. "I ran the kitchen tonight, so I'll be hearing the complaints."

His eyes move down my body slowly like he is inspecting a cut of meat in a butcher shop. I cross my arms over my chest and spread my feet hip-width apart. "So, was there an issue with the food? I'd love to correct any problems."

"Soup was cold." He nudges his empty bowl to the center of the table with three fingers. "The portions were too small, and I ordered my steak medium-rare, not raw."

Every plate on the table is empty. Not a single crumb in sight. Apparently, the issues were not bad enough he couldn't finish his meal.

"Do you have any of the steak left?" I ask, making a show of looking around the table. "If one of my cooks undercooked the meat, I'd like to be able to inform them."

"If? I just told you the meet was undercooked. Are you doubting me?"

"Of course not," I say. *Yes, absolutely I am.* "It is just that if the meat was undercooked, I do not understand why you waited until you'd eaten everything to inform me of the problem?"

The man looks around the table at his companions. They are all smiling, and I can practically see them sharpening their teeth, preparing to rip me to shreds. When he turns back to me, his smile is acidic, deadly. "How did you get this position—sous chef? Surely not by skill. You are pretty, which I'm sure did you a favor. Did you sleep with the chef? Maybe—" he moves his hand in an obscene gesture— "'service' the boss to earn your place in the kitchen? Surely your 'talent' didn't get you the job, seeing as how you have none."

I physically bite my tongue and then take a deep breath. "If you'd like me to remake anything for you or bring out a complimentary dessert, I'm happy to do that. If not, I apologize for the issues and hope you will not hold it against us. We'd love to have you again."

Lies. Lies. Lies. I'm smiling and being friendly the way I was taught in culinary school. I actually took a class on dealing with customers, and this man is being even more outrageous than the overexaggerated angry customer played by my professor.

"Why would I want more food from you if the things you already sent out were terrible?" He snorts and shakes his head. "I see you do not have a ring on. That is no surprise. Men like a woman who can cook. Men don't care if you know your way around a professional kitchen if you don't know your way around a dinner plate."

The older gentleman is speaking, but I hear my father's words in my head. *You do not need to go to culinary school to find a husband, Eve. Your aunties can teach you to cook good food for your man.*

My entire life has been preparation for finding a husband. The validity of every hobby is judged by whether it will fetch me a suitor or not. My father wants me to be happy, but he mostly wants me to be married. Single, I'm a disappointment. Married, I'm a vessel for future Furino mafia members.

Years of anger and resentment begin to bubble and hiss inside of me until I'm boiling. My hands are shaking, and I can feel adrenaline pulsing through me, lighting every inch of me on fire. This time, I don't bite my tongue.

"I'd rather die alone than spent another minute near a man like you," I spit, stepping forward and laying my palms flat on the table. "The fact that you ate all of the food you apparently hated shows you are a pig in more ways than one."

In the back of my mind, I recognize that my voice is echoing around the restaurant and the chatter in the rest of the room has gone quiet, but blood is whirring in my ears, and I can't stop. I've stayed quiet and docile for too long. Now, it is my turn to speak my mind.

"You and your friends may be wealthy and respected, but I see you for what you are—spineless, cowardly assholes who are so insecure they have to take their rage out on everybody else."

I want to spin on my heel and storm away, making a grand exit, but in classic Eve fashion, my heel catches on the tablecloth, and I nearly trip. I fall sideways and throw an arm out to catch myself, knocking a nearly full bottle of wine on the table over. The glass shatters and red wine splashes across the tablecloth and onto the guests in the booth like a river of blood.

I pause long enough to note the old Russian man's shirt is splattered like he has been shot before I continue my exit and head straight for the doors.

I suck in the night air. The evening is warm and humid, summer strangling the city in its hold, and I want to rip off my clothes for some relief. I feel like I'm being strangled. Like there is a hand around my neck, squeezing the life out of me.

Breathing in and out slowly helps, but as the physical panic begins to ebb away, emotional panic flows in.

What have I done? Cal Higgs is going to find out about the altercation any minute, and then what? Will he fire me? And if he does, will I ever be able to get another chef position? I was only offered this position because of my father, and I doubt he will help me earn another kitchen position, especially since I'm no closer to finding a boyfriend (or husband) since I left for culinary school.

Despite it all, I want to call my dad. He has always made it clear he will move heaven and earth to take care of me, to make sure no one is mean to me, and I want his support right now. But the support he offered me when a girl tripped me during soccer practice and made me miss the net won't apply here. He will tell me to come home. To put down my apron and knife and focus on more meaningful pursuits. And that is the last thing I want to hear right now.

I pull out my phone and scroll through my contacts list, hoping to see a spark of hope amidst the names, but there is nothing. I've lost touch with everyone since I started culinary school. There hasn't been time for friends.

This is probably the kind of situation where most girls would turn to their moms, but she hasn't been in the picture since I was six years old. Even if I had her number, I wouldn't call her. Dad hasn't always been perfect, but at least he was there. At least he cared enough to stay.

I untie my apron and pull it over my head, leaning back against the brick side of the restaurant.

"Take it off, baby!"

I look up and see a man on a motorcycle with his hair in a bun parked along the curb. He is waggling his eyebrows at me like I'm supposed to fall in love with him for harassing me on the street, and the fire that filled my veins inside hasn't died out yet. The embers are still there, burning under the skin, and I step towards him, lips pulled back in a smile.

He looks surprised, and I'm sure he is. That move has probably never worked for him before. He smiles back at me, his tongue darting out to lick his lower lip.

"Is that your bike?" I purr.

He nods. "Want a ride?"

My voice is still sticky sweet as I respond, "So sweet of you to offer. I'd rather choke and die on that grease ball you call a man bun, but thanks anyway, hon."

It takes him a second to realize my words don't match the tone. When it hits him, he snarls, "Bitch."

"Asshole." I flip him the bird over my shoulder and start the long walk home.

∼

Click here to keep reading BROKEN VOWS.

MAILING LIST

Sign up to my mailing list!
New subscribers receive a FREE steamy bad boy romance novel.

Click the link below to join.
https://sendfox.com/nicolefox